Published by Frankenstein Pickles
First published 21 September 2015

www.jojette.com

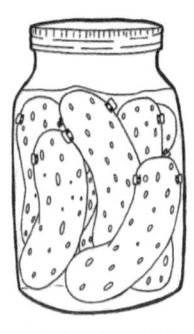

published by
Frankenstein Pickles

For Joshua.
Thank you for putting up with my neverending
nonsense.

And

Richard 'Farquar' Adams for being French in his spare
time.

CHAPTER ONE

Girl overboard

The waves lashed against the girl as she clung to the side of the ship, gripping some wet rope with all her might. It was the only thing between her and the certain death that awaited her should she let go. Her long red hair hung in sodden tendrils around her face, and she was soaked to the bone. Silently she wished she had put on more than a singlet under her dark, hard leather corset that day. She might now have had something to shield her battered body against the rough weathered wood of the ship. Her light woolen trousers were now torn and stained black and red from the fight, though thankfully her heavy leather boots had somehow managed to keep her feet mostly dry.

Warm blood trickled down the left-hand side of her face from a deep cut on her forehead and smeared against her skin. She wiped it away roughly as it ran down her left cheek, and she realised that she had lost her eye patch. Scowling to herself she cursed silently at its loss. Absently she adjusted her hair so that it covered the scar tissue that sat in place of where her left eye should have been. She then scrambled to get a better grip on the rope as a large wave washed over her, smashing her into the side of the ship yet again. Screwing her right eye shut she was momentarily dazed. She shook her head and fought to stay conscious. A task made somewhat easier by the constant spray of the water hitting her face as she held tight to the only thing keeping her alive right now.

Opening her good eye briefly, she felt the salt water sting, but at least it was keeping her alert and thinking clearly. She couldn't stay in the freezing water much longer. Her fingers were stiff from the cold, and she was slowly losing feeling in them. Her already pale skin was taking on a cool blue hue, and her body was struggling to keep her blood warm. But she knew that if she could just hold on for a little bit longer, and let the battle going on above her play out, then she might have a chance of surviving.

While she waited it out, she mulled over what had happened to her in the last 18 months since she had left home. It was on the night of the Obliteration, as she called it. Nothing could have made her stay after that. After what she saw. She shuddered involuntarily at the memory. True she had never intended to join a pirate crew but then again at the time, and with her being a woman, there wasn't much choice - it was either a life of servitude as a maid to some Lord, the workhouse (or worse), or take to the sea. It hadn't been easy at first, and she had had to fight off more men than she would ever have bargained for, but eventually she had come to earn her place on the ship above her. It was also fortunate that her Captain, Bernard Mayhem, didn't harbor any superstitious ideas about women being bad luck on board his ship. He had taken her on as part of his crew without a second thought, and made her feel as though she was part of his family of absconders.

Life on the Severed Seas was rough at the best of times, but lately it had been more cutthroat than ever, with a bounty being put on many a Pirate Captain's head in an effort by the Aristocracy to thin out their number. The other Pirate Captains hadn't figured it out yet of course, and were happy enough to turn on each other and do the King's work in exchange for the gold. To them a bounty was a bounty and, as they often said, they owed no allegiance to anyone.

Before the girl had found herself hanging from the side of her Captain's besieged ship, they had been drinking a toast to the fact that her Captain now had the highest price on his head of any pirate that ever sailed. Everyone had been smiling and in a jolly mood before they got word from their lookout. A black ship was approaching. By the colours, it was the Riffraff, Captain Thaddeus Blackwatch's ship. Blackwatch prided himself on having one of the best-armed ships on the Severed Seas, with one of the hardest crews, and it was said that in order to secure a place on Blackwatch's ship you had to have done something pretty black hearted. Though as usual the details on this were a bit ambiguous. Blackwatch was well aware of the huge price on Mayhem's head and he had a mind to claim it, despite the fact that Mayhem would obviously prefer to keep his head on his shoulders. It was where he liked to keep his thoughts and make decisions.

The Riffraff sailed on towards Mayhem, its battle colours flying high above it's tattered, dirty canvas sails, but it was closing in on Mayhem at a speed that no wind powered boat could hope to achieve. A fact not lost on Captain Mayhem.

'He must have turbo thrusters on that thing!' Mayhem screamed, 'and he flies the flag of war - man the cannons men, prepare for boarding!'

The Captain's rage was well-founded. Turbo charging your ship was frowned upon by most on the Severed Seas, but was accepted as long as it was utilized for escape from the hated Aristocrats. However using it against a fellow pirate on the open seas would mark you as the lowest of the low.

Within a heartbeat Mayhem's crew were caught in a blur of activity, preparing their ship for battle. They could not believe that even a marauder like Blackwatch would stoop to using the enhanced power of his ship against a fellow pirate. It ran contrary to the code they all lived by, handed down from the Thirteen Bones, and enforced with the cutlass and dagger. The code had been put in place to stop such unscrupulous men from taking advantage of certain available technologies to gain advantage over each other. It was in short considered cheating, even by pirate standards.

Just as Mayhem's crew had managed to get the canon doors open, and raise their own flag, the Riffraff was upon them, guns blazing. Blackwatch's ship pulled alongside Mayhem, and his crew made quick work of boarding his ship. Landing on the deck with their swords drawn and flintlocks at the ready within moments all was lost within a haze of chaos and confusion, smoke and gunfire. Blackwatch's men seemed to come aboard in an endless procession, and indeed Blackwatch had brought extra men with him. He had no illusions about the skill of his crew in comparison to Mayhem's and he wanted to stack an uneven deck in his favour. Under such an overwhelming onslaught, it wasn't long before Mayhem's men began to fall, including the girl. Through the smoke, as he cut down Blackwatch's men, Mayhem had somehow found her, lying on the deck clutching her head. Ordering her to stay out of sight until either he came to retrieve her or Blackwatch's ship had left, he had picked her up, put the rope in her hands and tossed her over the side of the ship like a rag doll. She had flown through the air for a moment as if she weighed nothing, before gravity unceremoniously pulled her back down. There the water caught her and cruelly slammed her into the side of the ship. Blinking back tears from her good eye, she refused to cry. It was not the time to fall apart if you wanted to live.

Now clinging on to the rope in the wet and cold, she could hear the distant roar of Mayhem and his men fighting, even as the water continued to smash her into the side of the ship again and again.

Above her on the ship things were not going well for Mayhem and his men. Eventually and inevitably they were overpowered simply by the sheer numbers of Blackwatch's crew. Falling to his knees on the deck with more wounds than he cared to count, Mayhem heard Blackwatch order his men to leave none alive, and watched as his protagonist strolled towards him with the air of someone to whom victory is a forgone conclusion. Exhausted and broken, Mayhem knew his time had come, and he almost welcomed it. With one slash of his cutlass, Blackwatch separated Mayhem's head from his body. He now had all he needed to claim the bounty. Looking around at the destruction and litter of fallen bodies, Blackwatch signalled for his remaining men.

'Loot the ship, then send her to the deep!' he roared, dissolving into a hearty laugh that would have terrified a more sane group of men, 'then return to the Riffraff and we depart as one. You have 10 minutes!'

As his men went to work once more, Blackwatch took a moment to smile at his triumph before he jumped up onto the boarding plank and stalked back across to his ship.

In the water time dragged on as the girl's muscles groaned with the cold and the pain of holding on to the rough, water soaked rope. Looking up she could just see the sun high above the main mast. Nearly an hour must have passed since Blackwatch had attacked. Given how much time had elapsed, and as she had seen no faces peering over the side looking for her, she guessed that her Captain must be dead. She strained to hear what was going on above her, over the wash of the waves and the occasional plaint of a gull. She could hear a man shouting, and though she could make out nothing he said she could guess. The sounds of battle had been replaced by the scratchings and scrapings of Blackwatch and his men as, she surmised, they looted the ship. She also knew that their next move would be to sink Mayhem's ship when they were done. Given the underhanded way in which Blackwatch had conducted his business with them today, he would not want to leave behind any evidence of his treachery. It was bad for the reputation. He couldn't be too much longer though, and it was then that she would have to make her move.

As she waited in the shadow of the ship, a small dull explosion sounded somewhere off to her right, on the other side of the ship, and immediately it's bearing shifted slightly as the vessel began to take on water. She knew she wouldn't have too long to pull herself up on board, and hoped that Blackwatch hadn't destroyed all the lifeboats. Patiently she waited as she felt the vessel pull itself over further. At least that will make it easier for me to pull myself back up onto the ship, she thought. She could only assume that Blackwatch was now making his getaway and wouldn't be sticking around to take in the last of the sunset and watch the ship go down.

Pulling with all her remaining strength the girl dragged herself inch by inch up the side of the ship, her frozen hands threatening to let go at any second. Passing the gunport she eventually reached the railing and pulled herself over it. Falling to the main deck she instantly slide across the rough wood towards the listing side of the ship. Thinking fast she swung her feet round in front of her and managed to catch herself up against the main mast. The ship had begun to list quite steeply and she was running out of time. Black smoke plumbed around her as fire began to spread from the Captain's quarters to the rest of the ship.

Surveying the mass of dead and bloody men that lay around her on deck, she could see no one moving – no one still alive. Then looking towards the bow she saw her Captain's headless body, partially hidden behind the raised hatch of the ship's hold. Turning away, she drew in a sharp breath to keep from crying out in despair, and with one hand on the deck she pushed herself up and struggled to her feet. She had to find a way off the doomed ship.

Stumbling through the smoking madness around her, she kept her focus on looking to see if any of the lifeboats had survived. She moved methodically from one small boat to the next, but they all seemed to be damaged in some way. She was beginning to lose hope. The nasty wound on her forehead continued to bleed, and her head throbbed with the dull pain of it, causing her to feel nauseous and dizzy. Stooping down quickly, she grabbed a scarf from one of the dead men, and tied it tightly around her head to cover the wound, positioning it to conceal the deformed space where her left eye should have been. It was such a small thing really, but from that moment she began to feel more in control. There was no point in panicking now. As the ship continued on to it's watery grave, she weighed up her options. If she could find something to float on, a barrel or a piece of wood from the ship, that might keep her alive for a while, but she knew she really needed something that would keep her out of the water and dry otherwise the cold salty deep would kill her.

Looking down again she grabbed a cutlass lying on the deck at her feet and wiped it on a dead man's shirt. Then spying something else she could use she put in some effort to wrestle a long, black leather jacket from another of the dead crew. This would do well to keep her warm. As the ship creaked threateningly and lurched over still further she made the choice to jump for it. She couldn't go down with the ship, and would have to make sure she was a safe distance before it finally went to it's final destination otherwise it would suck her down with it.

Running to the portside, which was now listing at almost 40 degrees to the water she found she now had a very good platform from which to dive into the sea and get a head start. She even thought she might be able to swim away from the ship, wait for it to sink and then return to see what of use floated back up to the surface.

Standing on the side of the ship she was about to jump, when in the afternoon light she saw it. One lone lifeboat floating out on the sea not to far from the ship, drifting lazily on it's own.

'Avast!' she cried to the wind without thinking, for if there was anyone aboard the small boat, there were equal chances that they were foe as well as friend, but no reply came. She had to take the chance it was empty or perhaps one of her crew were on board. In a moment of quick forethought, she returned to the damaged lifeboats to grab an oar. She didn't know if there would be one on the little boat on the sea, and oars were damned useful things to have in a small boat.

Leaping over the dead, she sprinted back to the side of the ship, and climbed up onto the railing. She balanced there for a moment and, before she lost her nerve, she threw the oar and the jacket into the water before following the items over the side herself. She might be on her own, but she wasn't dead yet!

The freezing water embraced her like an old friend, momentarily taking her breath away. If she had thought it was cold before it was like ice now! Reaching for the oar, she swam over to the little boat and threw it inside. Then exhausted and in pain, she pulled herself into the tiny vessel after it, but she wasn't out of trouble yet. She still had to clear a safe distance between her and the sinking ship. Taking stock of what was in the boat she found another oar, a bottle of rum, the canvas lifeboat cover, a small anchor, an old shirt and some rope. Setting the two oars into the loops on either side of the boat she began to row, with each stroke causing a worsening spasm of pain to shoot up her left arm. There was no time to check the injury now though, and she had to focus on getting as far away as she could from the flaming wreck that was Mayhem's ship before it went down.

Eventually she had to stop rowing as her arm finally gave out, but she figured that she was a safe distance from the sinking ship. Looking down she could see her arm had a fairly decent gash in it, which had been aggravated by her mad rowing. Something would have to be done about that. Reaching down she grabbed the man's shirt from the bottom of the boat and ripped one of the sleeves free, wrapping it round her wounded arm and tying it tightly. This would at least stem the blood flow and keep it clean until she could get it seen to. Grabbing the canvas boat cover she wrapped it round her thin frame to shield her from the wind, which had picked up and flung its weight around disapprovingly. She then spread the leather jacket out over the top, and though it was damp, it still provided another layer of warmth. Reaching for the rum she took a swig from the bottle, and threw the small anchor over the side. She didn't want to find herself drifting aimlessly on the ocean and she could feel herself slowly loosing consciousness. She didn't know how long she would be out for, but she imagined it might be at least a few hours.

When the girl woke again, she didn't know how much time had passed, but it was dark. She knew immediately she was no longer on the lifeboat. Sitting up and looking around she found herself in what she guessed to be the guest quarters of a large ship. The bed she was in was warm, soft and clean, and red velvet curtains billowed lazily round the cabin's porthole. Behind her mint striped wallpaper covered one wall, while two small lamps cast a yellow glow to her left and right. Deep purple carpet covered the floor, a strange luxury on a ship, further confusing the girl as to who could possibly have come to her rescue.

Throwing the covers back, she saw that she was now dressed in a clean nightshirt that hung down to her ankles. It was obviously someone else's shirt, someone who was much bigger than herself. To her left she could see her old leather corset hanging over the back of an ornately carved wooden chair along with some fresh, dark woolen trousers and a smaller long sleeve shirt. She swung her legs over the side of the bed and slowly got to her feet. Finding this felt good, she tried walking. She was a bit shaky. Maybe save that for later. She sat back down on the bed. Looking down at her arm she could see it had been dressed properly, and she could feel stitches under the bandage. Instinctively her hand wandered up to her face, where she could feel the hollow of her missing eye. Her hair was tied back from her face and swept back from her forehead, which was bandaged also. Pressing against the bandage on her head, she winced in pain, but at least she was still alive.

She turned her attention to the little beside table, and saw that it was 2 o'clock in the morning by the timepiece that sat there. Then she noticed the bottle of rum that had been left on the table for her. It was the bottle from the lifeboat. The girl poured herself a glass and downed it in one shot. The fire from the alcohol warmed her throat and as she breathed out she felt the heat spread out to her bones. Reaching over to the chair she grabbed the trousers and pulled them on roughly. Next she pulled on the shirt, and found it to be surprisingly soft against her skin. Finally she pulled on her boots, which were thankfully dry and sitting neatly side-by-side under the little table. Pouring herself another shot of rum for good measure, she looked towards the door and traced a finger over the silver Octopus that hung at her throat. There was nothing for it but to sit and wait for whomever it was that had picked her up to come find her awake. She needed answers, but she wasn't fool enough to go looking for them yet.

Before too long the door opened, and a man appeared in the frame. He wore the tricorne hat of a Captain, and had the bearing of a man who had seen too much in his time. On seeing his patient was awake, a great smile spread across his face, and he stepped forward into the light.

'You're awake! Grand, grand my girl! We were a bit worried about you for a while there. Been checking in on you every hour. I'm not sure what you think you were doing out there lassy. A shore boat is no place to sleep after going for a swim,' he paused for breath, 'I am Jessup Miserablesod, Captain of this fine ship, and who might you be?'

'I might be indebted to you for my rescue, and for the good work you have done to dress my wounds,' smiled the girl, 'my Captain's ship was attacked by Blackwatch for he wished to claim the bounty on his head... I am sad to say I am the only survivor.'

'Ahhh, I am sorry to hear that, but do I take it then that you are a lass of the sea?'

The girl nodded yes in response.

'Well in that case you may call me Captain, but by what name shall I refer to you?'

'You may call me... Blimey,' said the girl, who had heard the name somewhere before, and thought it was as good a name as any to start over with. Besides, she wanted to keep her past behind her.

'Well then, Miss ... Blimey, as a fellow pirate I welcome you to my ship!' extolled the Captain, smiling widely and sweeping his arm across his chest and then out in a wild gesture, 'perhaps I can even convince you to join my crew, if you have no immediate plans that is?'

Blimey smiled up at this strange man who had saved her life and now offered her a place to live and work.

'No plans that can't wait a few years,' she said simply.

CHAPTER TWO

Things don't always go as planned

That was a long time ago, and in the present day Miss Blimey had just awoken. Dressing quickly she pulled on a white singlet, black wool trousers, socks and her black buccaneer-style boots. Then it was time for some armor as she pulled on her dark brown, hard leather corset, which laced up both sides. A large silver skull and cross bones was emblazoned across the chest. Tying her long red hair back with a thin leather strap, she slipped on her black leather eye-patch and adjusted it so that covered the sunken place where her left eye should have been. Finally she threaded her favourite belt, with the silver crossed swords on the buckle, through the waist-loops of her trousers. Now all she needed was weaponry.

Any true pirate had to ensure their cutlass (sword), dagger, and flintlock, were in good working order. The last thing you wanted in a fight was for your gun to jam or your blade to be dull. It was such a concern for most Captains that it had eventually become part of code that all pirates lived by, and any pirate who knew what was good for them followed the code to the letter on this ship.

Today was a special day for Blimey for she was to be sworn in as second in command aboard the Avernus, a beautiful 3 mast rigged tall ship, 200 feet long if not by an inch. The sails of the ship were a deep emerald green, which matched the wonderfully detailed paintwork of the ship itself, and on the front of the ship was a beautifully carved wooden mermaid figurehead.

The Captain of the Avernus, Miserablesod, was a bit of a traditionalist when it came to pirating, and he had been Blimey's mentor and father figure ever since she joined his crew two years earlier. While at first many of his men had been against the idea of having a woman on board, over the months she had won their respect and now they all looked upon her as part of their large, scoundrelous family.

Miserablesod himself also came fully stocked with his own rambunctious reputation. He liked to dress as sharp as ripe cheese and was perhaps a little too fond of taking a swig from a bottle of the hard stuff, but at the end of the day there would not be many with more knowledge than he when it came to passing on the secrets of the pirate world.

Two weeks before Blimey had been voted in by the crew to become the new second in command on the ship, after the Avernus had lost its First Mate in a squirmish with a pirate named Captain Nouburg. Nouburg was generally known as one of the most underhanded men ever to set sail. The loss of Harrington had been a blow to Miserablesod, but then loosing any member of his crew always hit him hard, for he trained them all personally. However it did mean that a new First Mate had to be chosen.

Now some Captains simply preferred to appoint the First Mate themselves, but Miserablesod reasoned that as the First Mate was his second in command, he should put the decision to a crew vote. In this case the choice was unanimous, and Blimey was duly cast as the Captain's second. This created a bit of a conundrum for Miserablesod for rather than being happy that his surrogate daughter was to take on the role, for the first time in his pirate life he felt slightly anxious. No crewmember had ever had the whole crew standing behind them before, and the alarm bells screeched silently inside Miserablesod's head. The paranoia that so often accompanies positions of leadership settled in like a winter-bound squirrel, nibbling away at Miserablesod's mind as though it were nothing more than a store of crunchy acorns. Visions of mutiny played out over and over in his dreams, with himself ousted as Captain and Blimey taking the helm. However, if he had opened his eyes instead of internalizing this struggle, he would have seen that his fears could not have been further from the truth, and no one was more loyal to him than the girl.

Keeping such thoughts to himself however, Miserablesod had cheered along with his crew for Blimey's pending promotion. Preparations immediately began for the swearing in ceremony and the handing over of swords. A big party was also planned, with lots of drinking and dancing envisioned, and many songs to be sung. In a way the swearing in ceremony was akin to getting married, but instead you pledged your life to the sea.

Two days before the ceremony was to take place, a strange ship approached the Avernus, though it was clear from the lack of concern that he showed that Miserablesod knew who his visitor was. When he was within calling distance the approaching ship's Captain waved to Miserablesod, calling for him to come aboard. A gangplank was extended between the two vessels, and both Captains stepped up, meeting in the middle. The men smiled, shook hands, and pulled each other in for a warm hug, patting each other on the back in a show of manly affection. Then the strange Captain turned and returned to the deck of his ship followed by Miserablesod.

The hours passed and eventually Miserablesod re-appeared and headed back to his own ship, carrying what appeared to be a new cutlass. Rumour had reached the Avernus from the other ship that it was a gift from the strange Captain for Blimey, to be given to her upon her swearing in. Yet, the same rumourous whisperers also asked, how did this other man know that Blimey was being sworn in at all, and why had he really come?

A cloud settled on Miserablesod's face the following day and stayed there, with each moment it grew a little darker, like a tropical storm brewing. What the other Captain had told him now only served to confirm his fears that a mutiny was inevitable should Blimey become his First Mate, and he resolved to get the girl off his ship and out of his life immediately. The catch was, as he saw it, he would have to do it in such a way as not to upset the rest of his crew. Tricky waters to navigate, but then Miserablesod had been in this game for a long time.

As Blimey was downstairs adjusting her weaponry in the mirror, Miserablesod was putting his plan into action. Only one other person knew what was going to happen next. Miserablesod's resident mercenary, Charles Denver. On the main deck the crew gathered and waited for Blimey to appear. Miserablesod soon joined his crew, and he called them to gather closely round him. He then set his cards on the table.

'Men, as you know today we were to swear in Blimey as the new First Mate, but it pains me to say that this thing we cannot do in good tide,' he said.

'But why Captain?' called someone from the back.

'We have a traitor in our midst, one who has been dishonest about their intentions, their bloodline and their loyalties,' he answered solemnly, 'and as your Captain I cannot let this day continue a moment more without identifying them and bringing them to justice!'

A shocked silence fell on the men as they turned to one another, with questioning looks to their left and right. Who was it that had betrayed them? The doubt hung in the air like a pall.

At the same moment the Captain was breaking this news to his crew, his accomplice was calmly walking down the stairs and towards Blimey's quarters. Knocking on her door, Denver entered the room and, walking over to her, told her simply that she would be wanted on deck shortly. Blimey smiled back at him, it would never have crossed her mind that he meant her harm. As she turned back to the mirror she noticed to late the sudden movement, and before she knew what was happening Denver had placed a chloroform soaked rag over her mouth. The shock only caused her to breath more deeply and she sank to the ground, unconscious.

Denver knew he had to move quickly. Grabbing a rope he had tucked into his belt behind his back he tied Blimey up tightly, wrapping the thin rope round and round her slender frame. Then as instructed by Miserablesod, he removed her sword but left her other weapons in place. Frustratingly he now had to wait until she started to gain consciousness again before he took her up to his Captain. A dead weight was no easy thing to carry upstairs, and Denver had always been more of a reed than an oak. Too pass the time he went through Blimey's room looking for anything of value he could steal.

Around 20 minutes passed before Blimey opened her eyes. Her head felt like a hippo was taking a bath in there. Looking up at Denver she shot him a dirty look, but he merely responded with a smirk and helped her to her feet. Swaying for a moment, she caught her breath as Denver came round behind her and pushed her forward.

'Time to go.'

'What is this about Charles?'

'The quicker we get up them stairs, the quicker you'll find out,' he growled.

Resigning herself to the fact that she could do nothing for the moment, she started walking. Every nerve in her body screamed with rage at her imprisonment, but outwardly she showed no sign of rebellion. She had no idea what had happened or why she was being treated to this indignity, but she could guess from Denver's attitude that this was no prank. All her senses were attuned to looking for a way to escape.

Emerging bleary eyed into the sunshine Blimey was uneasy, uncomfortable and confused. It was clear from the look on the crew's faces that something was terribly wrong. As her eyes adjusted to the light several questions pulsed through her mind. Yes Denver had drugged her, but why? Had there been a Mutiny? Had he betrayed them to another Captain? She could only wait as the situation played out.

Denver directed Blimey clumsily along the main deck, and she soon recognised her Captain, who was neither captured nor mutinied. He stood on the quarterdeck, outside his quarters, apparently awaiting her arrival. To her left and right, the crew looked on – some with sad and some with angry expressions. They seemed unable to believe what they were seeing, but it was obvious that their anger was directed towards her and none would be moved to help her.

Denver propelled Blimey forward and she stumbled slightly, the tight rope wrapped around her making it difficult to walk. Stopping about a metre from the Captain, Blimey raised her chin defiantly and waited for whatever crazy explanation he had for her current situation.

'Blimey, today you were to be awarded the greatest honour this crew and Captain can bestow on you, but it is not to be. You have betrayed us, you have withheld information from us and as you know by the code this is grounds for death or marooning,' he announced grandly.

'I don't know what you are talking about,' replied Blimey tersely.

'Then I shall set it out for you. Is your father not a famed Pirate, and do you not wish to follow in his footsteps and Captain your own ship? And would you not see fit to mutiny your own Captain in exchange for such an opportunity?'

Blimey stood for a moment in shock, her voice lost, her jaw dropped. This was honestly news to her. As far as she knew her father was a Shaman back in the village she had fled from years earlier. There had to be some mistake.

'I don't know what you are talking about, my father is....' she began defiantly, taking the opportunity to defend herself.

'Your father was Gerald Bohnes, at one time one of the fiercest pirates on the Severed Seas,' Miserablesod cut her off in a thunder of rage, 'and that man who came to me yesterday came to tell me just this, and to pass on your father's sword – a gift for your promotion in light of today!'

'This is ridiculous. My father is a Shaman in a small village hundreds of leagues from here,' Blimey stated firmly, now finding her voice, 'that man must be mistaken. This is insane! My loyalty is to you, my Captain, and to this ship, and her crew!'

'Easy to say now when you have been found out. Gerald Bohnes is your father. This is your sword, and now your destiny awaits you at the bottom of the sea for I will no longer have you on my ship!'

'The Plank!' yelled Denver suddenly, before Blimey had a chance to protest further. All eyes were turned on her and the Captain and a great noise of agreement rose from the crew.

'You're not serious?' asked Blimey after the cheering finally died down.

'Yes, the plank,' confirmed Miserablesod firmly, 'but I will not be so heartless as to let you go without your sword, and so here it is finally,' he added taking the sword of Gerald Bohnes and placing it in the scabbard on her belt.

'Your fate will be as it may!' yelled the crew in unison as Denver produced the gangplank and placed it in position. It stuck out across the water and would have intimidated even the heartiest man.

With the help of two crewmembers Denver lifted Blimey up and placed her at the end of the gangplank. Pressing his flintlock into the small of Blimey's back he made a couple of nasty jabs and propelled her forward. Reaching the edge she looked down at the straight drop to the dark water below.

'You can't walk me off the plank' Blimey protested again, 'I refuse to die by cliché!'

'You have no choice, do you now?' smirked Denver.

He then turned and left her standing at the end of the thin platform. She had never felt more alone. Now Miserablesod approached her and it was clear that he meant to dispose of her himself.

'I am sorry it had to end this way,' he said, and with one great shove he sent her toppling into the awaiting cold darkness of the sea below.

CHAPTER THREE

The bottom of the deep blue sea

The water caressed Blimey with its icy embrace as she sank into the salty black. Instantly her blood turned to ice, and she slowly began to loose sight of the gentle sunlit glow coming from above. Kicking her legs below her, she maneuvered herself towards the ships stern. She did not want to break the surface without making sure she would not be seen first, and the back of the ship would provide her the most protection from view. With any luck Miserablesod and his men would assume she had sunk like a stone when she did not bob back up to the surface straight away, and would make their way East as they had planned.

Inch by inch she made her way along the underside of the ship, almost reaching the end before she began to run out of air. She would have to risk heading upwards. Still unable to free her arms she kicked her way up to the surface, and after what seemed like an eternity her head finally rose above the water. She gasped in air and tried not to immediately burst out coughing. Above her she could just hear Miserablesod rallying his men, and commanding his crew to set sail. She was also sure some mention of her being lost to Davy Jones locker for good would have been made, and hopefully no need to look over the side.

In the shadow of the great hulk of the Avernus, Blimey momentarily forgot to keep kicking her legs as she strained to listen to what was going on above, and instantly she slipped back down again into the inky black. Recovering quickly she kicked her way to the surface, but couldn't keep her head above water for more than a few moments. She couldn't keep going on this way forever, she was starting to tire and she knew that the only way out of this mess was to reach her cutlass.

Remaking her way to the surface for a third time, all the while keeping her eye on Miserablesod's ship in case someone should become curious and actually check as to whether she sank or swam, Blimey worked her fingers around the sword hilt. The rope cut into the back of her arm and her hand, breaking the skin and allowing a few drops of blood to disperse into the sea. This was not good. Sharks could smell blood from over a kilometre away, and they would soon be on their way to an easy meal if she could not get free.

As she continued to struggle with her bonds Blimey thought back to her childhood and the octopus she had kept as a pet. He would have been able to get her out of this. He was smart that way for an octopus. It was now Blimey realised that she never knew what had become of her childhood pet. Perhaps he had run away? Momentarily distracted, Blimey forgot where she was and sank below the waves again. She knew she was loosing the battle, and on her next ascent to the surface she took in a deep breath with a small side of salt water. As the light of the sun hit her face, she dissolved in a fit of coughing, which made the task of kicking her legs to stay afloat even that much more difficult. This was not good. She knew it in her bones that if she went down one more time she wouldn't come up again. She was exhausted. Struggling against her own waterlogged weight, Blimey felt more than before the cold waters encircling her throat, like the hands of a would be strangler. This must be what it feels like before the end, she thought as she felt the grip tighten, then relax, then tighten again but then slowly and unexpectedly it slipped away. Not long now, she sighed, and then it would be over.

Moments continued to pass, but she managed to stay above water even though her whole body screamed out against the struggle. It was unbearable. The cold, the pain and if she just gave into oblivion it would all go away. She stopped struggling and relaxed as her body drifted down deeper and deeper into the water. As she fell into the unfathomable somehow she felt the ropes binding her begin to loosen and pull away. But this was no time to question the hows and whys of good fortune, and summoning the last threads of her strength, she wriggled out of the rope, and thrashed her way towards the pale light above.

Breaking the surface, she felt a weight on her shoulder and thinking it was the end of the rope still hanging on to her she moved her hand up to brush it away. Blimey was immediately quite shocked to find the rope actually had a living organic quality, it was cold and a little bit slimy even, but it didn't budge. Twisting her head around to see what was what, Blimey was surprised to see a small, black octopus eye staring back into hers. 'What?' she started to say, but in the blink of an eye it was gone. Had she imagined it? Had an octopus really set her free or had she wriggled out of the rope herself? Was she perhaps a bit delirious from lack of oxygen and ingestion of salt water? Blimey breathed in slowly as she tread water.

'Well, for now I need to find something to float on otherwise I won't last long out here,' she mumbled to herself, casting her eye around her.

In the distance she could see something bobbing in the water, it didn't look like much but it was worth a shot. Swimming towards it, she soon reached what turned out to be a dilapidated old raft. Pulling herself on board, Blimey collapsed in a heap. The sun felt good on her back as it dried her clothing and warmed her tired bones. Looking towards Miserablesod's ship she could see it as moving away at speed. It looked like she was safe for now. As the familiar fog of unconsciousness descended on her, Blimey noticed a piece of ratty paper and an oar tied to one of the planks on the raft.

CHAPTER FOUR

A little help

The wind blew gently against Blimey's face, picking up strands of her long red hair so they tickled her nose. Pushing herself up on her elbows she looked around. Dusk was falling, and the sun was making its journey to light up the other side of the planet. Sitting up Blimey reached up and clutched her throat, but found only the silver octopus necklace she always wore. A gift from her father, the Shaman. But the living octopus was long gone, and perhaps, she thought, she had just dreamed it. Her eye then fell to the paper and the oar tied to the raft. Reaching over she snatched up the wrinkled paper, and read the scratchy scrawl.

*A little something to help you
on your way.*

Not one to look a gift raft in the wood grain, Blimey untied the oar and surveyed her surroundings. She had a vague idea of where she had been when unceremoniously pushed overboard by her mentor, and dropping the crumpled note overboard, she was able to see which direction she had been floating in for the past few hours or so. By her figuring she would reach some kind of land eventually. It was just a matter of when. For now she would just have to go with the ocean's flow, one oar would really only be good for getting into land.

As night drew on, Blimey was starting to get slightly anxious. Drifting around in the dark on a raft was not her idea of a fun time. Looking to her right, she saw a faint glow through the darkness, the light of a distant town or a passing ship. Either way she knew she had to get there. Picking up the oar finally she began to paddle....

CHAPTER FIVE

Any port in a storm

As her driftwood raft ran aground, Blimey jumped down into the cold, shallow water and made her way up the beach, treading lightly through the soft sand. Staking the oar in the sand, she tied the raft to it with a shaggy piece of rope. She didn't know which town she was headed into, or what she would find there and so for now she wanted to keep it handy in case she had to get away.

Straightening up she brushed herself down, and started out along the beach towards the lights of the town. To her left was the dock, where several ships were tied up for the night, and to her right a care-worn sign announced she was in the port of Worster. A town that, as she got closer, seemed to be composed of mostly one main street, and not much more. Heading up the unpaved road, to her right Blimey spotted the Athwart Tavern and counting the few galleons she had in her pocket, she decided a soul-warming drink and a bite to eat would do her good.

As Blimey headed towards the Athwart, she felt the dirt road steepen slightly as if going up a gentle incline. Buildings lined either side of the street. Above the front door of each hung a sign denoting the business there. The Apothecary, baker, tailor, bookmaker, blacksmith, jeweler - all set inside quaint wooden buildings, whose doors were locked and windows were dark. Everyone had closed up shop for the day except for the Tavern, which was the only lighted building in the street. The quiet buzz of conversation and merriment could be heard drifting out towards her on a gentle night breeze.

Reaching the tavern, Blimey pulled open the heavy wooden door, her ears instantly greeted by the din of a hundred conversations. The Athwart was a well-known card den, where a scoundrel could pick up a random game any night. The main floor comprised dusty, dark varnished wood floorboards, and was covered in square tables of varying sizes, set out in no particular pattern. At each table sat an assortment of ne'ar do wells, engrossed in their cards and betting their lives away. There were regular people, Octopods, Land Anglers, the occasional Sea Bassier and a number of other sea dwelling land species. The bar itself was dark polished oak, lightly dented from the thousands of glasses slammed down on it here and there over the years. Behind the bar, on shelves stacked up to the ceiling, stood bottle after bottle of single and blended malt whiskies, bourbons, vodka, gin, brightly coloured liquors, and of course a distinguished assortment of rum, including a full range of Blimey's favourite, Varn Clankston's. The barman himself was robust and mustached, well-dressed in a stripe shirt, waistcoat, dark trousers and suspenders. A crisp white apron was tied around his waist.

Not wanting to draw attention to herself, and ignoring the weird and wonderful people that made up her surroundings, Blimey headed straight to the bar and pulled up a stool. Smiling widely she nodded to the barman.

'What'll it be pretty lady?' asked the barman returning her smile as he wandered over to where she was sitting, and began wiping down a glass with a raggedy old piece of cloth.

'I'll have a glass of Varn Clankston's Cherry Cider please, and a chicken sandwich if you'd be so kind,' she answered.

'You got it,' said the barman, placing the cherry cider in front of Blimey and yelling out the back to his cook, 'Hey Bernard! One chicken double bread, please!'

'So, how would a stranger in town set about getting on a table?' Blimey asked the barman, taking a sip of her drink and thinking a quick game or two would be a good way to pick up some extra coin while passing the time until her next Captain slash adventure made itself obvious.

'You sure you wanna get involved with the likes a these scoundrels?' asked the barman in a friendly, concerned tone, all the while smiling at Blimey with a raised eyebrow.

'I can take care of myself, but thank you for asking,' she replied, smiling back at him as she picked up her cherry cider and headed for the nearest table with what looked like an available spot.

All eyes at the table were on her as she silently took her seat, including the table itself. Blimey glanced down at the wooden face in the table-top and blinked at the pale blue eyes regarding her with mild interest from the wood there. As she sat down the table smiled her way and winked. Custom grown eye-eye tables were common place in such establishments in these perilous times, and an absolute necessity for making sure the cheats stayed away. These tables kept an eye on each of the card players and if any should be caught cheating, it raised the alarm. The last thing a bar owner needed was a massive brawl, which would result in their place being smashed to pieces. Fights were expensive.

'Hello?' suggested Blimey as she looked around at her table companions. She instantly recognised an unwelcome face from her past but as he said nothing to her, she chose to let it pass for now. There would be another time.

'Ay miss, nice a yer to join us... Who's flag you been sailing under?' offered a giant Octopedded creature named Gnash. He was quite beautiful to look at with his brown spotted skin, and powder blue tentacles, his yellow and black eyes hiding in the shadow of his bowler hat.

'Does that matter?' offered Blimey as politely as she could. She knew such questions could go either way and was trying to deter any further probing.

'No, no, just making conversation,' smiled Gnash knowingly.

'So whom I be playing with and what's your game?' asked Blimey.

'I'm Gnash, this is Captain Bessie Smith and her fiancé, Captain Blackwatch, and finally to your left is Frysk - we're playing 3 Anchors High with a minimum or equivalent.'

As Blimey received her first hand of cards, and threw in her first bet, her food arrived. Taking a bite of her sandwich thoughtfully, Blimey observed her fellow gamblers. Frysk had his hat pulled low over his eyes and hunched into his jacket, as though he was hiding from the world and not just the table, whereas Bessie was a beautiful, but hard looking woman of about 30, with long dark hair, tanned skin and sharp green eyes. She was dressed much in the same way as Blimey. Leather corset decorated with a filigree of red stitching, plain white shirt, dark wool trousers and heavy boots. Blackwatch on the other hand was tall and black-bearded, with dark eyes and a mean look. An overly regal tricorne hat sat pitched over his long black hair, which was tied back with a black ribbon and he wore a black cotton shirt over black pinstripe wool trousers, while his long leather jacket hung over the back of the chair for it was a warm evening.

Round after round of cards and cherry ciders later, and Blimey's fortunes had gone up and down, and finally evened out when the barman made his call for the last card to fall. It was now quite late after all. As this was the last hand of the night, the entire bar started making ridiculous, ill-thought bets - souls, be your slave for a day, houses and other very valuable items. Blimey's small table was no different. Gnash had put up a nice pile of galleons, Frysk a pair of steel flintlocks that 'shot more than bullets' as he slyly put it, and Bessie... well she was a little drunk.

'I'll see your John Silver and raise you my ship, the Raven, and I'll even throw in me arms and head for good measure,' she slurred ever so slightly.

'Hmph... Well that be too rich for me. I'm out,' stated Gnash.

'I too must admit defeat,' stated Frysk, before unceremoniously falling off his chair and passing out on the floor.

'Well, if ye be that sure of yer hand my love, then there be no point in challengin' you, you've never lost your head before,' said Captain Blackwatch, looking adoringly at Bessie before throwing down his cards.

'Looks like it's between you and me eh Bessie? I'll see your ship and limbs and raise you me own fine vessel. Now if you would be so kind as to show us your hand...' said Blimey, fibbing her heart out. She knew she was being overly generous in her 'ships' description, but she also had a feeling that she had the best hand out of a bad deck.

Bessie lay her cards down on the table with a flourish, so sure was she that she'd won. Blimey looked at the cards and laughed, then threw down her own cards, and it was clear she held the unbeatable hand. At that moment a chill breeze blew between the card players at the table, and Bessie's smile fell from her face. She knew what was coming next, though unfortunately Blimey didn't. As the clock struck midnight, Bessie's head toppled from her shoulders and hit the floor, followed closely by her arms. The other players at the table jumped back in alarm. No one wanted to see that. It was traumatizing.

'What is this? What's happened? I don't want her limbs, and she can keep her head – the ship'll do fine!' Blimey shouted, mortified.

'It's too late for that now, them's the rules of the game an' she knew it all too well. All bets are settled at the end of the day, and there's naught anyone can do about it. Now do yourself a favour and be off before I decide to avenge me lady, I'll see to this .... no wait you stupid Octopeed! Don't touch her arm!' shouted Blackwatch at Gnash in alarm.

But it was too late, and as Gnash bent down to pick up Bessie's arms he found out just why Blackwatch had tried to stop him. The betting of limbs, fingers and so on was quite common at the Athwart Tavern, and so some time ago a charm had been put on the tavern, which worked thus - if someone looses a bet involving a limb, when all bets were settled that limb falls off immediately, but only temporarily as of course no one really wants to make off with someone else's big toe, forefinger or left ear. After a few seconds the limbs will automatically re-attach, however for the rest of the unfortunate loser's life they will bear dark scars around the temporarily lost limb to remind them not to do such a daft thing again. Unfortunately, through some quirk of fate as Gnash happened to touch Bessie's arms, they swapped with two of his tentacles. It all happened in a flash, the tentacles attached themselves to Bessie, but luckily her own head returned to her shoulders. As for Gnash, he now had two new human arms, complete with fingers and opposable thumbs. He was none too pleased, but there was not much he could do about it, and so crossing his new arms he sat down in a huff. Bessie in turn now sported two pale blue tentacles for her troubles.

Blimey took this as her cue to leave. Moving slowly and quietly, not wanting to draw attention to herself, she casually buckled the flintlocks on to her belt, and snatched the rolled up deed to the Raven from the table top, sliding it into her back pocket. As she turned to leave, her movement finally caught the attention of Blackwatch and the re-headed newly-tentacled Bessie, who with a look to each other decided that someone was to pay for this armed mix up, and that person was going to be the lady Blimey. Blimey looked up innocently, sliding her hand around to one of her new guns. The movement was so slight, you wouldn't have noticed it unless you had been staring at her hands.

'Stop right there girl!' snapped Blackwatch.

'Now what be this treachery? I won this table fair an' square an' I want no trouble for it,' stated Blimey in consternation.

'Oh it's far too late for that m'dear. You see this is my town an' I won't see me lady made a fool of by no switch of a girl like you,' he continued.

With this statement Captain Blackwatch took a swipe at Blimey with his cutlass. Deftly she jumped out of the way, and at the same time drew one of her guns. Sizing up the room, Blimey decided that there was a time for fighting and a time for living to fight another day, but before she could take these thoughts any further, the Barman rang the closing bell, providing a split second distraction. Seizing the moment Blimey ran for the door, and with one fast glance behind her, headed out into the street and made for the dock.

CHAPTER SIX

A quick getaway

Reaching the dock, Blimey wasted no time in heading straight for the Raven. It wasn't hard to find. As the moon peeked out from behind the clouds, she stopped for the briefest moment and in that second drank in every detail. The ship itself was made of the darkest mahogany, stained almost black. Years of sailing meant that it was a little worse for wear in places but she was still a beauty. Following the curve of the bow upwards her eyes fixed on the giant black bird carved out of the wood. Its mouth open in an angry red scream it screeched into the dark swollen sky as its wings furled down the sides of the ship. As her eyes followed one wing along the ship she could just make out the deep blood-red of the sails.

This quiet admiration of her latest acquisition was cut short as the angry roar of an enraged mob made its way toward her on the breeze. Taking the gangplank at a sprint and hauling it up behind her, Blimey ran to the helm and slammed her palm down on a round black button. Immediately the mooring line began to reel itself in, freeing her from the dock. Over the sound of the waves sloshing at the sides of the Raven, she could hear the rumblings of Blackwatch and his angry mob as they made their way down to the dock, and she could only assume they were not coming to throw her a casting off party.

Grasping the beautiful wooden helm she looked over the rectangular panel next to it, taking a second or two to get herself acquainted with the configuration, she pressed the button to retract the anchor. A further series of buttons then unfurled the sails and prepared the ship for sea. It was almost the standard for all ships to have these computerized conveniences fitted these days, as not every Captain wanted nor could afford to carry a crew. Everything could be managed

31

from a control panel next to the helm, from manning the cannons to raising the sails. Navigation was also a snap with the ship being able to follow any coordinates set, though right now the only destination Blimey had in mind was away from here. There was one catch. While her new ship was one of the best-outfitted ships on the Severed Seas, it was still reliant on the wind for power. The success of her escape now lay in the hands of the wind Gods.

Luck was on her side tonight and the wind suddenly picked up a gale. She knew that if she could get out of the harbour before Blackwatch got to his ship he'd be loathe to sail out of the bay in harsh weather, and the water was already beginning to work itself into a frenzy. As the ship made its way out of the bay on angry waves, the Raven's new Captain looked back, the wind whipping her hair around her face as it continued it's violent assault on everything it touched. She could vaguely make out a group of figures rushing to one of the ships, while another who towered over them all cursed the sky with a shaken fist. It seemed for a moment that Blackwatch might just be mad enough to follow her. It was true that she had a pretty good head start, and the Raven was a fast ship by all accounts, but she also didn't know enough about Blackwatch's own ship to make any assumptions in regards to her escape. Not wanting to be caught off guard, Blimey began to prepare the ship for battle, punching in the sequence on the control panel to remotely man the ship's guns and cannons. Just in case.

Moments passed in tense expectation, as Blimey sailed further out onto the open ocean. She could only wait to see what happened next. The ill wind continued to blow, but tonight the luck of the devil was surely on Blimey's side as the storm changed direction, altering her course by a sharp 35 degrees. The ship lurched violently on the waves as the sails whipped angrily. Gripping the helm with all her might in one hand, she stabbed at buttons on the control panel, altering the turn on the sails slightly. All the better catch the wind and stabilize the Raven. She may not have had an engine to drive the ship, but from the helm she could harness the wind from any direction she needed.

Looking back towards where she had come from, she realized that this sudden change in weather would be enough to ensure Blackwatch would have a hard time getting out of the hooked curve of the bay, giving her a good head start. All she wanted to do now was sail as far away as possible, and hope that if she ever saw Blackwatch or Bessie again, they had calmed down a bit.

Out on the open ocean, the moon glowed brightly in the sky as it found another break in the clouds. The wild wind continued to buffet the ship from side to side, and the sea seemed to roar like trapped dragon. Water sprayed over the deck, while fat drops of rain began to fall from the sky. Blimey gripped the helm and steered the ship on, a smile spreading across her face as she fought with the sea and sky to keep control of the Raven. Nothing could alarm her now though, and every sense in her body was thrilling to the freedom of being out on the sea, in command of her own ship. To go from near death to Captain of your own ship within a matter of hours was unthinkable, yet it had happened.

She sailed on through the night until lack of sleep began to take its toll. As the dawn began to break and the sky glowed orange, she knew she would need to set anchor somewhere soon or risk falling asleep at the wheel. Getting her bearings, she realized she was only about a half hours sail from the little island of Evileen, a place she had not been for a long time and for good reason.

Evileen was a gnarly port, attracting only the worst type of scum and villainy, but it would also be the last place anyone would look for her. Pulling into the dock, she dropped anchor and went to see the portmaster to pay the docking fee and request she be left alone. Dropping some coins into the palm of his hand, she thanked him quickly and then turned back to her ship, hanging a Do Not Disturb sign on the mooring post as she passed it. Dragging herself back up the gangplank of the Raven, she turned to her right and stomped up the stairs to the Captain's quarters. Flopping down on the bed she grabbed at the thin woolen blanket at the end of the bed and pulled it across herself, falling asleep as soon as her head hit the pillow.

Blimey woke in the late afternoon, with the sun streaming in through the window. She sat up and took a long luxurious stretch. She had slept in her clothes so there was no need to change or dress. Pirates rarely slept in pjyamas, it always paid to be on your toes. Getting out of bed she wandered out into the sun and raised her hands to the sky. It was such a nice warm day. Down on the main deck she turned sharply left and pulled open the hatch that led below decks, and skipped down the stairs. As her eyes adjusted to the gloom, it was obvious to her that Bessie hadn't been spending too much time aboard the ship lately. Dust had settled everywhere – where had the dust even come from! Heading down the dark hallway, she turned right into the galley, looking for coffee and a bite to eat. She was immediately aware that she hadn't had time yet to take stock of her new ship, and she was pretty sure Bessie was not the type who would keep life's essentials on hand. Looking through each of the cupboards, and the chill box, it soon became obvious she had been right about Bessie. There was nothing on the shelves except a jar of instant coffee and an open packet of crisps. Not exactly appetizing. Sighing to herself she knew she would have to go into Evileen for supplies. This might be the last chance she would have for a while and so it would not make sense to miss the opportunity just because she wanted to avoid the town. Thanks to her win the previous night she now had plenty of cash to spend.

Turning on her heel she stopped in the doorway and looked up and down the hall. The will to go exploring was overwhelming, but she also knew that given the lateness of the day she had better get her butt into town, and to the shops before they shut. Sighing in disappointment, she stalked back up stairs and out of the hatch into the sun again.

Out on the deck she took a moment to drink in the beauty of her ship in the light of day. She had heard many tales about the Raven, aside from it being one of the fastest and most well equipped ships on the Severed Seas. The railing was ornately fixed, with each bolster carved to look like an Octopus tentacle, while the main rail around the ship featured the crossed bones at 30cm intervals. Each of the three masts, though worn, had been carved to look as though each had been hewn from sea dragon scales. The sails themselves were blood red with a black skull and cross bones visible on the first of the main sails. Throughout the ship were hidden swords and daggers, placed at what Blimey guessed were strategic points, laid on just in case some scoundrel managed to corner one of the crew during a battle. Looking over the side Blimey could see the cannons were at the moment hidden, but could tell where they would make an appearance when needed as a menacing skull marked their hatches. Finally she came to the bow, where she could see the wondrous head of the giant carved black bird, with it's wings outstretched, spreading down each side of the ship. The Raven truly was, by all accounts, an ocean bound beauty.

Walking down the gangplank, she tipped her hat to the portmaster, and explained she was going into town to get some supplies, before she would be headed back out to sea. The portmaster nodded as she walked by. He was not used to such courtesy and appreciated it. Blimey turned left as she reached the end of the dock, and headed for the town's centre. It was just as she remembered it. The small city spanned out from the dock, which was the centre of town life. The buildings were set close together, tall and slightly rickety, for it was an old place. The city smelled of life and not necessarily the good parts. It was at turns musty, and out of the open spaces where the wisps of breeze could flow you could smell the sea. Turning through the tiny streets, she kept her wits about her as she headed for Carbunkle's General Store. At least the old man would be pleased to see her, he never forgot a face - especially the face of those small few who had ever beaten him at chess. Reaching the store, she marched through the doors and straight up to the counter, and smiled down at the sleepy face that greeted her. Mr Carbunkle suffered from narcolepsy, a condition that caused him to fall asleep at random moments. No one would have dreamed of stealing from the store though. Carbunkle's loyal blue macaw saw to that. Not only could the thing screech and yell like there was no tomorrow, but it had a little gun of it's very own that Carbunkle had taught it to fire. It wasn't enough to kill, but it would give you one hell of a sting.

Blimey bowed ever so slightly and said hello to the parrot, who cawed in reply, as she gently shook Mr Carbunkle's shoulder to wake him. Sitting up slowly, Carbunkle looked at the girl who had woken him, his sleep weary face breaking in to a smile as he recognized her.

'Well I'll be a sunken treasure, Blimey in'it?'

'That's right,' she replied with a smile.

'What can I do for you?'

'I've just come into my own command, but I need supplies. I also happen to be dying for a coffee... Do you have anything you can recommend?'

'Well congratulations my young Captain. I'm sure I can rustle you up a cup of the black stuff. You start rounding up what you need and I'll be back in a minute.'

'Thanks, I'd like that,' replied Blimey turning towards the shelves and racks of clothing behind her. Carbunkle really did keep a well-stocked store, and as she fingered the gold in her pocket she thanked lady luck profusely.

Twenty minutes later she had amassed quite a pile of stores and equipment on the counter. Aside from the food, she took the chance to pick up some new clothes, including some new boots (that came up just below the knee, steel-capped round toe, delicious black leather with a small chunky heel and large buckle on the side at the top of the boot), a couple of shirts and singlet's, and she also picked out a pair of leather brocade trousers in a dark blue and a pair in black. Next she grabbed a new hard leather armored corset, dark brown, which laced up the front. This one had a silver metal octopus coming up from over the left hip, it's tentacles winding up across the front. Finally she picked up an armored sleeve, also in dark brown to match the corset. It buckled over her right arm in 4 places, with a further final piece that went over the shoulder and bucked around the neck.

She then picked out a beautiful wet-stone for sharpening her cutlass and dagger, some lengths of rope, and a new compass that fastened to a leather band she could wear on her wrist like a watch. Next, looking down at the flintlocks she had won in the card game, which were now at her side, she knew she should also get some bullets. She pulled one out of its holster and looked at it properly for the first time. She had never seen anything quite like it before. They didn't seem to be made to take conventional bullets at all. As she was trying to figure out how to open the thing, Mr Carbunkle returned with the coffee.

'What you got there?' he asked, seeing the perplexed look on her face.

'I thought they were a pair of flintlocks, but now I don't really know what they are. I'm normally pretty good at figuring this stuff out, but I've never seen these before. I won them in a card game,' she explained.

'Can I see them?'

'Of course,' she smiled, handing the guns over, and watching as Carbunkle looked them over quickly before pressing one of the little silver skulls in the handle. The gun then neatly split in two, exposing its inner workings.

'Oh my!' he exclaimed, his face lighting up, 'you've scored well there lass. These are very special guns indeed, and very rare. Only the Thirteen Bones ever carried these. Rarely need new ammunition these, but it be hard to find it once you run out. Ha! Lucky for you I just happen to have what you need in stock,'

'But why are they so special?' asked Blimey, intrigued.

'Come out the back and I'll show you. We need a bit of room for this one,' smiled Carbunkle, walking out the back and grabbing a small box on his way past. Blimey followed him, looking back to make sure the parrot had an eye on the store. Walking through the shop, and on through the small house Carbunkle called home, once they were out the back Blimey found herself in a large, overgrown yard.

'Now watch this very carefully Miss, as I'm only going to show yer once. These things cause too much of a kerfuffle as it is an' I don't want the locals to think there's some kinda to-do over at ol' Carbunkle's,' he said, taking a small silver ball from the little box he had picked up on his way out and loading the gun. Then aiming carefully at a stack of ale bottles sitting on a rough wooden table next to his smoking chair in the garden, he pulled the trigger. A small green spark appeared next to the gun barrel, and Carbunkle let out a loud whoop as he knew what was coming next. A small red ball flew out of the muzzle, a tiny spark from a tiny fuse in the ball just visible in the fading light of the afternoon. As the bullet hit the bottles it exploded in a flash of flame and a puff of smoke.

'Cherry bombs!' yelled Mr Carbunkle, doing a little jig in delight, 'I haven't fired one of these in many a year. You wouldn't want to sell these here bazookas to me now would you?' he asked hopefully, raising an eyebrow.

'Sorry Carbunkle, not on your life now I've never seen what they can do! These I plan on keeping,' Blimey laughed.

'Spoken like a true pirate,' smiled Carbunkle, handing over the shooter as they walked back into the shop, 'look I'll give ye the last of me stock of bullets for 'em – but one box I have is right spesh – a box a stun pellets. They won't kill anyfink, but they'll knock 'em right out. Sometimes you need to leave someone alive to answer questions,' he winked.

'So they can fire different ammunition then?'

'Oh yes, and you can even put in a few different types at once, and if you turn this here dial on the side, you can select what you want 'em to fire – cherry bombs, stun pellets, regular bullets, knock out gas, poison gas, tiny arrows and it'll even shoot out a thin wire rope for lassoing folks – I'll give you ammunition for all.'

'Wow! They really are special then, but which fires what on the dial?'

'I'll write it down for ya, but essentially it's like this – the star for cherry bombs, the lightening bolt for stunning folks, the skull for poison gas, the X for regular bullets, the cloud for knock out gas, the arrow for the arrows and the infinity loop for the rope.'

'Lots to remember, but still amazing,' marveled Blimey, 'how does it all work?'

'Gallifreyan technology, Gandalf magic,' answered Carbunkle moving back behind the store counter, 'I'm not rightly sure, but I don't tend to question something if it works for me.'

'Good advice,' smiled Blimey as she reached the other side of the counter, 'now what do I owe you?'

After Blimey paid for her supplies, including the boxes of ammunition for her new guns, she hoisted as much as she could carry in a pack and slung it over her back. Leaning over the counter she kissed Mr Carbunkle on the cheek and thanked him for his help, promising to come back again and say hello one day. Mr Carbunkle in turn promised to have the rest of her purchases promptly delivered to her ship. He knew Evileen was not the sort of place she would want to hang around, and couldn't blame her. Thanking Mr Carbunkle, Blimey headed out the door, stopping only to turn back and wave to her old friend and his parrot.

CHAPTER SEVEN

Betty hates Veronica

On her way back towards the Raven with the sun low in the sky, Blimey stalked past the Tired Axolotl Tavern. Crossing her arms and shivering as she passed under a shadow, something caught her eye in the yard down the side of the building. Crouching in the corner under a makeshift shelter was a girl, her long white hair slightly matted and grey with dirt. Her clothes a little more than rags. As Blimey approached the girl, she scuttled back into the shadows further, clearly afraid of contact with people. It was then that Blimey saw she was chained to a pole in the yard, which - as Blimey followed her line of sight upwards - was crossed by another pole at about shoulder height to form a large T. On each arm of the letter T were metal locking wrist cuffs, and as Blimey looked more closely at the girl she could see the tell tale signs these cuffs had left round the girls wrists. It did not take much imagination for her to piece together the scene in her head, which was only too soon confirmed when the girl turned her back to her and several large red welts were visible on her back through her torn clothing. A small sign nearby even promoted the Tavern's favourite form of entertainment – Whip the Girl, 3 Lashes for a Piece of Silver.

Blimey felt her blood begin to boil as the colour rose to her cheeks like she had just eaten a small garden full of hot peppers. Growling in guttural anger, Blimey let her breath out slowly in a low hiss, her temper barely hanging on by a thread. She knew what she had to do. She could not stand by and see the disgusting treatment of this beautiful creature continue.

With her face set in a grimace of fury, Blimey turned abruptly and stormed off round the side of the building, slamming through the doors of the Tired Axolotl. Inside she was met with a cacophony of noise as the bar's early evening crowd settled in for a night of wine, beer and song with the occasional fight thrown in for good measure. The barman watched the angry woman approaching him with a vague smile and an air of amusement. Trouble often came calling at this bar, but as the barman knew trouble also found itself immediately and unceremoniously kicked out the door again - much to the delight of the locals. So when Blimey approached him and bluntly stated she would be removing his star attraction, the barman openly laughed in her face. Blimey bristled. She had expected an argument, but not ridicule. The barman in turn felt he had the upper hand and so nothing to fear. He was about to find out just how wrong he was about a lot of things.

'I don't see why you think this is so amusing, you must know I am perfectly serious or are you simply to stupid to figure it out? I am taking the girl and you can accept it graciously or suffer the consequences,' she reiterated in a voice so low and calm it was frightening.

'Oh I can see you are serious, but there is no way a waif like you is taking my Betty away, the patrons will be most upset,' smiled the barman, indicating to the whole room with a sweep of his hand. At this movement there was a mass scraping of chair legs on the floor behind her, and what seemed like the entire bar got to its feet to back up the barman.

'You see?' he continued with a smirk, 'and now most unfortunately for you, I think you will have to either join her out there in the dirt, or die. What is it to be?'

Blimey sighed. She had warned him, and he had ignored her. Why did these men always feel that they had the upper hand? As if she would just bow down and accept her fate as the new whipping toy. Slowly she turned to face the angry mob behind her, using the few precious moments before anything happened to size up her opponents. Absently she patted one of the flintlocks at her side, grateful for it's comforting weight, though she hoped she would not need to use them as shooting wasn't really her style.

'Get her!' yelled the barman suddenly.

Blimey did not flinch. In a blur of fists and cutlasses, they came at her with everything they had. However things don't always go as planned, and several yelps of surprise could be heard as one by one the miscreants in the bar fell heavily to the floor. Amidst the settling dust of broken furniture and spilt drinks, blood and the moans of the wounded, Blimey turned back to face the barman. The only man left standing in the room. Looking him up and down in disdain, she wondered what he would do now, every nerve in her body tingling with adrenalin as she made ready to fight to the last. The barman in turn took one look at all the bloodied bodies on the floor, and shaking with fear, anger and humiliation he threw a set of keys at the pirate girl before turning towards the back of the bar and making a run for it out the door. Blimey let him go. She had what she wanted and she also felt it couldn't do any harm for him to spread this story and stake her reputation as a pirate you did not mess with.

Putting the keys in her pocket, Blimey grabbed a bar rag lying on the counter and wiped down her cutlass before putting it back in it's sheath. A pirate always made sure their weapons were in good, clean working order. Without a backward glance, she headed back outside to retrieve the girl.

Rounding the corner of the building, she approached the alley down the side, where she could just make out the girl hiding in the shadows. The young girl watch fearfully as Blimey approached, tears welling in her pale, almond-shaped eyes. She knew what was coming next, and in silent acceptance she tensed in expectation of the sharp bite the whip would bring. But the sting never came and instead Blimey reached under the girl's arms and lifted her to her feet, where she swayed a little but didn't utter a sound. Blimey reached into her pocket and pulled out the barman's keys, shaking them out and choosing the one that looked like it would fit best. As she twisted the key in the lock it cracked open with a click, and Blimey gently removed the metal collar from around the girl's neck. As she dropped it, the chain clattered to the ground, leaving the girl free for the first time in as long as she could remember. The girl rubbed her neck slowly. It was red and raw from where the metal collar had chaffed against it. Looking up at the woman who had released her, the girl smiled so brightly that it lit up the dark, and then she fainted, crumpling in a heap on the ground. Not wanting to waste time in case the barman managed to rustle up some more men to follow her, Blimey bent down and lifted up the girl in one movement, hoisting her up over her shoulder. Shifting her feet under the weight, she turned away from the tavern and started off towards the docks. It was time to get out of this town.

Running as fast as she could with the girl over her shoulder and the pack of supplies on her back, Blimey made for the dock, just hoping that Mr Carbunkle had been able to get her goods delivered to her ship. If not she wagered she may have to leave them behind. The important thing was to get the girl away safely. Without a glance at anyone around the dock, Blimey bolted up the gangplank, noticing happily that a number of parcels, boxes and barrels we're sitting on the deck. Mr Carbunkle had been as good as his word. Then she noticed the note, tied to a soft, old and worn dark leather jacket, which had been thrown over one of the barrels on the deck. Lowering the girl gently and placing her on the wood of the deck, Blimey snatched off the note, and read it as fast as her eyeballs would move across the page.

Well my lady it seems you haven't changed a bit. Be kind to the girl, Betty hates Veronica, as she has been through much. But nay tarry no longer as the town has been alerted to occurrences at the Tired Axolotl and the barman is rounding up a posse to come for you. Hopefully our paths will cross again soon
– your friend, Adelaide Carbunkle

'Betty hates Veronica?' Blimey whispered under her breath, looking down at the unconscious girl, 'well there's no time to query that now, we better get out of here,' and leaving Betty on the deck she rushed to the helm and soon had the Raven sailing out into the open ocean.

When she felt they were a safe enough distance out to sea, Blimey set the ship on an even course and went to check on her charge. The girl was still dead to the world and so Blimey gently lifted her off the deck and carried her downstairs to the First Mates quarters, where she placed her on the bed. Pulling a blanket over the girl, she turned to leave, closing the door quietly behind her before heading back up on deck to have a glass of whisky and watch the sun set. Pulling on the jacket that Carbunkle had left her to guard against the evening chill, she marveled at how perfectly it fit, and promised herself she would go back to thank the old man as soon as she could.

CHAPTER EIGHT

A pirate's worth

That had been three years ago to the day, and as Betty hates Veronica had recovered from her wounds they became firm friends, with Betty hates Veronica eventually asking if she could stay on and become the ship's First Mate. Blimey of course accepted at once, and over time Blimey had trained her to fight with fists, sword and flintlock, and with the long dagger, which was now Betty hates Veronica's favourite weapon. She had also learned how to run the ship, and the two lasses had become a force to be reckoned with on the Severed Seas. As a result they often received regular random challenges from na'er do wells and pirates alike.

Blimey stepped away from the helm of the Raven, which was leisurely sailing through the calm and misty seas, and turned on the auto-pirate. The auto-pirate was a fairly new addition to the Raven. Blimey had never been one to trust entirely in technology, but she was also tired of spilling her coffee while she tried to steer the Raven on its chosen course. The auto-pirate also freed up Betty's time, so they could spend time together and enjoy their friendship rather than sticking to ship bound protocol.

The ships speed was a steady 20 bows (girls don't sail in knots, they sail in bows, remember that) and for the moment not another ship could be seen on the horizon. Blimey skipped down the steps from the helm and joined Betty hates Veronica on the main deck.

'Would you mind taking a look around?' she asked Betty H.V handing her the spyglass. Something didn't feel quite right, and though she couldn't see anything approaching them herself, she wanted a second pair of eyes on the matter.

Betty Hates Veronica took the telescope and made a sweeping circle of the ship. She couldn't see anything out of the ordinary either, but she now shared the bad feeling that her Captain had about this. Absently she pushed back on the leather and brass goggles she was wearing over her leather aviator cap, and looked up at Blimey. She shook her head and shrugged her shoulders, causing strands of her white hair to be picked up by the breeze and blow about her face. It was at that moment that an annoying bleeping sound started emanating from the helm.

'Damn! What is it now?' asked Blimey.

'Well unless you actually take a look you'll never know, it sounds like the radar picked up something,' stated Betty H.V matter of factly.

'Thanks for the tip,' called Blimey over her shoulder as she ran back up the stairs to the helm deck and looked over the control panel next to the helm.

'Looks like we've got trouble heading our way!' called out Blimey as Betty hates Veronica turned to see what the news would be.

'What is it?' she asked. It seemed like a natural question.

'Looks to be a strange ship in the vicinity, from the signal it could be ......' Blimey trailed off.

'Could be .... what?' asked Betty hates Veronica, concern entering her question half way through.

'I thought .... no, no it can't be that, anyway we'll find out soon enough, it's coming in pretty quick,' replied Blimey, and she was right.

Moments passed tensely in expectation, and then over the horizon came a ship flying a strange flag. It looked like two crossed scalpels under a stethoscope. Blimey and Betty H.V both stood by the helm as the ship approached. The Captain of the strange ship hailed them.

'Ahoy! You there! We have come for your medical supplies!'

'What do you want?' yelled back Blimey in consternation.

'Your medical supplies!' repeated the Captain.

'Who the hell are you?' returned Blimey.

'I am Doctor Mean,' replied the strange Captain as his ship coasted along side the Raven, 'and we urgently need your medical supplies.'

'Why?' asked Blimey, suspiciously. No ship ever attacked another simply for its medical supplies, but she would let this play out a little longer.

'Um......" trailed off Doctor Mean. He honestly had not been expecting that question.

'Not the right answer,' said Blimey, 'now what do you really want?'

'Ok, fine, we have come for you, I mean to say we've been sent to bring you in, there's a large bounty on your head and I want to claim it,' replied Doctor Mean.

'A bounty? What in the name of Copernicus? Who put this bounty on my head?' asked Blimey, genuinely confused. Surely she had not become that notorious.

'How the hell should I know?' countered Doctor Mean angrily, 'but YOU are both coming with me!'

'What makes you think it'll be that easy? Why would we simply come with you? You think just because we're women we're a pushover?' asked Betty H.V stepping forward menacingly as her voice rose in anger, her cutlass drawn.

'Ah look... Just come quietly and everything will be fine,' Doctor Mean said soothingly, suddenly losing confidence and trying to change tack. He seemed to realize that he was now only a few seconds away from loosing complete control of the situation.

'Never!' shouted Blimey as she and Betty hates Veronica swung aboard the Doctor's ship.

Doctor Mean's crew immediately decided they wanted not a bar of this craziness and simply backed away from the two girls. They weren't getting paid enough gold to be willing to die for it. Doctor Mean had promised them an easy catch and when it looked like this wasn't going to happen, they simply couldn't be bothered, and went off to take turns sipping from a rum bottle at the other end of the ship, away from the confrontation. Nodding to the crew, Blimey advanced on their Captain and soon had him pinned up against the main mast.

'Cowards!' called Doctor Mean to his crew, who diligently ignored him.

'Who sent you?' demanded Blimey, her cutlass at his throat.

'I can't tell you,' replied Doctor Mean.

'Of course you can, and you will or your fate will await you at the bottom of the sea,' replied Blimey viciously.

'Fine, what do I care really, as long as I get out of here, it was Captain James Blade. He's looking for you,' answered Doctor Mean with a sigh.

'Blade? But I haven't seen him in over a year.... What would he want to hunt me down for....' Blimey trailed off.

'I don't know, but judging by that look on your face I'm sure we'll be finding out quite soon,' piped up Betty H.V.

'When you see him, you tell that bastard Blade I'm coming for him,' growled Blimey, and knocked Doctor Mean out.

'Time to go?' suggested Betty hates Veronica and together they jumped back aboard the Raven. Running for the helm she looked at the map laid out on a small table. She was looking for the nearest port, which happened to be Worster. The way Blimey saw it, Blade had known exactly where she would be and had sent Doctor Mean out directly to bring her back. That meant he must have been following her for a while, and it also meant that he wouldn't be too far away.

CHAPTER NINE

Even Worster trouble

The Raven docked hard against the short pier. Blimey cursed under her breath, she hadn't meant to pull the ship in so fast but she was in a hurry. Someone she had once been close to had put a price on her head and she needed to find out why. Betty hates Veronica joined her by the helm and they both looked at the port of Worster together in silence. Blimey adjusted her heavy weapon's belt over her fitted black leather brocade trousers, and as she looked towards the town, absently twisted the leather laces of her skull stitched corset, which was worn over a simple white singlet as the day was warm. Beside her Betty hates Veronica was wearing a sleeveless shirt under a black leather corset that did up the front with a series of silver buckles. Her dark blue pin stripe trousers were tucked into chunky black boots that came nearly to the knee. She had customized the right boot recently so that she could sheath her favourite dagger on the outside of it. On her head she wore her favourite leather aviator skullcap and her leather and brass goggles. She liked to have those with her at all times for the days when the sun was too bright. Her pale eyes were quite sensitive, and she found the dark tint of the goggles helped. Plus at night she could turn them on to infrared and see in the dark, which was always handy.

Looking at each other for a moment, neither of them needed to say anything. For some strange reason fate had brought Blimey back to this evil little town and it made the two girls uneasy.

'Where to?' asked Betty H.V.

'The Athwart Tavern,' Blimey replied with a sigh, and together they walked down the gangplank to the wooden dock. Turning left, they headed towards the town, trudging on with a feeling of dread weighing heavily on their shoulders.

It only being late afternoon, the Athwart was fairly empty when Blimey pushed hard on the heavy front door, and stomped in. There were no need for niceties in this place and so she headed straight for the new barman. Betty hates Veronica wandered in slowly after her, and stood silently in the background taking in the details of the bar in case anything bad went down. Windows, doors, chairs, tables, available weapons. Check, check, check, check and sadly none to be seen.

'Where's Blade?' Blimey got right to the point.

'You must be that Blimey bird, we was told you'd be showin' up here,' answered the barman. They didn't get too many women in the bar at this time of day, so it was a fair guess.

'Yes I'm that "Blimey bird", now where is he?' Blimey repeated her question coldly.

'Ha! Feisty... He's in the back room, back there to the left,' smiled the barman hoisting his thumb over his shoulder in the direction of away.

'Fine..... Betty H.V, you wait here, you'll be OK won't you?' asked Blimey of her First Mate.

'Sure, you know I will,' smiled Betty H.V reaching down and taking her favourite dagger out of her boot, and stabbing it fiercely into the bar top in a deliberate display of don't mess with me.

Blimey smiled at her friend and strolled out towards the back of the bar, shortly reaching a dirty wooden door. She didn't bother to knock, storming straight in. There he was, lounging in a plush leather chair in a corner. His long brown hair hung in strands around his face, which looked like it could do with some sleep. He was dressed in a white shirt, unbuttoned past his collarbone, under a dark blue leather vest that hung open. His heavy dark wool trousers were tucked into a pair of dark, jaunty leather boots and he looked every part the rouge that he was. The lazy afternoon sun broke from behind a cheeky cloud, and streamed in through the open window, passing its beams over an ornate table on which sat a bottle of red wine with two glasses. The sun was chased by a subtle breeze, slightly salted, that cleared the stale air of the room.

'I knew you'd come here looking for me,' stated Blade, getting to his feet and crossing to the table. Uncorking the wine he poured its luscious velvety redness into the two glasses.

'Yes, I suppose you did, Blade,' replied Blimey, 'but what I don't understand is why you would put a bounty on my head …. Or where you even got the money to do so…' she trailed off.

'Oh that, well, that was nothing, a joke, a laugh, I didn't really have the cash,' explained Blade passing her one of the glasses but no longer looking so smug.

'A joke?' she asked, taking a sip of the wine before grimacing at its tart flavour. Suddenly she threw the glass against the wall in anger and frustration, as she exploded at the man standing in front of her.

'You really are an infuriating twit Blade! I came here to kill you! Did you know that? Maybe I should just kill you, how do I know you're telling the truth? That idiot Doctor Mean was planning to kill us!'

'No, he wouldn't have dared, I paid him to bring you in alive,' justified Blade.

'With what money? You didn't have any cash remember? What does that even mean? I have enemies you know, enemies who would be more than happy to see my head on a spike in Scoundrels Alley!' countered Blimey.

'I'd never want to see your head on a spike,' smiled Blade sheepishly as he stepped forward casually, brushing his hand against her cheek and leaning in for a kiss.

'Oh no you don't Blade, that was a long time ago, I have no intention of being sucked into that tractor beam again. What are you really up to?' she asked as she deftly smacked his hand away and dodged his affections.

'Ouch,' smiled Captain Blade, turning away and looking guilty.

'Blade, just tell me why you are sending these miscreants to kidnap me,' asked Blimey exasperated, taking the now empty seat and picking up the other glass of wine, taking a swig.

'Look, I just wanted to see you again, and I knew that if I sent word to you, you wouldn't answer after what I did last time, so I figured this way you couldn't avoid me,' answered Blade finally. He was staring at the floor unable to look Blimey in the eye.

'Blade, what do you want me to say? First you left me high and dry at Portfino, then you stole my ship and tried to trade the Raven for a wheel barrow…. I nearly lost her, if Betty H.V hadn't found you in time I'd have been left sailing around someone's garden right now!' replied Blimey.

'I know, I made a mistake, but I miss you,' said Blade quietly, scuffing the toe of his boot on the floor and looking genuinely sorry, but he had played his last card out of hand.

'That may be the case Blade, but right now I need to get out of this place, and I'm taking you with me until I can figure out how to deal with you, come on,' decided Blimey and grabbed Blade by the wrist, dragging him out into the bar and picking up Betty hates Veronica on the way to the door.

'What's he coming with us for?' asked Betty H.V coldly.

'That's what I'm still trying to figure out,' replied Blimey grimly. But she knew that if Blade was that desperate to find her there was a lot more to the story, and she wanted to find out what that was.

Once back on board the Raven, Captain Blade plonked himself down in one of the comfy chairs in the Captain's lounge, a glass of chilled white wine held loosely in his right hand, his left was hung gracelessly over the arm of the chair. Blimey wandered into the room and sat down across from Blade. She hated white wine, and wondered where he had brought it from. She didn't normally allow it on the ship.

'Hi there pretty lady,' Blade greeted her.

'Can it Blade, I know you're in trouble again, so just tell me what you've done this time and we'll get you out of it,' stated Blimey

'Hey, hey, hey, relax. It's all under control, don't worry about it,' replied Blade.

'You're an infuriating fool Blade! It is not under control at all if you have to put a bounty on my head so I will come and find you!' challenged Blimey.

'Oh that, I thought we'd moved on from that situation,' replied Blade, looking down at the floor awkwardly.

'No, we haven't,' sighed Blimey, '... what am I going to do with you Blade? You keep popping up in my life, causing havoc and then disappearing. I can't have it.'

'Uh, yeah, sorry.....' Blade trailed off.

'So what happened this time?' continued Blimey.

'It was these guys see, we were playing cards nice and casual like and then we started playing for ships, you know the score, that's how you ended up with this baby isn't it,' explained Blade, gesturing to the Raven.

'We're focusing on your problem right now if you please, now let me guess, you were drinking that spiced rum again?' asked Blimey.

'Ah, yeah I suppose I was, and ... well not that it matters now anyway, because I lost,' replied Blade.

'So who has your ship?' asked Blimey.

'Doctor Mean,' said Blade simply.

'But you sent him after me you idiot! Why couldn't you just get it back from him?' asked Blimey.

'Well, he wouldn't take a cheque from me, and I thought if I sent him after you that you'd kill him and then ... well, problem solved!' finished Blade.

'So that's what you see me as? Some kind of convenient mercenary?' sighed an exhausted Blimey. Blade could be very tiring with his constant jaunts and capers.

'No, ah no it wasn't really like that!' justified Blade, 'I knew you'd come after me when you'd finished off Mean.'

'Oh really,' smiled Blimey, 'figured we'd have a little reunion did you? Ha! I don't think of you that way anymore Blade, too many broken promises and broken hearts left in your wake, but now we still have the problem of getting your ship back.'

'Sorry honey,' replied Blade, who knew he had hurt Blimey more times than he should, 'you know I appreciate you helping me.'

'Don't call me honey, and don't worry,' she said, 'I'll get your ship back, but then you best be on your way I think. I can't do this anymore with you Blade. It's too hard.'

She got up suddenly and stalked out of the room before anything like her old feelings for him got in the way. However Blade himself, though confused, was undaunted. True he had not thought the situation would play out this way, but he still felt he could win Blimey over and back into his arms sooner or later. Blimey meanwhile had headed straight up to the helm to where Betty hates Veronica was staring stonily at the sea.

'So?' asked Betty H.V. a bit too haughtily.

'We have to get his ship back, and that is all,' answered Blimey sternly, picking up on her friend's disapproval.

'Good. I don't like him, and I don't know what you ever saw in him,' replied Betty hates Veronica.

'I know you don't, because you're a good friend, and to be

51

honest I don't know what I saw in him either, but the sooner we find his ship the sooner we can send him on his way.... he brings up bad memories,' replied Blimey, folding her arms and rubbing them against the chill that just rolled over her bones. Turning to the navigation computer she began to plot their course, and then they were off once more to find Doctor Mean.

CHAPTER TEN

To catch a crook

'Found him!' shouted Betty hates Veronica triumphantly some time later, 'I took the ship's signature, which we had captured earlier, and triangulated it against his last known location.'

'Excellent, nice thinking, where is he?' asked Blimey

'Off the coast or Beighe.'

'Damn it! I hate that town, everything is so dull and boring, and no one seems to have any fun at all,' sighed Blimey before turning to Captain Blade, who had made his way up on to the deck at last. 'Mean is in Beighe, are you sure you're ready for this? It's a tough town, boring, but tough.'

'Sure Blimey, you know me, I'm ready for anything,' replied Blade flicking his hair out of his face with a roguish grin.

'That's what worries me most.'

Taking the helm roughly Blimey turned her ship towards Beighe, home to the more conservative miscreants, criminals and general nasties. It would take a number of hours to get there from their current position.

On they sailed, through the evening and into the night. The weather stayed fair as the waves crested beneath the bow of the Raven. The salt wind felt good on their faces, and for a moment they forgot they were headed for trouble. At around 1am they set the ship to auto-pirate and went to get some sleep. Dawn would be on them all to quickly, and they needed to make sure they were rested and prepared for anything. As the sun rose, Blimey skipped up on to the deck in time to see Beighe coming into view. They sailed into port and moored the Raven next to what Blimey recognised immediately as Blade's ship, the Nevermore. As she dropped anchor and set about brewing up a fresh pot of coffee, her shipmates stirred from their slumber and one by one joined her on deck.

'There she is!' cried Blade, a large smile breaking across his handsome face as he stepped bleary eyed out into the sun and spotted his ship.

Blimey couldn't help but smile at his childish joy. She understood what it was like to see your own ship from afar, and the feeling of freedom it inspired.

'Yes, but we can't just take her Blade, I know what you're thinking, we have to see Doctor Mean first and settle this properly,' stated Blimey firmly, absently wiping down her cutlass, ready for a scuffle.

'Fine with me,' replied a happy Blade, whom Blimey suspected of having early morning drinkies, which were not really conducive to a battle.

Based on the information Betty H.V had gathered, Blimey figured that Doctor Mean would be at the Ten Toads tavern for the annual, 24-hour Black Jack tournament, so that's where they headed first. They left the Raven at the dock and headed into the town. Leaving the main drag after about 200 metres, they turned left then right, and then right again as they followed Blimey down several small and rickety streets. The houses on either side of them were tall and narrow, and packed tightly together making it hard for the sun to reach it's sunny tendrils down to warm the street and the residents below. Betty hates Veronica rubbed her arms for warmth as the lack of sunlight started to get to her and she wished she had brought her jacket.

Walking down another dingy alleyway, they came to an open space where a tall, old bluestone building stood surrounded by a small but tidy garden. The sun shone down on them briefly, warming their bones, before it thought better of it and flitted away behind some light clouds. A wooden sign above the door featured ten carved toads, which appeared to writhe with constant movement. Blimey looked to her companions and nodded. This was the place.

Skipping up a small set of stone stairs, Blimey pushed open the door and surveyed the room, which was indeed set up for a card tournament. Several small circular tables were arranged around the room, at which sat pirates, scoundrels and characters of all kinds. The din of conversation rent the air, as card after card fell, and glass after glass was raised along with the stakes. Looking round Blimey soon spotted Mean.

She approached him slowly, and calmly tried to resolve the situation peacefully first. She didn't want to cause a scene and interrupt the games afoot.

'Hello again, Doctor Mean' she said quietly.

'Hmph,' said Mean, trying to be cool about the situation even though it was clear to everyone at his table that it was brown trousers time.

'Doctor Mean, I'll get to the point, will you return Blade's ship in exchange for fair payment of his debt?' she enquired.

'You foolish female, have you seen his ship? It is far superior to my own clapped out old bunkle, as if I would return it now. She's mine fair an' square.'

'True it is a pretty vessel, but come now, we don't want any trouble here. You're ship is a fine vessel, and it suits you. Surely you can give Blade back his ship, and we can settle this matter without having to paint the floor a new shade of crimson?'

'You may rule the seas Blimey, but here on land I have the upper hand so do yourself a flavour and clear off, if you know what is good for you,' he replied haughtily, leaning back in his chair and smirking to his fellow card players.

'I take it that is a No then? Fair enough... as you wish,' sighed Blimey and drew her sword, letting it hang loosely at her side. She still hoped Mean might change his mind, she had fully intended to pay him for the ship and what she offered was a fair deal, but disappointingly Doctor Mean turned and laughed at her, getting to his feet. The rest of the bar instantly fell silent. Doctor Mean also drew his sword, and without a word swung it swiftly at Blimey's neck. Leaning backwards out of the way of the steel, she did not flinch and kept her ground. A flicker of fear scooted across Mean's face, but just as soon it was gone. In response Blimey raised her lip in a happy sneer. All bets were off now. He had clearly thrown the first blow, and Blimey was free to defend herself without fear of being called out for robbing the man of his winnings.

Sensing his peril, Mean quickly swung at Blimey again, but this time she struck back and as her blade clashed with his the rest of the players at the table jumped to Doctor Mean's defense. It was their folly, and within moments they discovered they were clearly no match for the trio of Blimey, Betty H.V and Captain James Blade. Standing back to back they took on each man in the bar as they rushed towards them in a blur of steel. The bar was filled with the noise of metal chinking on metal, metal slicing through flesh, an agony of screams and a scuffle of footwork as the trio split finally to finish off the job. For those who had stepped into the battle and not lived to tell the tale it, was bad news all round, and for those who were injured but still remained alive (or who had chosen not to get involved) the barman was frantically indicating a safe haven could be found in the back parlour. As the bar emptied, Doctor Mean finally fell to the ground, clutching his arm as he bled out slowly. The game was over.

Wiping her sword on the sleeve of one of the dead, Blimey nodded to Betty H.V and Blade that it was time to leave. Walking on ahead of them back to the dock, Blimey was deep in thought. Once there she knew she would be saying good-bye to Blade yet again, which was not a problem in itself, but it still stirred up old emotions she thought she had long since forgotten. Sighing to herself she decided that she wouldn't let it get to her. She had finished hitching her wagon to Blade's crazy train years ago, and while some of the time they had been together had been fun, a great deal more of it had been tears and disappointments. As they reached the dock she turned to face Blade.

'OK, there you go, now you have your ship back I would appreciate it if you could do your best to keep her this time,' smiled Blimey.

'Yes Miss,' smiled Blade, bowing gallantly, 'and thank you,' he added stepping forward to give her an awkward hug, before pulling away slowly and staring down at her, keeping hold of her hand.

'See ya round Blade,' added Betty, breaking the moment swiftly and waving to Blade as she turned to walk up the gangplank to the Raven. She had no wish to speak with him further, he was infuriating and Betty H.V felt wasting time on this man was time very ill spent.

'Make sure you do,' said Blimey retrieving her hand and stepping back from Blade, 'I'll see you around, Blade,' she added, turning away and heading for her ship.

Walking the gangplank to the Raven, Blimey turned and waved to Blade, smiling to herself and shaking her head as he swilled from a newly opened bottle of spiced rum, and stalked off back to the Nevermore. On the Raven, Betty hates

Veronica did not hide her relief that Blade was out of their lives again. In truth she had never liked him - there was just a feeling about the man that was bad news.

CHAPTER ELEVEN

The Hollows of Korpus

The seas had turned rough well into the night, and the Raven was bearing the brunt of it. Water crashed over the decking as Blimey slept badly. The girls had been forewarned of the storm in the evening and had battened down the hatches so to speak. Below deck on the Raven everything was watertight and sealed off from anything above so there was no fear of flooding.

Rolling over in her sleep, a dangerous frown creased Blimey's forehead as she slipped deeper into her dreams, but they were not of the happy variety. Nightmares had plagued her since her run-in with Blade days before, dredging up old memories and feelings, not for the rogue himself but rather those surrounding the events that caused Blimey to flee her home so long ago. Lightening streaked across the sky outside Blimey's cabin window, closely followed by a tremendous clap of thunder. Blimey sat bolt upright in bed, clutching the bed sheets in balled fists, a look of fear and sadness on her face. It took her a moment to recall where she was, and then turning to the window she looked out upon the black moonless night, as rain pelted against the glass portal. She knew what she had to do. She couldn't go on with these night terrors, if he was still out there she had to find him. She took the dreams as a sign that it was not yet over. She just hoped Betty hates Veronica would understand this temporary glitch in their plans.

Dressing in the dark, she waited until the storm seemed to ease off, then she headed out to the helm. The rain was still falling but the ferocity had abated and now it was more of a blatting drizzle. With a sigh she plugged the coordinates into the navigation system.

Blimey sailed on through the remainder of the night, lost

only to her thoughts and the feeling of the sea beneath the ship. The rain had passed around dawn, when Betty hates Veronica awoke and came above with coffee for them both. She knew immediately by the position of the rising sun that the ship had changed course in the night, but waited patiently for her friend to tell her why – be it the storm or the will of the Captain.

Taking a cup of coffee from her friend, Blimey set the ship on auto-pirate and joined her on the deck.

'I've changed course towards Korpus,' explained Blimey, 'I keep dreaming of him… you know the one I told you about? I just have this feeling that he is still out there – that he did not perish and I have to be sure… I can't go on with these dreams and this doubt.'

'I know. I just wish…'

'I had told you. Yes, and I am sorry about that, it wasn't fair to take the decision without speaking to you first but I was running on lack of sleep and instinct, and the bad feelings that seeing Blade again brought up.'

'I understand. How far off are we?' asked Betty hates Veronica.

'A days sail, no more… we will be there by nightfall,'

'Don't trust to hope. I don't want to see you disappointed again, do you really think it is possible he survived?'

'Anything is possible my friend,' replied Blimey wistfully as she looked off into the distance.

***

It was not long dark when the Raven docked quietly in Korpus, and all that could be seen were the faint lights of the town. Blimey had not been back to this place for a very long time and the faint sounds she could hear drifting towards them from the little city sent her reeling back as she tried to force the memories of what had happened here out of her mind. At the touch of a button the anchor dropped with a splash into the water, while the gangplank extended down to the dock.

'We'll need to be very careful,' Blimey warned Betty hates Veronica as they descended down the gangplank, 'bad things happened here… and I don't know think anyone would be happy to see us snooping around.'

'Don't worry, you've told me enough about this place to

keep me on my toes until we take our leave,' responded Betty hates Veronica, as they continued on towards the source of the lights.

In another lifetime, before Blimey had fled to the sea, a tragedy had befallen the quiet village of Korpus. Long before she became a Captain, when she had spent her days in humdrum contentment as simply another unknown inhabitant of the bordering town of Credonmere. Not quite out of her teenage years, she had fallen in love with a boy from Korpus, which under normal circumstances and in a normal world would not have been an issue, but of course there was a problem.

The boy she had fallen in love with was a Hollow, which in the language of Korpus meant 'one whom death has returned'. All of the inhabitants of Korpus were Hollows, and anyone who came into the contact with the soil there was granted not only renewed life but also a much longer life. The Hollows of Korpus had actually come to re-live there by accident, after the neighboring Credonmerians first buried their dead there. Initially there was an understanding and rapport between the towns, but this soon broke down when the religious right began campaigning for the separation of humans and Hollows, and no more dead were buried there. The Credonmerians thought that these poor people were an abomination against the will of their God, but the people of Korpus were not evil and there was no way they could escape their fate. However this meant that the population of Korpus had since settled and only rarely expanded when someone left a beloved friend or family member inside the Korpus town limits. This was a fairly stupid move on behalf of the grieving because they would not be able to see their loved one ever again, but grief does give people illogical ideas. For their part the Korpussians took these new folks in and made them feel welcome. After all, they had all been there themselves.

Now unlike Zombies, Hollows are not flesh-eating freaks obsessed with cranial fillers, so put that thought out of your head. Sometimes people who die are just fortunate (or unfortunate) enough to come back to life. This did not stop the Credonmerians spreading the 'fear' about the people of Korpus being monsters, and over time the icy truce became more and more strained as the living became more and more fearful over what was essentially nothing.

Over time certain laws had also been put in place to discourage interaction between the two, and now Credonmerians and Korpussians were forbidden from even looking at each other, let alone uttering a word in polite conversation. In fact the people of Credonmere so despised their neighbours that they built a rather long, tall and spikey wall between the two townships. The Korpussians were cool with that though, as these days they didn't want to have anything to do with the Credonmerians either.

From time to time though, curiosity would get the better of some of the young people in both villages and they would find a way through the wall to check out their neighbours. When caught the cheeky party would simply be returned to their village with a stern warning. These little annoyances were tolerated in order to keep the peace between the two towns. It was in a similar way that Blimey had met Vincent Blackshadow. She had been hiding away in her favourite place, in a little arbour next to a particularly spikey place in the wall, but in this place the wall had cracked and long since split leaving a rather large hole. On the day she met him, she was sitting quietly and reading a book on advanced cutlass techniques, lost in her own thoughts. She did not see the Hollow boy watching her from his side of the wall. Together they sat there for some time in silence, before she developed that eerie feeling we all get sooner or later as we realise that someone is watching us. Not wanting to appear startled, Blimey purposefully didn't look up, but instead asked the young man what he wanted.

'Oh!' he said, caught off guard, 'nothing really... I was just curious to see your side of the wall, that's all.'

'My side of the.... wall?' responded Blimey looking up sharply, immediately drawn to the pitch black eyes of the Hollow, which was common of his kind.

'Errr, yes, your side,' he said again, smiling.

She had smiled back. She didn't think she had ever seen a more handsome face. From his aquiline nose to his long dark hair, which hung casually across his forehead, and occasionally covered his eyes, at which point he would roughly push the hair away. It only served to make him more striking.

'Is it true you can't cross over to our land?' she asked,

knowing something of the lore surrounding the Hollows of Korpus.

'Yes, but there are places where our soil mixes with yours and we can walk on that... we cannot go far though.'

'How old are you really... if you don't mind me asking?'

'I'm fairly young by Korpus standards, and was only left here a few years ago, though we age so slowly once we get here, it's hard to tell. I think I am about 24 or 25, in your years.'

'Interesting. What's your name?'

'Vincent... and you?'

'Jeanne,' she replied, as her hand moved up to her face to check that the hollow where her eye should have been was covered. She was quite self-conscious about it and had not yet taken to wearing an eye-patch, choosing instead to hide it behind a wall of long red hair.

'Why do you hide your face like that?' asked Vincent, noticing the movement.

'I'm deformed,' she smiled sadly, looking down in shame. She was used to being teased by the other children in her town, and so she expected Vincent to do just the same, 'see?' she added angrily pulling back her hair roughly and exposing her missing left eye.

'I think you look beautiful,' Vincent smiled, taking it all in his stride, after all he was used to seeing strange things in Korpus all the time, this was nothing by those standards.

'Gee, thanks....' she smiled brightly, 'no one has ever said that before, that's for sure, except maybe my mum so that doesn't count,' she laughed.

'Don't worry about it,' he said dismissively, trying to be cool, 'what are you reading?'

And so their conversation went on, and that day they spent the whole afternoon together, talking of everything and nothing, and from then on they met at least every second day in the same spot. Both had to be very careful not to be caught by their respective villages, and slowly over the course of months they knew that they had fallen in love, and that the only way they could be together was for Jeanne to join Vincent in Korpus, for he could not ever leave the town. They made plans to kill Jeanne, and leave her in Korpus to be resurrected. Even though technically she could have simply moved to the other side, they both knew that the Korpussians would never let her stay while she was conventionally alive.

As the big day approached, in their excitement they were a bit careless and her father discovered their plans. The people of Credonmere were not happy, they could foresee this becoming a 'thing' between their young folks and wanted it halted for good. It was about time, they felt, that they showed their neighbours the true meaning of life for trying to turn one of their own. For their part the Hollows of Korpus were confused. Never had a living person ever wanted to voluntarily suffer their fate, and so they chose to ignore the situation. It was something that a lot of them would not live to regret.

Three nights later, the men of Credonmere made their move. In the darkness of a moonless night, they snuck through the wall and prepared their attack with sword and fire. Many Korpussians died twice that night, never to walk again, and word soon reached Blimey that not only had Vincent perished, but it had been their plans to be together that sparked the cruel slaughter of the Hollows to begin with. Unable to face her father, and with her heart thoroughly ground down into a thousand million pieces, Blimey had decided then and there to flee to the ocean, where she began her life a new as the most feared pirate on the Severed Seas... though at this point in time she was not there quite yet.

Back in the here and now, Blimey and Betty hates Veronica strode towards the town of Korpus. Betty H.V didn't know exactly why Blimey had felt compelled to come back here, and was worried that all she would face was disappointment. They headed for the bright lights of the main street and found the nearest seedy looking bar. Slowly opening the doors, they entered the atmospheric gloom inside and found the barman rotting away quite contentedly behind the bar. He was obviously one of the oldest Korpussians, or simply unlucky to come back to life in a state of semi-putrefaction. Catching a sniff of fresh flesh, the barman looked up and was surprised to see the two very much alive girls approaching him. He opened his mouth in shock, but it was immediately clear that Blimey would be the one to do the talking. The barman had lost his tongue.

'Where can I find Vincent Blackshadow?' asked Blimey softly. The barman looked up at her, unable to speak, his mouth still hanging open like a rotten cavern yawning before her. He raised his hand slowly and pointed to a corner as a voice growled from the shadows.

'Who wants to know?'

Blimey turned on her heel and stalked over in the direction from which the voice came, leaving Betty H.V to try and order something to drink from the barman, which was proving more difficult by the minute as the barman's ears had also apparently fallen off. In the dark corner at a small table sat a man, handsome in his own disheveled way, his long black hair hanging across his forehead and around his face in a very familiar way. Blimey sat down at the table and looked up at this scarred creature. He said nothing and stared at the table, refusing to look at her.

'Vincent?' asked Blimey quietly.

'Yes, but who are you?' he asked, still refusing to look directly at her.

'You don't know my voice? Look at me,' Blimey stated, reaching over the table to lift up his chin.

Vincent looked into her face, but said nothing. It seemed he was not even breathing. In the silence as he sat frozen in his chair, time dragged on awkwardly. Long seconds passed, and still nothing. Not knowing what else to do, Blimey stood up to go. Perhaps she had been wrong. It had been such a long time.

'Wait, I... please sit down,' he started, reaching for her arm to stop her from leaving, but he didn't say anything further.

Sitting back down in the rickety chair opposite Vincent, she knew her time there was short. It would not be long before word got out that she and Betty were there and the people would not be happy about it.

'I came back for you,' she said, 'I had to see if you were still ... alive. I had this feeling that maybe you hadn't been destroyed by... by those fools from Credonmere, and I had to see if it was true, I'm... so sorry,' said Blimey, hanging her head.

Vincent moved quickly round the table and lifter her up into his arms, holding her close and kissing her forehead. She looked up and met his lips with hers.

'Jeanne, I have missed you more than you can ever know, like I have been living in slow motion,' he said pulling away, 'I can't believe what happened to my people after they found out about us. I tried so hard to hate you too, as I hated the others, but I couldn't - it wasn't your fault. I even tried to look for you after it all went down, but then I heard you had run away.'

'I had to go! I thought you were gone, burned with the others, and I couldn't stay knowing what I had caused, what my father had done to your people,' she replied.

'Don't blame yourself, please... but you can't stay here, look over there, the other man who was here when you came in has gone. He will have told the whole town that you are here by now, and they will already be on their way to come for you. Their hatred is still very much intact since the massacre, and they have sworn vengeance on any one who is not Hollow born - you have to go!' said Vincent urgently.

'Come with me,' stated Blimey standing up and boldly grabbing Vincent's hand, pulling him towards the door.

'We both know I can't leave, and what keeps me here, I'm bound by it,' replied Vincent, in turn pushing the girls along.

'I'll come back for you then!'

'Then I'll be waiting for you, so you better, now come on Jeanne, it's time to go!' Vincent replied, moving her towards the door and motioning for Betty hates Veronica to follow.

'She calls herself Blimey now,' piped up Betty H.V from behind them, 'ha! Jeanne! No wonder you wouldn't tell me, even after all this time!'

'This is no time to discuss my moniker!' laughed Blimey, who couldn't help herself even though they really were in stupid amounts of danger. Turning back to her friend she added, 'and there is nothing wrong with Jeanne thank you very much!'

On they ran, as Vincent rushed them outside. Betty stumbled slightly on a loose paving stone, but before she could fall Vincent had steadied her.

'How did you move that fast?' she exclaimed in surprise.

'No time! Now come on both of you!' Vincent insisted, grabbing Betty by the hand and dragging her along so they could catch up with Blimey, 'it's time to go, they are coming!'

Once they had made it partly out of the town towards the docks, they could hear the rumblings of trouble heading their way, enunciated by a choir of angry voices that grew ever louder as they approached.

'Now go!' yelled Vincent, coming to an abrupt halt, 'I'll hold them up here and buy you some time.'

'You don't need to do that!' Blimey said in alarm as she skidded to a halt and turned back towards Vincent, 'please, they'll beat you and lock you up or something, I don't want to risk loosing you again, just go and hide somewhere, no one need know you helped us escape. There's a time to fight and a time to fly!'

'I'll do whatever you ask – now please, just go!' pleaded Vincent growing ever anxious.

Blimey grabbed Vincent's hand and pulled him towards her, brushing her lips against his in a swift goodbye, before turning back towards the dock. She took off in a sprint, tapping Betty hates Veronica on the shoulder as she passed to signal her to pick it up and follow.

'I'll return!' she yelled to the wind, though she didn't take time to look back as they sped on towards the safety of the Raven, she couldn't risk tripping over her own boots and being captured.

Once they reached the ship, they burst up the gangplank, and only then did she grab her spyglass and look back to see Vincent disappearing in the distance, away from the mob of Hollows that was still headed their way. With lightening skill the two pirate girls had the ship under sail and out of the harbor, but a new weight settled on Blimey's heart as she steered the Raven out onto the open sea.

CHAPTER TWELVE

Rawkous

Two days after their visit to Korpus and Blimey was still feeling unsettled and maudlin. Betty hates Veronica had spent the best part of two hours trying to think of something to do to snap her out of the doldrums. Blimey stepped away from the helm and sat down hard on the planks of the helm deck, letting out a huge sigh. Betty hates Veronica looked up at her friend from the main deck below and decided that she would find something fun to take her mind off their recent troubles. She walked past her Captain to the horizon scanner mounted near the helm, and started looking for any other ships or blips or blips of ships that may be in the vicinity. Maybe a good old-fashioned skirmish was what they needed. True they were not the types who went looking for trouble, but must needs as the pirate sails they say.

It didn't take long for Betty to spot a promising ship, it was about 5 miles from their current position and swift sailing would bring them to this possible foe in no time at all. She set the course in the navigation computer and they were off. Blimey was so distracted by her dark emotional state that she didn't even question their change in direction.

A short while later they came upon the object of their search, which turned out to be an old Junk ship. These were a rare sight on the high seas these days, and legend told of them being wonderful vessels carrying all sorts of oddities and treasures which could be bought at a reasonable price. Betty hates Veronica jumped up and down clapping her hands in an extraordinary display of excitement.

'Look, Blimey! A Junk! Have you ever seen one before? I've always wanted to shop on one, I hear they have heaps of weird stuff on them!' she chirped away like a hyperactive child, releasing the anchor.

'Really? A Junk?' asked Blimey, getting to her feet and squinting into the sun and immediately forgetting she was meant to be feeling sad. The Captain of the other ship soon noticed them as they drifted alongside his motley vessel until the anchor hit the sea floor, and pulled them to a stop.

'Ahoy!' yelled the Captain of the Junk, 'come aboard and view the strange wares I have collected from all over the world, Ya har!'

Blimey raised an eyebrow and looked at her friend, 'what a fruit loop,' she whispered, before jumping deftly across to the Junk ship from the railing of the Raven. Betty followed and once they were both on board they began looking over the piles of claptrap, riches, strangeness and beauty that was piled up in every corner, and hidden in every nook and cranny of the Junk. The Junk itself had the air of an antique shop under sail. Mingled with the salt smell of the sea was a musty, worn smell of old things. The sails themselves were yellowed with age, crinkly in places between the battens. Down one end, near the helm was set up a little table with an old cash register upon it, a small set of scales, an abacus and a glass of red wine.

Walking in and out between the piles of trash and treasures, they had never seen so much stuff in one place before, and although it was wondrous, Blimey still felt her unhappiness eating away at the edges, nagging at the back of her mind like a restless squirrel. The Captain of the Junk came over and stood next to Blimey as she sifted through a pile of old cutlasses.

'Ye seem to be missing something,' he stated.

'Perhaps... yes that's what it feels like,' smiled Blimey ruefully.

'Well perhaps what ye need is a parrot, they're good companions, and not bad for conversation once they be learnin' a few words, I have several over there if ye be interested?' suggested the Junk Captain.

'A parrot? Never thought about it really,' mused Blimey, 'I always thought they were a bit clichéd for pirates.'

'Yes, true, an' that may be so lassy, but then why do you think so many pirates have parrots? It's not as though ye have a uniform,' justified the other Captain.

'That be true, I guess I never thought of it that way. Indeed, I will take a look at your parrots,' replied Blimey, feeling more cheerful already. She wandered over to the area where the parrots were kept, some in large cages, others tethered to their perches by delicate silver chains, but after checking out the birds she found that she felt worse. She hated to see such beautiful creatures tied down when they should be flying on the wind.

Sitting on a nearby bench in disappointment, she flopped her arms down on her knees and sighed. Looking across at a small, half open box under the parrot cages she spied a plume of red feathers. Curious, she got to her feet and bent over, walking forward, trying to figure out what it was she might be seeing. Reaching the box she gently lifted the lid fully open and looked inside. The feathers belonged to a small macaw. It did not move and appeared to be quite dead indeed. Blimey reached into the box and pulled out the parrot. It didn't flinch, and no heartbeat could be felt. Looking the red macaw over carefully, she curiously noticed what appeared to be a small clockwork key sticking out of its back, between its wings. Blimey smiled, intrigued by this odd clockwork creature. Would it work if she wound the key? There was only one way to find out. Blimey grasped the silver key between her fingers, and was just about to wind it round when the Junk Captain came bolting over.

'Nooooooo!' he yelled dramatically, 'ye can't, stop! Don't wind that key, you don't know what ye be lettin' yourself in for!'

'Why? It's just a wind up bird?" queried Blimey, a perplexed line creasing her brow.

'No, no, it's not" said the shaken Captain, 'you'll be sorry if you wake that thing up!'

'That sounds like a dare,' laughed Blimey, 'all right then I'll buy it from you, then it's my problem, how much do you want for it?'

'So ye ignore me warning girl? Fine be it on your head, take the damn thing, I want no coin for it, you'll soon see what I mean.'

'Stop being so dramatic, but thank you,' said Blimey before turning to her First Mate, "come on, it's time we we're going.'

The Junk Captain watched the two girls climb back on board their ship, and smiled to himself as he watched them sail away. Sometimes, he thought to himself a little bit out loud, the only way to get people to take what they need is to tell them they can't have it.

Returning to the Raven the way they came, Blimey stared at her new pet. The Junk Captain's words had startled her, but curiosity was always going to get the better of her. She turned the feathery thing over and over in her hands, and then slowly wound the key.

'Are you sure you want to be doing that after what that man said?' asked Betty H.V.

'No', laughed Blimey, 'but I can't not wind it up now can I? I can't see what could be so bad about a wind-up parrot...'

Blimey wound the key until it clicked to a stop, which told her it could be wound no more, then she placed the bird on the deck, and waited. Beside her Betty hates Veronica watched intently. Slowly the macaw began to stir. A little stiffly at first, and then as its gears warmed up the bird snapped into life.

'%#*^%#@*!' it screeched.

'What the sugar-puff sandwiches did that thing just say?' asked Betty H.V alarmed, 'it sounded like the worst cursing I've heard in a long while.'

'Harrr arrrgh! I love it already!' laughed Blimey heartily as the little bird got to its feet, 'a filthy mouthed parrot, just what I've always wanted.'

The little parrot stood up and shook itself gently, extending one wing and then the other as though it was stretching after waking up from a long nap. Then it stretched each of its claws and tilted its head from side to side, before screeching blue murder again.

'I don't know if I want that thing F-ing and jeffing all over the ship,' said Betty H.V slowly as she watched its weird feathery calisthenics in action, 'how long does that winding mechanism last do you think?'

'It'll be great, don't worry, I'm sure it's just some waking up type swearing... but as for how long before we have to wind it up again, we'll just have to wait and see,' replied Blimey, turning sharply to look at her new pet as it spoke to them, which was completely unexpected.

'I only need winding once every month, and I only cursed because you wound me to tightly,' said the parrot eloquently.

'Haha! Fantastic, you speak! What's your name little man?'

'You may call me Rawkous,' replied Rawkous, taking a small bow.

'Why are you called Rawkous?' asked Betty hates Veronica.

'How the hell should I know? Qwaurk,' snapped Rawkous.

'Now, now bird, please don't speak to my First Mate that way, I shouldn't want to have to throw you overboard when you've just arrived,' scolded Blimey, though she still had a smile on her face.

'Sorry Captain, I guess I'm still a little wound up, swoo whoo,' apologised the bird, 'and at any rate I can fly you know,' he added and with that flew up to the crow's nest, perching on the platform quite proudly.

'This is the best day ever! A talking, cursing, flying wind up parrot is just what I needed,' said Blimey hugging her friend and laughing as Rawkous flew back down and came to rest on her shoulder.

CHAPTER THIRTEEN

Farquar of the Severed Seas

Neither Blimey nor Betty hates Veronica knew exactly when the Raven had sprung a leak, but they had been steadily taking on water for the past few days and it was getting to the point where the piramatic pumps were no longer able to keep the water down to a manageable level. They had to admit they were in trouble and find a port where they could get repairs made to the ship before they started to sink good and proper. It was all part and parcel of living on the open seas, and leaks were bound to happen sooner or later, though Blimey sorely wished it were later as she had been planning to hold a party for her First Mate. They had even sent out the invitations and were expecting the rabble of guests to arrive within the next few hours. Blimey knew that she had two options. Either she cancel the festivities at the eleventh hour or the guests got wet feet. Neither was very appealing.

The outlook seemed bleak but fate was on her side today, and at that moment a strange ship appeared on the horizon. A wondrous vessel, it was almost as beautiful as it was illogical. The main sail featured upon it two crossed severed arms, whose hands clutched many golden doubloons, a signature Blimey did not recognise from any of the fully registered pirates she knew sailed the Severed Seas. Reaching for a hardbound book on a small table next to the helm she consulted the *Pirates Book of Flags*, but she couldn't find this particular motif in that comprehensive tomb either. Furrowing her brow she looked to her First Mate, who shrugged, thoroughly perplexed.

As the ship approached Blimey could make out the helm wheel, which appeared to be carved out of amber and glinted invitingly in the sun. Blimey had always wanted an amber helm, but had not been able to reach to the extravagance. Her gaze then fell on the Captain of the ship, a tall, finely dressed, bearded man who seemed to be doing some kind of sailing jig as he steered his ship closer to the Raven. The ship itself was painted a voluminous candy apple red, with watermelon green trim. The figurehead at the bow was an ornately carved seagull, its head pointed to the sky.

Blimey held back the urge to giggle at his antics and waited solemnly for him to hail her ship. Presently he did so.

'Lo fair pirate-ess of the Severed Seas, what brings ye to these waters and why the look of solemnity? Do ye hath no liquor or sailing songs with which to cure this curse which prevails upon you?' he cried out.

'You what?' replied Blimey, obviously taken aback.

'Well now, it would seem that thee has a look of suspicion about thee, which I have heard can be dissolved with a cherry cider or a red rum?' replied the Captain.

'Quite possibly,' countered Blimey, smiling against her will as the Captain's verbose manner struck accord, 'but who are you may I enquire, before I commit to losing this so-called suspicious air?'

'Aha! Why I am Farquar of the Severed Seas, and I am a native to these fair parts,' he answered.

'Indeed, but where are you headed and for what purpose?' enquired Blimey.

'I am headed nowhere and have no purpose except to sup from the subtle nectars of the ale and be French in my spare time!' he laughed in reply as his ship pulled alongside the Raven.

'You're intent, is it peaceable?' snorted Blimey, unable to help herself as the words left her mouth.

'But of course it is,' he replied, 'though it appears that thy Pirate's ship is in fair buggery and need of some repair, she sits to low in the water for such a fine vessel.'

'Yes, indeed my ship, the Raven, is in strife and I need to get her to some port nearby to get her mended, and quickly as I have organised a birthday party for my First Mate and it begins within the next few hours!' replied Blimey.

'Never fear,' said Farquar, 'my men are famed for their skills in ship repair while on the fair sea and they will repair your wondrous vessel, the Raven, on the condition that we may all attend this shin-dig you speak of.'

'Brilliant!' yelled Blimey, happily, 'then verily you will be our guests of honour if this thing you can do!'

Farquar's men swung over to the Raven, joined by their Captain, who then directed them below decks to find the leak and seal it up. While they were working he told Blimey and Betty hates Veronica his tale.

'I was once a pillaging, rampaging, bloodletting, baby-eating pirate,' he began, 'I had my own ship, my own band of scurvy sea dogs and, for a while, I even had a parrot... until I ate him!' he rumbled leaning menacingly towards the girls and growling, then breaking down into a haze of cackles.

Blimey and Betty hates Veronica looked sideways at each other and giggled.

'I travelled the Severed Seas,' he continued, 'leaving a trail of unheard of destruction behind me on account of my parents not hugging me enough as a child. I planned to pirate the WHOLE world, from port to port, bay to bay and yacht club to yacht club. I would take all as my own and leave nothing for those who fell before my fearful wrath... And I would have done it too, if it wasn't for my treacherous Cabin Boy, Oily Pete,'

'Oily Pete?'

'Yay, for you see, Oily Pete had long since wanted to be a pirate; a rapscallion king of the seas and had been making plans a long time hence. It was he that turned my crew against me, and it was he who held a dagger to my throat when I awoke that fateful morning, but it was not my day to die, and out of what I can only guess was a nostalgic reverential he cast me from the ship. Exiled from my own vessel, so there I was, abandoned to the unmerciful inclinations of the tide with nothing but a dead seagull to balance on. That's right, my friends, not even a boat did he leave me, just the surprisingly buoyant carcass of a sea bird.'

'That explains his ship's figurehead...' whispered Betty out the side of her mouth, before Farquar continued speaking over the top of her.

'Long did I stand tip toed upon that cursed creature; alone; un-owned and waiting for deaths clammy hands to come take me,' he went on, 'but, to my surprise, those hands did not come my friends. Pulling myself together, I made an outboard motor from passing debris and rode that seagull corpse to dry land! You know, if it hadn't been for that dear, defunct creature, I would not be here today. In fact, I still have that dead seagull mounted on my helm deck, I call him... Motorarse! From that day on I swore to do good deeds and be the man who stood behind those who could not stand for thee-selves, which is how I then came by my namesake, for many of my fellow scurvy dogs did find my new ways quite amusing and they called me the Reverend. To them I was akin to a padre or 'do-gooder', but in truth there is no master I follow except my conscience and my heart.'

'An interesting tale you have told us, that is not to doubt,' said Blimey after a moments pause, 'but I hope we can trust you not to eat our ship's parrot!'

'Dear me no,' replied the Reverend Farquar, 'a clockwork parrot would give me indigestion, wouldn't it now Rawkous?' he asked as the parrot flew down and landed on the deck in front of him.

'How do you know our bird?' asked Betty H.V frowning.

'I know many things fair and foul on the Severed Seas, but it has been an age since I have seen this little master. Last I saw him he was with Captain Rantillian, but that was many leagues ago now.'

'Rawwwwk – yes swoohoo... And then I was on that damnable Junk for the longest time,' answered the macaw, turning his head to the side and looking inquisitorially at the man before him.

'Yes, well it looks as though you have landed on a good ship now,' he said rubbing the bird under his chin affectionately.

'Aye,' said the bird, flying up to land on Blimey's shoulder.

'Yes....' Farquar trailed off.

At that moment, the developing awkward situation was interrupted by one of Farquar's men, who appeared on deck to let them know the leak had been sealed and the last of the water was being pumped out of the ship.

Blimey smiled up at the man and thanked him, and Farquar for their help. At that same moment the guests for Betty hates Veronica's party began to arrive, and true to her word Blimey invited Farquar and his men to stay as guests of honour. The cherry cider soon flowed freely and they drank in the sunset.

CHAPTER FOURTEEN

A rude awakening

Betty hates Veronica's guests had filtered away back to their own ships in the early hours of the morning, as Blimey sat deep in conversation with Farquar. They finally gave in to sleep themselves at around 4am. Farquar was full of cherry cider and in no state to return to his own ship, so Blimey kindly offered him one of the guest cabin's on her own vessel. There he could bed down for the night and get some rest.

Blimey awoke to a loud screeching around mid-morning. Rawkous was walking around in a tight little circle on one of her pillows, clearly in a bit of a state.

'What is it bird?' she asked blearily, pushing herself up on one elbow to get a better look at her alarmed feathered friend.

'Kwarrrk... there's a nasty looking ship headed our way. The main sail features a skull and crossbones on a large black beetle,'

'Blackwatch!' exclaimed Blimey sitting up so fast that a startled Rawkous flew off in indignation, coming to rest on one of the elegant chairs in the room, 'what can he be up to.... how far away would you say he is Rawkous? An hour?'

'I wager about half that... there's not enough time to flee without the risk of him catching us sooner or later, and the guests from last night have all left... only Farquar's ship remains.'

'I'm not one to run away from a battle, but by that same token I don't see the point in engaging in war just for sport,' Blimey said as she got out of bed and began to dress, 'half an hour you say... that gives us enough time to ready the ship and also enough time to get the Reverend and his men off safely. I will not involve them in my quarrels.'

Hurriedly she dressed, buckling on her sword and guns, and tucking her favourite dagger inside her boot. Taking the hall at a run she none to gently woke Betty H.V and the Reverend.

'We have a bit of a situation,' she explained, as she raced up to the main deck a few minutes later and her crew and guest huddled over a hot cup of coffee each, 'there's a nasty piece of work headed our way, Captain Blackwatch's ship will be here within the next 20 minutes. Farquar, there's enough time for you and your crew to leave. Blackwatch's quarrel is with me, and I don't want to drag you in to my battles.'

'Are you sure he is coming for you?' asked Farquar, raising an eyebrow in a knowing fashion.

'Why do you ask?' questioned Betty H.V, slowly turning to look at their guest, a frown creasing her forehead.

'Blackwatch is not a popular man on the Severed Seas, and has many enemies. If I met him in anger now, it would not be for the first time... or I wager, the last,' replied Farquar.

'Whether he has come in search of you or I is not a question I wish to take a chance in answering, though given the coordinates of last nights festivities, my location is the obvious give away as it would have been easy information to come by, so I believe I can safely assume he is looking for the Raven... especially given it was formerly owned by his lady. No, it is best you head off now Farquar and leave us to deal with this.'

'But there are only two of you against his whole miscreant crew?!' stated Farquar alarmed.

'Don't forget our gallant parrot,' smiled Betty hates Veronica sardonically.

'Even so, I would like to stay and see where the cards fall... I feel that my presence could be somewhat... helpful,' said Farquar.

'This isn't a game of gin rummy Farquar, Blackwatch may very well mean serious business here.'

'Blimey,' said Farquar, walking slowly away from the girls, 'I must confess it was not simple fate that crossed our paths yesterday. I have been searching for you these past few months. I have some important information to impart to you. It is time you knew of your legacy... and of your real parents.'

Dropping her gaze, Blimey's eyes followed him, as he walked slowly around the deck. In the stunned silence that followed such a statement her brain whirred with what he could be saying, and if it could in fact be true.

'What do you mean my real parents?' she asked quietly,

slowly lifting her head to look Farquar in the eye as he turned to face her.

'Swoo hoo,' squawked Rawkous breaking the spell, and interrupting the eerie scene developing before everyone forgot what was headed towards them, 'begging your pardon human people, but Blackwatch approaches, time is racing and a decision about Farquar's crew needs to be made if they are to get away.'

'He's right Blimey,' conceded Betty H.V, stepping forward and touching her Captain on the shoulder.

'All right, fine. Farquar stays and his ship goes. If we live through the next hour I will expect to hear everything our new friend has to tell us, but in the meantime prepare for what may come,' growled Blimey, stalking off to the helm.

Farquar turned towards his ship and signalled for it to leave with an intricate wave of his hand, as if this scenario had been planned earlier. His First Mate saluted him in return and within minutes Farquar's ship was disappearing from view. They had just enough time to get far enough away not to present a worthwhile target for Blackwatch if the crew of the Raven didn't survive.

Back on the Raven, Blimey was brooding over Farquar's revelation, while through her spyglass she watched Blackwatch's ship approach. If his intention was open battle, this really would be a tremendously arrogant and ill thought first move as he was flying towards her over open water, giving her plenty of time to prepare a full scale retaliation. He must want something else, she thought. Anxiously she bit her lip, her mind a storm of confusion. What could Blackwatch want? And if they survived, what would Farquar tell her and how would it change her life?

The seconds ticked by like time bombs as they waited. The law of the Severed Seas laid out very clearly the rules for engagement should two ships meet, and that no ship should fire on another without an open threat. But were they threatened? What did Blackwatch mean by following them across the wide ocean? Blackwatch knew that Blimey and Betty hates Veronica sailed alone, and Blimey knew that he, like the more arrogant men of the sea, assumed that two waifs on their own would be no match for a fully armed crew, never entertaining the thought that lack of skill on their behalf might present the real challenge.

'We'll wait to see if the full colours are flying, then we'll know more about his intentions,' stated Blimey finally.

'He's never been known to be one to play fair me lass, if you don't mind me adding my thoughts,' said Farquar.

'Nevertheless Farquar, this is how I run my ship and we keep to the code of battle. I have no doubt this will not end well, but it will not be because I simply open fire on every near-do-well I meet on the high seas, if that were the case there would not be many pirates left sailing now!'

They continued their silent watch as Blackwatch's ship approached, and a wary air settled on the Raven. While it seemed at this moment that Blackwatch only wanted a quiet word, this could change at any second. He was not known for his personal stability.

Finally Blackwatch's ship pulled up alongside the Raven and dropped anchor. Blackwatch appeared at the side of his ship and made his intentions clear.

'Blimey, I have needs to speak with your guest - may I come aboard?'

'My guest?' replied Blimey, slightly confused, but mostly surprised, turning to look at Farquar.

'I did say he might be looking for me,' stated Farquar calmly, 'but with all fair warning and with full disclosure in mind, it is not just me he has come to find.'

'Right, of course, that makes perfect sense,' responded Blimey with just a hint of sarcasm, before turning to address Blackwatch, 'you alone may come aboard Blackwatch, your crew and your weapons must stay behind!'

'I will meet those terms,' replied Blackwatch as his First Mate extended a gangplank to connect the two ships. Stepping up on the wood, Blackwatch stormed across to the Raven with the air of a man on a mission. Hitting the deck of the Raven, he walked straight past Blimey and up to Farquar.

'Is she the one?' Blackwatch demanded directly of Farquar, rudely ignoring Blimey and any form of pirate ship-to-ship etiquette.

'Yes, and before you ask me again, I can tell you I am sure of it,' sighed Farquar, knowing that what would come next would determine the fate of his new friends.

'How did I ever miss this juicy fact,' Blackwatch sneered,

walking in a slow circle around Blimey and looking her up and down in a lecherous way she had not experienced from her enemies before. What it meant she wasn't sure, but she knew she didn't like it and that she would make Blackwatch pay for this outrageous behaviour.

'She must come with me, dead or alive,' Blackwatch finished coming to a halt in front of the two girls.

'I don't think it will be as easy as that my old foe,' replied Farquar.

'Excuse me,' interrupted Blimey, a scowl marring her face, 'but the decision as to whether or not I leave my ship, and what my fate thereafter may be, will not be decided by either of you.'

Ignoring her the two men began to circle each other on the deck.

'How did you figure it out?' Blackwatch asked Farquar.

'I must admit it took me a while,' he mused, 'she's not an easy one to track down. After she left her foster parents care, she simply disappeared, and I could find no trace of her, for years, even with my connections. In that respect I grossly underestimated her. She is more like her mother than I expected.'

'Foster parents?' Betty hates Veronica said quietly under her breath, desperately trying to ascertain what would happen next.

'What are you talking about?' demanded Blimey, 'my father is a Shaman!'

'You poor deluded girl, you really have no idea? Your mother, your real mother, I mean, is a wanted criminal.'

'Blackwatch that is clearly open for debate, you cannot go round casting aspersions based on hearsay!' Farquar stepped in, his voice rising suddenly.

'And as such,' Blackwatch continued ignoring Farquar, 'my client has asked me to return with you as assurance that your mother will turn herself in... though my client did not stipulate what state you need be in on delivery,' he finished, a nasty sneer crossing his face.

'And what has my so called real mother supposedly done to your client, Blackwatch?'

'That is none of your concern, now you will come with me.'

'Blackwatch, this is all ancient history, what can Vainglorious want with Elizabeth's daughter now?'

'I don't know, he's a rich idiot, but an idiot who pays me well, and I do like my work... perhaps he plans to marry the daughter as revenge for being left at the altar by her mother? What do I care?'

'This madness ends now, the girl Jeanne is not yours to take, return to your ship and be gone,' warned Farquar, losing patience.

'Or what? You three plus parrot will make me sorry? Arrrrrgh har har har... you always were well known for your jests Farquar.'

'He's not joking now Blackwatch,' growled Blimey, whose temper was fraying faster by the minute.

'You are mine!' stated Blackwatch stepping forward and trying to grab Blimey by the arm.

It was not a good move. Within a heartbeat Blimey had turned the tables on Blackwatch, grabbing his hand and bending his fingers back before snapping his arm up and around behind him, then forcing him to the ground, which had the effect of incapacitating him in a not un-painful way.

'Do we get the hint now Blackwatch?' she snarled, lifting his arm higher to reinforce her point more painfully.

'Yes, fine, I'll go. Release me!' Blackwatch thundered, completely caught off guard.

Blimey let him go slowly, but as she did so she shoved him over with a kick from her boot in disgust. Getting back to his feet, Blackwatch straightened himself up to his full height and brushed himself off, desperately trying to regain some part of his dignity.

'She will regret that,' he mumbled mostly to himself as he turned towards the plank connecting their ships, looking for all intents and purposes as if he was going to return to his ship, but things are never this easy of course.

As he reached the edge of the Raven, Captain Blackwatch raised his hand above his head and waved down. To Blimey it appeared as though he were waving a sarcastic farewell, but to Blackwatch's crew it meant something else entirely more sinister. As his arm hit his side, Blackwatch's men loosed their battle cry and from nowhere produced further gangways, which they threw down to bridge their ship and the Raven.

While his First Mate lead the boarding party, still more

men let loose a barrage of grenades, creating a smoking haze through which the men ran. Blackwatch turned on his heel to face the crew of the Raven, and began to walk back towards them, sword drawn. As his men landed on the deck behind him, he thought to himself, this should be fun.

'Blackwatch you will pay for this insult! I have been cordial with you long enough!' Blimey roared as she watched Blackwatch's men landing on her ship. Drawing her sword, she felt the anger in her rise until a calm fury overtook her. A cold smile played at her lips.

Taking their cue from Blimey, Betty hates Veronica and Farquar drew their own weapons, and as Blackwatch and his men met them on deck, soon all was a haze of swords, screams, smoke and fury. Suddenly the easy victory Blackwatch had predicted was not looking so likely as Blimey and her two comrades fought with a fierceness that he had not expected. In truth Blackwatch had never met Blimey in battle before, and had dispelled as rumour the tales of her proficiency with a cutlass. Unfortunately for him he was finding out first hand that the stories were true.

As Betty hates Veronica and Farquar made short work of Blackwatch's crew, Blimey made a decisive movement towards Blackwatch. She surmised correctly that if she could kill or at least injure their leader, then his men would scamper like rats back to their own vessel. Cutting aside members of Blackwatch's crew in her wake she made her way towards where he stood, watching proceedings from a safe distance.

'Blackwatch you are a true coward, leaving your men to fight your battle while you cower in a corner of MY ship, now take up your sword and fight me!' she yelled above the battle, her voice like slow rolling thunder.

'As you wish Blimey,' returned Blackwatch, who thought he still had a few more tricks up his sleeve. Dead or alive Vainglorious had said, and if it was to be dead so be it.

As Blimey reached Blackwatch they crossed swords, while behind her the melee continued. Blackwatch's men continued to fall, but Betty H.V and Farquar were slowly beginning to tire. Blimey knew she had to end this quickly. As she and Blackwatch fought on, Blimey didn't see Blackwatch's First Mate sneaking up behind her, but Betty H.V did. Screaming for Rawkous, she directed the bird to intervene, and just as

Blackwatch's man was about to run Blimey through the back with his sword, Rawkous caught him by surprise digging his not insubstantial claws deep into the sides of the man's head. As he yelled out in pain and shock, Rawkous disengaged and Blimey swiveled on her heel, and ducking a cheap shot from Blackwatch donkey-kicked him square in the groin causing him to double over in pain. With her next move she ran the First Mate through with her sword. As she pulled her blade free, he fell backwards, now out of the game. Wiping down her sword with a bloody rag, Blimey turned back to Blackwatch, who still hadn't recovered wholly from the blow he had been dealt. Sweeping her sword round, she caught him with her sword just above the elbow, the blade going deep and nearly severing the ligaments, instantly rendering his sword arm useless. Blackwatch started back, howling in pain, deciding quite rightly that things had now gone very badly for him.

'Men! Retreat!' he screamed as Blimey made to cause him further injury. Lurching past her he ran for the safety of his own ship, followed by what men he had left alive.

Traditionally the Pirate who won the battle took the other Captain prisoner, either to deal out further humiliation later or to ransom for a stack of gold. They also kept the other Captain's ship, but Blimey let Blackwatch go. She knew it would be more trouble than it was worth to try and keep him prisoner, and she had never liked his ship anyway. It was a flashy thing that literally announced to the world that he was not well endowed. For his part, Blackwatch took advantage of her mercy and set sail as fast as he could away from the Raven and her crew.

'This victory may be yours woman, but it will not be the last you see of me, or hear of my client,' Blackwatch yelled from the side of his ship as it moved away.

'You would do well to keep your threats to yourself before you are a safe distance from the range of my canons,' Blimey returned the volley, 'and keep it always in your mind that I let you go free today Blackwatch.'

Blimey, Farquar and Betty hates Veronica watched in silence as Blackwatch's ship sailed off. When she felt there was enough ocean between them, Blimey set Rawkous on watch and turned finally to survey the damage done to her ship, and the carnage this latest encounter with Blackwatch had left.

83

'This is why you should always take your battles away from home,' she sighed to herself, 'what a mess.'

'Well, this is going to take some time to clean up so we better get stuck into it, shall we just dump the dead over the side for the sharks?' asked Betty H.V.

'My ladies, there is no need for us to clean this up,' interrupted Farquar.

'What do you mean?' asked Blimey suspiciously. She was understandably wary of their new shipmate, who still had some secrets to share with them.

'A modern pirate often doesn't have time to waste returning their ship to an orderly state after an affray and so there are people you can call on to "clean house" for you. Let me engage the services of the Three Corpsateers, they are the best cleaners in the business. It would be an honour for me to pay for this. I owe you at least this much to begin with, and then while they are sorting out this mess, we can take some time to talk of your past,' he offered.

CHAPTER FIFTEEN

The Thirteen Bones

While up on deck the Three Corpsateers set to work cleaning the ship and removing the dead, Blimey, her First Mate and Farquar settled into some easy chairs in the Captain's lounge. As they shared a bottle of Red Rum between them, Rawkous stomped restlessly back and forth across the room's mantle, his sharp claws scratching lines the paint. He didn't like being cooped up inside, but he also didn't want to miss out on whatever was going on here.

'Alright Farquar, here we are, a captive audience, now tell me what it is about my lineage that is so important that you have brought such wrath down upon my ship to impart.'

'Well,' Farquar began and settled in to recount the tale of the Thirteen Bones...

'The tale I am about to tell you is not a happy one by all accounts, but it is the truth and fair in its facts. Your mother, your birth mother I mean Jeanne, was the most feared pirate of her time, and leader of the fearsome Thirteen Bones. Her married name was Elizabeth Bohnes, which would make you Jeanne Bohnes. I must admit though, I did not expect you to take on the namesake Blimey, which is why it took me so long to track you down. I have been looking for you since you ran away, and after you changed your name you became nothing more than a whisper for the longest time. Your foster parents, gentle misguided souls though they may be, do care for you very much and love you as their own child. Your disappearance has been a heavy burden for them. I have now sent word to them that you are alive and well and to worry no more. I trust that one day soon you will see it in your heart to write to them at least? The sadness at Korpus was not their doing, and was beyond their control to stop, so it will not do to have them living on in the shadow of blame for this. They are good people, and agreed to help me in troubled times though it put their own lives at risk. On this matter I must be firm, for they are old friends of mine.'

Blimey looked down at her boots, and nodded. She had not thought of her parents for the longest time, and had never given a thought to how her running away must have affected them.

'Your birth mother, Captain Elizabeth Bohnes, ruled the high seas with sword and saccharine humour in hand, with her own path to piracy leading from betrayal and a longing to avenge both the death of your father and your grandparents. I am sorry to say this, truly for I know it is a lot to take in, and you will never know your father, though he too be a good man when all debts are settled...'

Blimey nodded again, and reached for the bottle of Varn Clankston's Red Rum that Betty H.V now passed to her. Taking a swig she gestured for Farquar to continue, and handed him the bottle.

'Your father, Captain Gerald Bohnes, was also a pirate, and a noble man. I never knew him to turn down someone in need, nor give his last doubloon where it could help. In fact that is how he met your mother. Her parents, the poor trusting Everlone's, asked Gerald to take Elizabeth into his care and help her escape what they saw as a fate worse than death for their daughter. Elizabeth's proposed marriage to their employer. Lord Vainglorious. A disgusting brute of a man, as arrogant and mean as he is wealthy and stupid. I guess it is easy to tell I do not think much of the man. This request the kind hearted Gerald undertook, but the Everlone's paid for it dearly. Vainglorious took their actions as a personal betrayal and murdered the Everlone's himself in a fit of rage. Their poor frail bodies felt the sting of his lash over and over again before they finally gave in to the sweet relief of death. Elizabeth had no way of knowing this had occurred of course, as by this time she was dressed as a boy, and spirited away on Gerald's ship, hidden in plain sight as a member of the crew. Only Gerald knew her secret. She proved to be a good sailor, a good pirate, and quite handy in a battle, but eventually she would be found out. Luckily for both Gerald and Elizabeth, who had fallen in love, the crew of Gerald's ship – the Rapscallion – agreed Elizabeth could stay on, even though she was a woman.

'All was well and not long after this Elizabeth revealed she was going to have a child, and so your father suggested they get married. This is where I came in, for you see it was I that married them. They came to stay with me on my Island, Edevane, and once the baby was born it was agreed that Elizabeth would stay on with me, while Gerald returned to his life at sea. The baby born was you, my dear Jeanne. Months went by, and after your birth, Gerald returned to the sea while your mother stayed with me. However your father's first sail set would not end happily. Vainglorious had put a bounty on your father's head equal to a kings ransom, and every pirate on the Severed Seas was out to claim it – even those he had called friend in fairer times. It was not long before Captain Blackwatch found them, and openly attacked Gerald's ship. In the ensuing battle, Blackwatch ran Gerald through the back with his sword, just as he tried to do with you today. The blow was fatal. Having accomplished this treachery, and with the photos to prove it, Blackwatch ordered his men to depart, leaving the crew of the Rapscallion to tend to their fallen Captain. Gerald's dying wish was for his first mate, William, to ensure you and your mother's safety.

'William and the crew of your father's ship then set sail to return to Edevane, in the hope that they would reach me before Blackwatch. However unbeknownst to anyone, Blackwatch now had an unfair advantage. One of Gerald's own crew had betrayed him in exchange for a place on Blackwatch's ship, and a cut of the loot. It was the cabin boy, only just 11 years old and already showing signs of the double-dealing cad he would eventually become, James Blade...'

At the sound of Blade's name Blimey turned pale. Her fingers tightened around the arms of her chair, so much so that her knucklebones poked whitely through her skin, and the muscles in her face tightened, as her jaw clenched in anger. She could not believe her ears. Getting to her feet she ran to the room's portal and shoving it wide open, she pushed her head outside and threw up violently. Straightening up, she wiped her mouth as she looked out across the ocean, her face a mask of stone. She had always known Blade was a scoundrel, and of course he could never have known that Gerald Bohnes was her father, but nevertheless she vowed that he would pay for this betrayal. She would see to it. However for now, this anger would need to be buried, deep. There was more to hear from Farquar yet, and revenge is a dish best served so cold it was almost frozen, stabbed through the heart like a dagger made of ice.

'Are you alright?' asked Farquar as Blimey turned back to them and returned to her chair. She still looked as though she had seen a ghost.

'Yes, yes. Well, I will be. It's just so much to take in,' she replied, deliberately avoiding Betty hates Veronica's questioning gaze.

'Shall I go on? Do you need some time to ... recover from what I have already told you? I'm so sorry my dear, I know this must be hard for you to hear.'

'No, no please do go on Farquar, I must know it all,' encouraged Blimey.

'But...,' began Betty H.V and Rawkous at the same time.

'That,' stated Blimey coldly with a look that would strike dread into anyone who saw it, 'can wait for another time.'

'Very well...' started Farquar hesitantly, unsure what the other's were trying to say and unable to read the quizzical looks on their faces, 'Blackwatch sailed for Edevane as soon as he had left Gerald for dead and he arrived there within the day. His men rounded up all the villagers, including the children. Anyone who resisted was killed, or at the very least badly wounded. To avoid any further bloodshed, Elizabeth bravely volunteered to return to Vainglorious with Blackwatch and his crew. At this stage they did not know that Elizabeth was your mother, and they had no cause to suspect that she had a child at all, especially as I was holding the baby you at the time. Elizabeth might have left as a prisoner that day, but Blackwatch left us in peace, and so she saved many lives. The sorrow for your mother is that she did not even get to kiss you good-bye as it would have been too dangerous. After several days at sea, they had returned to your mother's hometown, Hallvard, and Blackwatch delivered Elizabeth to Vainglorious. It was then that she discovered the fate of her parents, as well as your father, and she swore vengeance. She was also told that plans were underway for her upcoming wedding to Vainglorious, more unwelcome news. But your mother was clever, and she used the opportunity to take over the planning of the nuptials herself. This way she could secretly divert some of the money that would have been spent on the wedding preparations towards purchasing her very own ship. She even had the seamstress who was making her wedding gown run up some beautiful black sails for the ship. The ship itself was also painted black and named the Reprisal. At the bow was a carved warrior maiden, holding a sword in one hand and in the other holding aloft the severed head of a longhaired man that clearly looked like Vainglorious. Elizabeth meant business.

'The day of the wedding approached, and all was in place. As she walked down the aisle in a flowing white gown, Elizabeth nodded to Vainglorious' Butler, whom had assisted her in her plans with the provision that Elizabeth take him and his family with her to a safe place to start a new life. As Elizabeth approached the arrogant fool Vainglorious and the minister, she swung aside a layer of her dress to reveal a very well armed maiden indeed, with a pistol in one hand and a sword in another. Yet rather than shoot Vainglorious on the spot Elizabeth had other ideas. Instead she jammed the gun under his chin and took him hostage, using him as a shield to make her way safely out of this theatre of grotesquery.

'I'll hunt you down and make you pay for this you harlot,' growled Vainglorious through clenched teeth.

'That be if you live through this. I decide whether you live or die in this moment so I would keep my thoughts to myself if I were you, you treacherous bastard!' returned the ferocious bride, as she forced her way through the crowd. No one dared to stop her, and Vainglorious' men could only look on in angry silence. It was no secret how much Elizabeth Bohnes hated Vainglorious, but few had seen such a powerful woman before, and in truth they were so stunned that many of them would not have been able to move even if they wanted to.

'Shoving Vainglorious into a carriage, where the Butler and his family awaited, Elizabeth sped towards the dock and the freedom that awaited her there. Arriving at the port she was met by William and the crew of the Rapscallion, who would sail with her out of the harbour and then rendezvous with their own ship. Forcing Vainglorious up the gangplank and onto her ship, the Reprisal, Elizabeth left him under the watchful gaze of the Butler so that she could man the helm and get her ship under sail, however it was then that Vainglorious made his move, and grabbing the Butler, he scared him into letting him go with threats to forever hunt him down and kill his family. As the Reprisal pulled out into the open sea, Vainglorious jumped ship and swam back to shore. Realising it was to late to turn back and stop him, Elizabeth had no choice but let him go. However she swore that one-day she would have her revenge on both Vainglorious and Blackwatch for what they had taken from her. She also kept good on her word to the Butler, who was dropped off on a small island, much like Edevane, with his family.

'Your mother then went on to become one of the most ferocious pirates on the Severed Seas, creating the Circle of Thirteen Bones, sometimes sailing alongside the Rapscallion, but often alone. She was a protector of those who could not protect themselves from the greed and evil that people do, but she never did get to take revenge for the loss of Gerald, her parents and missing out on watching you grow up. She always felt she would put you in danger if she returned for you, but I kept in touch with her for as long as I could, to let her know how you were getting on, though I haven't spoken to her for what seems like an age now,' sighed Farquar, leaning back in his chair as he reached the end of his tale.

'But, what happened to Elizabeth, my mother?' asked Blimey.

'Well that is the curious thing,' began Farquar slowly, 'For 16 years your mother ruled the Severed Seas, following Blackwatch to the farthest corner's of the globe, but fate seemed to be on Blackwatch's side, and every time your mother managed to track him down by the time she arrived, he had already left. I suppose eventually these constant near misses may have frustrated your mother, and perhaps she decided to give up her pirate life and her quest, and just settle down somewhere sunny. I really can't say with any certainty. I lost track of her around nine years ago. She simply disappeared and no one seems to have any idea of what happened to her, or where she may have sailed too. This latest brush with Blackwatch puzzles me though, as no one knew about you other than the crew of the Rapscallion and the Thirteen Bones themselves, and me of course. But how did Vainglorious find out about you... this I think I need to discover as soon as possible and then I will put an end to this madness for good... and so if I could trouble you for a lifeboat, and some oars, I will be on my merry way.'

Farquar got to his feet, smoothed down his vest, and looked expectantly at Blimey. She was deep in thought. To say that she was in shock was underplaying the situation. She had just been told not only that her parents were not her real parents, but that her father and grandparents had been murdered, she had been betrayed by Captain Blade and her real mother might still be alive some place.

'Oh no you don't mister,' stated Blimey, looking up finally, 'you don't land on my ship, lay all this on me, and then think you're just gonna take my landing boat and row off into the sunset to find my mother, or take out Blackwatch and Vainglorious – or whatever you're planning! No way – uh uh! If there's a chance that my real mother is still alive out there somewhere than I want to find her before Blackwatch does. I guarantee you that will be his next move. If he can't present me to Vainglorious he'll still want to take back someone, and he may just think my mother an easier target now that he knows I'm no pushover. But I want you to come with me. I need someone who knows what she looks like, plus I think you owe me that for leadin' Blackwatch to me in the first place – it seems to me like he's been following you for a while, waiting for his chance.'

'Very well, that may be so, and to be honest I wouldn't have expected anything less from Gerald Bohnes' daughter,' Farquar smiled.

'Betty hates Veronica, Rawkous, what do you think – are you in?' asked Blimey, getting to her feet.

'You know we are,' Betty H.V smiled, speaking for her and Rawkous as she stood up to face them.

'So where do you think we should start Farquar?'

'Well... I would say we should try to track down the Thirteen Bones, if any of them are still alive, as I said I have not heard anything of your mother in these many years past, but I do know where some of the Bones may be, and they should give us a compass point at least to begin with.'

'Alright then, lets get this boat under sail!'

CHAPTER SIXTEEN

A Hollow on the run

Vincent Blackshadow, the Hollow love of Blimey's past, was sitting at the same table in the Korpus Tavern as he had been when she had suddenly returned to his life. He had been brooding over her sudden appearance and re-disappearance for the past month or so. He couldn't seem to get her out of his head.

It had only been a brief encounter, with Vincent hurrying Blimey and her First Mate out of the town to protect them. Hatred of the living ran strong in Korpus, and the Hollow folk who dwelt there would not hesitate to destroy any living person they encountered. At the time Vincent had wanted to follow Blimey to the Raven, and the freedom of the open seas, but he was kept in the small town by the same misfortune that kept all the other villagers captive. By a strange twist of fate, it was actually the very soil of the town that kept the Hollow inhabitants in a state of suspended mortality, causing them to re-animate after they had been buried there. This soil possessed some strange magical properties that had not only brought the dead back to life but then allowed them to stay that way. However, should any of the Hollows stray outside the perimeter of Korpus, then their life force would simply fade away and they would die a second time. Vincent had cursed his entrapment here every day since Blimey's return, but it did not seem there was a way around the rules. Until now.

Vincent had been thinking, night after night, of a way around this dilemma. How could he leave but still stay "alive" and harness the power of the town's earth? Eventually an idea came to him and he went to see the local Blacksmith with a strange request. What Vincent wanted was an amulet, cast in steel, but with the soil of the area smelted into it, running through it. Vincent hoped that by always carrying the soil of Korpus with him, it would give him both the freedom and power he needed to track down his lady. The Blacksmith was intrigued by this strange request, but he saw in Vincent's eyes the look of a man who will not rest until he has conquered his demons, so the amulet was made.

Vincent placed the amulet, which the Blacksmith had shaped like a star, around his neck on a strong silver chain and walked to the edge of the town. When he reached the border he stopped, breathing heavily. A great fear weighed on his broad shoulders. What if this should not work, and he should perish... again? What then? Vincent had no answers, and only his life to loose, and so taking a deep breath, more for effect than anything, he stepped into unknown territory.

He stood paralysed for several minutes unable to move, only able to stare at the stars in the sky and wait for oblivion to grab him by the throat and pull him down, but nothing happened. He waited what seemed like an insurmountable time longer, and still he continued to stand. It seemed to Vincent that he had accomplished the impossible, and what no other Hollow of Korpus had been able to do. He had gotten out. Now all that remained for him to do was to gain passage on a ship somewhere, anywhere, and find Blimey. A simple enough plan, however Vincent first had to find the nearest port.

The night was cold, but Vincent didn't feel it as he walked through the forest towards the town of Ginshel, where he knew many ships came to get supplies before heading off to far stranger lands. Vincent reached the town's centre within a few hours, and headed for the dock. In the dark he did not stand out so much from the other pale townsfolk, and was able to walk quite freely through the cobbled streets. But Vincent knew as soon as the sun pierced the sky with its amber glow his appearance would begin to attract unwanted attention.

He hurried on, the glow of the moon telling him that his time was running short and he must get passage on a ship very soon. At the port he looked around for any likely ships that would accept him. Most of the ships were simple trading vessels, and not one flew the flag of a scoundrel. Vincent began to loose hope of getting out of the town that night, and was contemplating finding a place to stay during the day, when he finally spotted a ship that might suit him. It was the

Nevermore, and though he did not know it at the time Vincent was about to sign on board a ship captained by his former rival for Blimey's heart, James Blade.

Vincent approached the ship as if in slow motion, he did not know what to expect from the crew or the Captain, and hoped no one would notice the pallor of his skin or stare too deeply into his dark eyes, which were for the most part, pure black. He hoped things would go smoothly, and he could use this vessel to get away from his homeland and begin his quest. In fact all Vincent had at this stage was hope.

Sitting on the main deck of his ship in the dark, savoring the last drop from a bottle of wine he had begun drinking not too long ago, Captain Blade noticed the dark stranger heading up the gangplank of his ship and jumped up to meet him. He was just drunk enough to be looking for someone to talk too, and too drunk to care who that was. The curse of the high functioning alcoholic.

'Ahoy there, what can I do for you friend?' he asked jovially, ignoring the fact that this man may indeed be one of his enemies, of whom he had made many over the years. Blade was not known for thinking things through.

'I wish to gain work on your ship so that I may get clear of this land,' replied Vincent, bowing low.

'In trouble eh?' laughed Blade, who was not above running from situations himself.

'Not so much trouble... as just a basic need to get away,' replied Vincent speaking in vague half-truths.

'Not to worry, come aboard, we have no steady work and sail where we may, often with no destination in mind, but I can at least get you on your way,' smiled Blade.

'Thanks!' returned Vincent, 'but don't you want to know... '

But Blade cut him off with a wave of his hand. 'No, I don't want to know anything, it's late, and the night is too short for such boring stories, why not come and share some wine with me?'

In the dark, Vincent raised his eyebrows. He was surprised and not a little concerned by Blade's lack of curiosity, though in truth he would have reacted the same way himself if he had been as drunk. Sometimes the only way to survive in this world is by not knowing the reality of things, and Blade had lived by this ideal for most of his life so far.

'Ahh, and it feels as though we're just casting off, so no turning back now, I hope that's OK?' laughed Blade as he poured himself another glass of wine and the Nevermore drifted out into the harbour.

'So where are you headed this night?' Vincent turned to Blade in the moonlight, 'and at such an early hour?' He thought it wise to at least find out their headed direction if not their destination, so he could plan his own next steps if he was to find Blimey. A faint voice in the back of his mind had warned him not to ask Blade her whereabouts directly.

'Ah my life is uncomplicated, and I go where the wind takes me, I leave a town early as I stay up late and then get bored, and I just have to keep moving - there is too much to see and do to stay in one place too long, that is why this life I lead suits me,' said Blade without really answering.

'You must have a very interesting life,' said Vincent, momentarily forgetting himself and leaning into the candlelight a little to far. For a second the flame flickered brightly against his black eyes.

'My stars!' exclaimed Blade, starting back, and nearly drunkenly falling out of his chair, 'were you locked up somewhere boy? You're skin is white as marble and your eyes black like the devil's night!'

'Do not be alarmed,' soothed Vincent, knowing it would be better to skirt the truth further at this point, 'yes, I was trapped for many years, I only managed to escape tonight, I have been kept down for so long I forget how my looks might startle the average folk.'

'Who you callin' average?' laughed Blade, immediately recovering his jovial ways, 'it not be my business what has happened to you, but you best get some sun if you don't want people staring at you or running from you in horror!'

'Thanks for the tip,' laughed Vincent in relief, glad that he had managed to cover his tracks. Though Blade's words struck a chord of fear in his mind. Did he really look that alarming to the outside world? Could he really pull this off and find Blimey? Or was he living in a fool's fantasy? Well it was too late to turn back now.

CHAPTER SEVENTEEN

Out to sea

The Nevermore had been out on the open ocean for three days and Vincent, at the suggestion of Captain Blade, had been working the ship at night so as not to alarm the other crewmembers with his pale as death complexion. Vincent enjoyed working at night, and though he missed feeling the warmth of the sunlight on his skin, he could see the merit in Blade's idea. He wanted no trouble on this voyage. He knew he would encounter it soon enough. Besides, Blade was always up to all hours drinking and looking for conversation, so the night's were never boring. Blade's wild stories and adventures kept Vincent amused while he worked, though truth be told so far the night's had all ended with the two men drinking and laughing merrily instead of doing actual work.

Vincent was realising that he could quite happily make the sea his home, but first there was the question of his girl. He had been dreaming of her for too long now, though his dreams of late were troubled. In them he could see Blimey screaming out to him, as though terrified of something. But of what? He hadn't been able to figure that out. He always awoke as he turned to see what was causing her fear. Waking to find the last rays of daylight creeping through his window, he would shiver in his bed and glance out at the sunset. As he dressed and headed up on deck to work, the uneasy tendrils of the dream stayed with him, clutching at him like cold fingers in the dark.

That following evening the Nevermore pulled briefly into the port of Evileen, dropping Vincent off there at his request. Something had drawn him to this place and he felt it best to trust his instinct. It was all he had to go on at this stage. Blade was sorry to see Vincent go, but he knew better than to try and dissuade a man on a mission. Vincent turned to wave goodbye to Blade and the Nevermore as he headed towards the town and the nearest Tavern. Perchance it was the same tavern that Blimey had rescued Betty hates Veronica from years before. Pushing open the doors of the Tavern he headed straight for the bar, where he caught the eye of the barman right away. When your skin is as pale as walking death, and your eyes as black as sin, it's easy to attract attention. The barman scuttled over and gruffly asked what Vincent wanted.

'I'm looking for someone,' replied Vincent.

'Be that as it may,' said the barman, 'but I'm not talkin' to ye anymore lest you buy a drink.'

'Fine, I'll have a bottle of Shanty's lager,' answered Vincent, thinking to himself that the barman was a tad childish, 'now could you tell me where I could find a certain female pirate round these parts? Name of Blimey?'

As the words left Vincent's mouth the room fell silent.

'Why do you want to know where that harlot is?' asked the barman.

Vincent bristled at hearing his lady called a harlot, but he was smart enough to know that if he caused trouble now he would never find her. Very quietly Vincent answered the barman's question with a lie.

'I need to find her... so I can kill her.'

'Ahhhh,' smiled the barman, 'then in that case, she flies a ship called the Raven, doesn't come into this port no more - she's not welcome here and knows as much. Best way to find her is put out word you want her dead and she'll find ye soon enough.'

'That seems like a lot of trouble and would kind of ruin the surprise of it all,' murmured Vincent to himself, before adding 'what I mean to say is I don't want her to know I'm comin' after her, so I need to find her first.'

'Well sir, then the best thing you can do is get yourself a ship and go out looking for her. Last I heard she was headed South West, but that was many moons ago and is unfortunately the best I can do for directions,' said the barman.

'Thanks anyway,' replied Vincent, taking a sip of his beer, and flipping a gold coin at the barman, 'can I take this with me?'

'Sure, just don't let the constabulary know you got it from me,' smiled the barman, thinking to himself what a nice young man he was and that it was sad that he would soon probably find himself sleeping with the fishes after being on the wrong end of Blimey's sword.

It was time Vincent went and found himself a ship. Taking his beer with him, he went out into the night and turning his back on Evileen, headed down to the dock to survey the vessels moored there. Surely there was one he could easily steal. Vincent figured that as long as he was chasing a pirate he may as well become a pirate himself, and the few days he had spent at sea with Blade had at least given him a basic understanding of how to run a ship. He just needed to find one that was heavily automated.

Creeping like a bat out of hell towards the last ship on the dock, which would be the easiest one to get out of port, Vincent spied what in time would become his other love. She was beautiful and had curves in all the right places. Vincent had just caught sight of the Obscurity. A ship as black as night, and just as mysterious. Many had heard tales of the Obscurity and her captain Etype Jagwar. Etype was well known both for his violence and his love of jam fancies (little jam filled biscuits normally served with a cup of tea). This didn't matter to Vincent at this moment as he untied the ship and stalked up the gangway. All that he wanted now was to get this ship out onto the ocean before anyone noticed what was going on. As stealthy as he was being, what Vincent didn't know was that Etype was watching this little act of thievery in disbelief with his crew from the shore, but he was too far away to do much about it at this point and he knew it. By the time he or any of his crew made it to the harbour, Vincent would be long gone. The Obscurity was a fast ship. This didn't stop Etype from swearing his revenge quite loudly, and to anyone within listening distance. By morning Etype would be shipped up, crewed up and on his way to get his ship back.

Hitting the helm in a blur of adrenalin, Vincent punched the controls to get the ship in motion. The last few days with Blade serving him well on this next part of his adventure. Flying out of the harbour, the Obscurity sliced through the dark waters of the sea much like an apple cart doesn't. Vincent felt the night winds caress his face gently. He inhaled the salty air and thought he might explode with happiness. So this was what having your own ship felt like. Vincent had never experienced anything quite like it. The closest thing he could compare it to was a kiss from Blimey herself. Now he understood why she lived for this freedom, and why she could never return to her old life. Vincent couldn't go back now either. Instinctively he reached for the amulet that hung around his neck. Clutching it in his fist briefly to reassure himself. Despite this new happiness he couldn't help worrying about what would happen should it come loose and fall from his neck.

Vincent's distraction was short lived as the moon drifted out from behind the clouds where it had been hiding. It's light casting a silvery glow over everything, bringing Vincent back to reality and returning his focus to the task at hand. It dawned on him that some decisions would have to be made. Including where he was actually going. He had not sailed before and whilst his amateur skills and natural feel for the ship would keep him afloat on the open ocean, sooner or later he would have to pull into a harbour, and Vincent wasn't sure he would be able to pull that one off without breaking something. Navigation was not another one of his strong points at this stage either, and so for now he would have to be content with randomly sailing through the ocean, going where the wind willed.

Vincent was about to catch a break in a big way however, when the Raven appeared on the horizon the following day. Blimey had found him first.

CHAPTER EIGHTEEN

Hello again

Two days after Blimey had decided that she would go to find her mother, she and Betty H.V were sparring with sword and dagger on the deck of the Raven. After a rather energetic lunge, which Blimey expertly parried, Betty hates Veronica spun off dizzyingly before running into the side of the ship. Looking up and out to sea she spotted something that was enough to ruin anybody's early morning cutlass practice.

'Bloody Heck! The Obscurity's heading our way!' yelled Betty hates Veronica to her Captain.

'What? it can't be, I heard Etype was on holiday,' growled Blimey, not at all impressed.

'Well unless someone has stolen his ship I'd say he very much means business - he's comin' this way fast,' replied Betty hates Veronica.

'That na'er do well, he spoils everything that's good and pure. Just be ready for him, if he's drunk we might be able to sail right past him,' advised Blimey.

The girls both made their way up to the helm where they could get a good view of the Obscurity and watch for signs of likely inebriation. Slowly and a little crookedly, the ship moved towards them. Blimey sighed in relief. It seemed that Etype may be drunk after all and would probably coast right past them. Etype was well known on the seas for booking no peace with any crew, fighting with anyone for reasons unknown and firing cannons at seagulls for fun. But at least he had the common decency to fly the colours and give warning of an approaching battle. Blimey was heartened to see his flag was not currently flying. This respite was short lived, however, when Blimey soon realised that the drunken fool at the helm of the Obscurity would soon sail his ship right into the Raven if he did not change course. He was approaching much to fast to maneuver out of the way.

'Watch out!' Blimey hailed the other ship via loudspeaker.

'Ahhhhhh!' screamed the captain of the Obscurity in reply, who they could now see was obviously not Etype, though they could not exactly see who it was yet.

'Betty H.V, take the helm, I have to get over to that damned boat and steer her away!' ordered Blimey in alarm.

Diving over the side of the Raven, she swam out to the ship. She knew she didn't have much time. Grabbing onto some rigging hanging over the side of the Obscurity, she pulled herself up out of the icy water and began climbing up the side of the ship. Hauling herself over the side and on to the deck, she landed on her feet and sprinted for the helm. Shoving Vincent roughly out of the way, Blimey grabbed the helm and pulled the wheel to the left with all her strength. The boat groaned outwardly as it began to swerve sharply out of the way of the Raven. Blimey wrestled with the ship as though they were both locked in a battle to the death. The Raven was more important to her than anything right now and she was not going to let it get damaged by some idiotic drunk driver. Meanwhile Vincent, who had lost his footing after Blimey had thrown him aside, had fallen down the short set of stairs that led up to the helm deck, and rolled across the hard wood of the main deck, crashing into the main mast. He moaned softly, and then consciousness left his mind to it's own black devices.

Back on the Raven, Betty hates Veronica was struggling to undertake evasive maneuvers of her own, steering the Raven sharply to the right. Alarmed by the sharp movement of the ship, Farquar bounded up the stairs from below deck, making his way to the helm, gripping the stair rail for dear life as Betty H.V pulled the Raven out of harms way. Lost in the moment, Betty H.V had no time to think, and no time to explain. Finally, as the Raven sailed out of trouble, out of the corner of her eye she could see her Captain at the helm of the Obscurity, and sighed in relief as the opposing boat finally slid away past the Raven, just missing her by a thread. It was close.

Now they had avoided collision, Blimey threw the lever that released the anchor, stopping the Obscurity gently in her sail. She then turned to the ships Captain, who was slumped against the main mast, seemingly in a drunken stupor. She still did not know whom she had thrown aside in her haste as there had been no time to waste. Now as she stormed over to the unconscious form, she was not in a very generous mood.

As she approached his sunken form, her pace began to slow as she caught sight of the man's face. She realized she was looking down on Vincent Blackshadow. As this washed over her, her heart beat in her chest like a drum. Running over to him and dropping to the floor, she cradled his head in her hands. A rush of happiness coursed through her, as she stared into his handsome face, and slowly his eyes opened.

'Welcome back. You nearly wrecked my ship,' she said gently as Vincent cupped her face in both his hands and kissed her.

Back aboard the Raven, Betty hates Veronica had also dropped anchor and was watching the scene unfold aboard the Obscurity. Her mouth dropped open in shock as she watched her captain kissing some strange man, who from this distance she still thought might be Etype Jagwar.

Blimey pulled away from Vincent and looked into his face again for a moment. She could not believe he was back with her. A million thoughts fought for control of her mouth, but none it seemed were capable of winning.

'But how? I thought you couldn't leave Korpus...' she said finally, fighting to hold back tears.

'My amulet,' answered Vincent, holding the star aloft, 'is cast from the earth of Korpus and so keeps me alive, but I guess it is now also my weakness. I hitched a ride on a ship called the Nevermore to the port of Evileen and then I stole this ship, though I'm not much of a Captain, yet.'

Vincent smiled, and Blimey kissed him again. Alarm bells rang gently in the back of her mind. The Nevermore. So Vincent had been with Blade. Did Blade know what Vincent's connection to her was? Where was Etype Jagwar? Surely he was missing his ship and would come looking for it, which would mean more trouble. She knew they had to get back aboard the Raven and figure out what to do next. Helping Vincent to his feet Blimey hugged him briefly for a moment and called to Betty hates Veronica.

'It's not Etype! It's Vincent!'

'Wait, what? How?' called back Betty H.V.

'We're coming back over, and I'll explain everything,' returned Blimey as she and Vincent laid a gangplank between the two ships, and walked across to the Raven.

Betty hates Veronica didn't quite know how she should react as they jumped down onto the Raven's main deck. On the one hand she was relieved that it was Vincent and not Etype who had been captaining the Obscurity, but on the other she knew that this meant a crazed evil villain would be heading their way to reclaim his ship. And what of their current mission? What did Vincent's sudden appearance in her Captain's life mean for that? Would he join them now? Betty H.V was still pondering these questions when Blimey rushed up and clapped a hand on her shoulder.

'Nice work saving the Raven,' she said.

'Thanks, you didn't do so badly yourself,' replied Betty hates Veronica smiling broadly at her friend, before turning her attention to Vincent, 'nice to see you again, Vincent.'

'Uh, thanks,' he replied somewhat bashfully, 'sorry about the bother... you know, nearly smashing into your ship.'

'Oh we're quite used to things like that,' smiled Betty H.V at his humbleness, 'I'll get us something to drink, I think we could all do with something strong,' she finished, before turning to run down to the galley.

'Well now I must say you make quite an entrance!' exclaimed Farquar, stepping forward and putting out his hand.

'It was not intended sir, I can assure you,' laughed Vincent shaking Farquar's outstretched limb, 'I am Vincent, and have known Jeanne here for a long time,'

'I see,' replied Farquar raising an eyebrow at the use of Blimey's real name, 'and you may call me Farquar, or the Reverend. Now then m'boy, you're a Hollow aren't you? From Korpus? I know your people well, and something of your... history, but how is it that you could leave there?'

'I found a way,' smiled Vincent, somewhat awkwardly, his hand automatically touching the amulet at his throat.

'Yes... I see,' started Farquar slowly, before Blimey interrupted them.

'Vincent, you took a great risk coming here, I have several enemies you know, and now so do you,' she stated.

'I know, but I don't care, I had to find you, ever since you came back to Korpus you're all I can think about. I love you,' explained Vincent in a rush of emotion, turning to Blimey and reaching for her hand, but his girl turned sharply away.

'Oh Vincent, you beautiful fool, you can't stay, it wouldn't work out. I have to get you back, I will not let you put your life on the line like this, you're too vulnerable,' she said to the wind, walking to the side of her ship and looking out to sea dramatically.

Vincent felt like he had been punched in the face, had a dagger stuck through his heart and had all his *Star Wars* toys confiscated. Her words hurt him that much.

'Well, think what you may, I'm not leaving you,' he stated pensively.

Blimey didn't answer him, but instead continued looking out to the sea. Tears threatened to escape her eyes and roll down her pale cheeks, but she would not let them. She had not spent the last few years learning not to care, just to have it all taken away from her now.

'You cannot send me away!' Vincent continued defiantly, and Blimey knew she owed him some kind of reply. Thoughts flew through her mind like razors, cutting here and there as she tried to formulate an answer that would not be a lie. She did want him to stay, but his life would always be in danger. Finally she turned to him.

'Very well, but if you stay I cannot guarantee your safety. This amulet you wear leaves you so very vulnerable. If you stay, your life is in your own hands, but I could not stand to lose you again.'

'You don't have to be so hard all the time. I knew what I was doing when I left, can't you just be happy to see me?' he asked, walking over to her, gently lifting her chin and looking into her eyes.

'Sure, I can,' she relented as the tears finally won, and rolled down her cheeks.

Hugging her tightly, Vincent kissed her forehead as Betty H.V returned with their drinks, breaking the silence. Blimey turned and wiped away her tears. This was the last time she would cry for a long time.

'So what's going on here besides the obvious lovers reunion?' asked Betty hates Veronica trying to dissolve the serious mood that had settled on the Raven. She did not care for seriousness, and often found it to be quite dull, unless it led to a fight of some sort.

Sensing this might not be the right moment to press his

questioning further, Farqaur grabbed one of the drinks on offer and all took a seat on the deck. Sipping their drinks thoughtfully, they all listened intently as Blimey explained to Vincent just exactly who's ship he had stolen and why they were all now in a bit of a hot mess. Blimey had heard much about the pirate Etype and wasn't entirely confident that they could beat him in battle. Strange things had happened to those who had faced him in the past. Some said he was a sea monster masquerading as a man, others said he was a demon, some still said he was a shape shifter who turned into a polar bear. While she believed none of these tales, her thoughts were still dark. They eventually decided that the best thing for them to do was to get rid of the ship and hope that Etype didn't put two and two together. Unfortunately they weren't counting on Vincent opposing this plan.

'I was actually thinking I might be able to keep the ship,' said Vincent, hopefully.

'What? Why? No! It's just mischief on water now,' replied Blimey in astonishment. She had never considered that Vincent actually liked the whole sailing around the ocean gig, and was in truth a bit put out that he would want a vessel of his own rather than sailing with her. I mean after all – he was on the Raven now – one of the most amazing ships on the sea! She did however understand the temptation of having your own ship, and to be honest couldn't really blame Vincent. The Obscurity was also a beautiful vessel.

'Oh,' Vincent looked down sadly.

'You must understand, Vincent, we have to leave this ship behind, Etype is no ordinary pirate, his crew are vicious. He is hunting you for his ship, even as we speak, and the easiest thing for us to do is leave the Obscurity somewhere that he will find it, and be done with it.'

'I understand, but I will miss her,' he replied.

'I know, but I will let you steer the Raven anytime you want,' Blimey offered soothingly, as she got up and walked over to the helm, kissing Vincent lightly on the cheek on her way.

Later that afternoon as Vincent was bringing lunch out to the girls they spotted a strange ship on the horizon. Blimey could sense who it was before she even saw the flag flying. It was Etype come to claim his ship. Calmly she took a bottle of Red Rum from a small table she had set out on the main deck, specifically to rest her rum on. Swigging from the bottle she turned to her crew, who were playing poker nearby.

'Damn his hide! We're out of time! I knew we should have cast off earlier, you know what this will probably come to now,' she stated grimly.

'Yep,' replied Betty hates Veronica stepping forward and taking the bottle from her Captain. Vincent stood also and wrapped his arm around Blimey's waist, staring off at the approaching ship. Farquar stood just a fraction behind them, deep in contemplation. It was he who had convinced them to stay a bit longer.

'I give us ten minutes,' said Blimey, signaling for Rawkous who flew down to perch on her shoulder.

'If things go pear shaped bird, you know what to do,' she said to the parrot.

'Swoo hoo, yes Cap'n,' replied the bird taking flight again and heading up to the crow's nest where he could watch events unfold from a safe distance.

The strange ship came upon them quickly, with it's colours flying. Blimey didn't recognize the flag, but she didn't care. The Captain of the opposing vessel hailed her.

'Where is the thief who has taken Etype's ship? I have him with me, and he has come to claim it!' he stated.

'I had kind of figured that one out for myself, but I will not give up the thief, for he did not mean to cause trouble,' responded Blimey, adrenalin coursing through her veins as she tried to assess the situation.

'That of course is up to you lass, but whether he meant harm or not is no matter to us, we will take the Obscurity and you will pay for this treachery,' returned the Captain of the other ship.

'This I also counted on, but first do me the courtesy of telling me who you are?' asked Blimey.

'I am Vanilla Kingston, and this is my ship, the Volvonte,' replied the Captain.

'And you're connection to Etype?'

'I deliver his biscuits,' answered Vanilla proudly.

'Right, so this is why he commandeered your vessel and came after me then, you're an easy mark with not much to do?' she summed up.

'Well..... er.... Yes, that would be a fair assessment,' he said.

At that moment Etype and his crew appeared along the side of the Volvonte. Swords raised in anger, and also in a vague kind of threatening way.

'I don't want to fight you Etype,' called Blimey, 'and so I will give you one more chance to do the honourable thing, take back your ship for we have no want of it, and leave now!'

'I would heartily like to my dear,' replied Etype, 'for I respect your skill with the blade, however I also realise the power I will be able to wield over every pirate on the seas after I have killed you. It'd be good for business, and also for my personal reputation.'

'As you wish,' replied Blimey coldly and drew her cutlass, behind her Betty hates Veronica, Farquar and Vincent did the same. They looked hopelessly outnumbered compared to the numbers of Vanilla and Etype's crews combined.

Tense moments passed with the two enemies facing each other over the watery divide. Someone coughed. It wasn't apparent who, but this it seemed was the cue for Etype and his men to board the Raven. Swords clashed and much scuffling was involved. One by one Etype's crew began to fall as Blimey and her loyal friends cut down the flotsam and jetsam around them, until finally Etype was the last man standing. It was at this moment that he chose to reveal his true form. He was indeed a giant white hairy thing masquerading as a man, but it was clear to all that he was some kind of monster, not a polar bear.

'Oh great, now I suppose we'll have to clean up your errant hairs as well as all this blood and gore your crew have left all over my ship!' snapped Blimey.

'I don't molt so easily,' growled Etype.

'I don't want to discuss your hair loss problems, just look at the mess your men have made of my deck!' returned the angry Blimey.

'I believe it was you who killed them,' retorted the monstrous Etype.

'We quibble over details ..... look, I will give you one more chance to leave this vessel in peace or I will be forced to take you down hairball,' she offered graciously.

'Don't test me girl, it is I who should be making you offers, though I be out numbered by your crew it will still be me who emerges the victor in this,' replied Etype.

'You arrogant bastard!' stated Betty hates Veronica, attracting Etype's attention and causing him to charge at her in a wrath of fur.

Betty H.V dived out of his way but he moved too fast and caught her arm with one of his claws, leaving a long gash. She screamed out in pain, falling heavily onto her side. Vincent grabbed her and quickly pulled her to safety. Etype skidded to a stop on the deck, leaving deep scratch marks in his wake. He turned to face Blimey, snarling briefly, his lip rising to reveal yellowed but sharp teeth. Blimey stalked towards Etype, the fury shining in her eyes as she glimpsed the blood dripping down her friend's arm, and the scratches in her wood veneer.

'You've ruined my deck!' she yelled, her cutlass at her side.

'Come on, it'll buff right out,' he laughed, before charging her. The two came together in a mess of flesh and fury. Betty H.V and Vincent watched on, their faces aghast, for Etype was easily three times the size of Blimey. They were fighting so fiercely, that the others were afraid to step in lest they accidentally hit her. All they could do was watch on. Suddenly Etype roared in pain as Blimey's sword found it's way to his heart, and she deftly stepped aside as Etype breathed his last and fell dead on the deck. She looked over at her friends. They were standing not far from her, Betty H.V clutching some cloth against the wound on her arm, as Vincent prepared to stitch up the deep gash underneath.

'So who wants to help me clean up this lot!' she smiled.

'Next time, we fight at their place, I hate cleaning up after the party,' complained Betty H.V. wincing in pain as Vincent put in the first stitch.

'Don't worry, I'll do it, I guess I owe you girls quite a favour,' said Vincent.

'Yes you do, but I'm not going to make you clean this mess up on your own. I'll just call the Three Corpsateers – Farquar will you do the honours?'

'The what now?' asked Vincent.

'The T.C, Farquar put us on to them. They show up quick smart when you call and cart all the bodies away, wash away the blood, make things all nice again and all for a very reasonable fee,' explained Betty H.V.

'Wow, that's handy. Looks like you pirates have just about everything figured out,' laughed Vincent.

Within a few hours the Raven was restored to her former glory. The T.C had done a marvellous job, and had hastily cleared away the mess left by Etype and his crew. Vanilla Kingston, the biscuit deliverer who had brought Etype Jagwar to Blimey had fled as soon as it looked like things were getting a bit, ah herm, hairy. And now the only problem left for Blimey and her crew to deal with was the Obscurity, the ship that Vincent had stolen, which had gotten them into this mess in the first place.

Blimey knew that Vincent wanted to keep the ship for himself, but she also knew that he did not have the skills yet needed to captain it on his own. Not only that, but the ship was well known as belonging to Etype, and people might ask them questions that they didn't want to answer, at least not right now. Better to let the word of Etype's death spread like whispers in the night from the lips of Vanilla Kingston. It would cause less ripples this way.

There was also the problem of Vincent's vulnerability. While the amulet around his neck was the only thing keeping him alive, Blimey didn't want him in harm's way lest it could be helped. His protection had been utmost in her mind during the scuffle with Etype and his men, and she had given Rawkous explicit instructions to make sure he put himself between Vincent and danger should it look like he was in trouble. The bird may have been small, but he was wily, and his claws packed a decent punch.

The only solution to the situation seemed to be for Vincent to stay with Blimey, at least for now, until he learned all he would need to pirate a ship on his own. He would find no better teacher surely, and Blimey was not one to keep a man from the sea. She knew herself how the lure of the open ocean captured your mind and forever drew you to her waters with the promise of sovereignty. She also knew that eventually Vincent would leave her to return for the Obscurity. It was indeed now his, and it would be cruel to deny him the chance to sail her on his own. Of course he would never be away for long and would always return to her. That was yet to come however, and they would have to hide the Obscurity for the time being. Preferably in some stereotypically isolated rocky sea cave. Then they could return for her when things had settled down a bit.

Blimey looked at Vincent and smiled to herself. He was standing on the bow, the wind picking up idle strands of his hair and tossing them this way and that. He was indeed a very handsome man. Lost in her thoughts for the moment she let her mind wander to what other troubles her beau may encounter. One by one she added them together, but the one that now stuck foremost in her mind was also one she dreaded most. Captain Blade. Vincent did not know about the past she shared with Blade, or the revenge she now planned to take against him for his role in the death of her father. True she hadn't seen him for weeks, but she had a feeling that he would be back in her life very soon. Like a bad penny he always seemed to turn up sooner or later.

CHAPTER NINETEEN

What you don't know

The following day, as the sun hid behind angry clouds, Blimey sailed the Obscurity, followed closely by the Raven, towards a set of three isolated, deep caves that she knew of. Called the Three Sisters, they had once been a well-known hiding place for pirate treasures, but they had long since fallen out of favour as the King's men discovered their whereabouts. Abandoned for many years now, Blimey had often come here when she needed to think, meditate and get away from the endless decisions and responsibilities that life threw at her.

Mooring the Obscurity in the left hand, and deepest of the caves, she dove into the dark waters and swam out towards the sunlight, where the Raven awaited. Overhead, the ceiling of the cave was covered with stalactites, which glowed with an eerie green light. It was a decent swim to get out of the cave, and without this guiding light, it would have been easy to get lost in any number of the watery side passages that veered off to the left and right.

Back on the Raven, and with the Obscurity safely tucked away, Vincent began settling in to life on the ship. Blimey also felt a sense of peace she had not experienced before. It worried her. It had been three days now since the clash with Etype, and almost a week since their meeting with Blackwatch, and no other pirates had crossed their path. Usually this would be cause for celebration, but in place of festivities there had developed a feeling of disconcertion. Focusing on the horizon ahead as she steered the Raven towards the coordinates Farquar had set into the ship's guidance system, she still wondered if she were doing the right thing. They were headed for a port that Farquar knew of, or a collection of miscreants as he called it, in the hope that they might gain some information on the whereabouts of the Thirteen Bones and Blimey's mother, Elizabeth. Betty hates Veronica joined her at the helm and stared out at the calm seas ahead of them.

'I don't like this calm. He's on his way isn't he?' she asked, 'I can feel the winds blowing ill every time he is about to show up again.'

'Yes,' was all Blimey would say, and so Betty hates Veronica felt it best to leave her alone with her thoughts. Blimey had yet to work up the courage to tell Vincent about Blade and the past she shared with him. She didn't know how to start the conversation. She was terrified that he would be hurt, or angry. That he would leave. All of the above.

Blimey subtly changed their course and sailed due east, away from the direction she instinctively knew Blade would be coming from. She had to buy herself some more time until she could figure out how to explain to Vincent why this scoundrel was chasing her across the ocean, and what Farquar had revealed to her about her former beau.

Betty hates Veronica stood a small distance from Blimey and stared at her Captain in a quiet contemplation all of her very own. The wind whipped her hair around her face, but she let it play its games. She knew Blimey was worried. Blade had been a part of her life for some time and you can't just shove your emotions around until they fit in a neat little package. Betty H.V was dreading Blade's arrival. She had never felt he deserved such a friend as he had in Blimey. He was a user of people, a vagabond, a joker, a cad and a liar. Silently she vowed to ensure that Blade would soon be out of their lives for good.

Blimey looked towards her first mate, and smiled thinly. It was time to settle this.

'I'm going to go and find Vincent,' she stated.

'Are you sure you want to do this now?' asked Betty H.V stepping up to take the helm, as Blimey strode towards the lower deck.

'I have no choice!' Blimey called back, disappearing below decks.

Vincent Blackshadow was sitting in a chair in the ship's library, quietly reading. A beam of sunlight flew in from the window suddenly, lighting his handsome face. Blimey's heart swelled, as she seemed to finally realise just how much this man had gone through to find her.

'Vincent, I have to tell you something,' she said breathlessly, breaking the silence.

Vincent's smile turned gently into a frown as the words left Blimey's lips. No conversation ever ended well that had begun with these words. He hated moments like this, it felt the same as when he had learnt that Blimey had run away all those years ago.

'Sure,' he said with a strained smile, 'come sit down.'

Taking a seat, Blimey began hesitatingly.

'I was ... seeing... this man... well he's not really a man... more of a rapscallion... well a pirate really. But it was so long ago now, and it's over... so definitely over. I promise, and I haven't seen him... like that... in that way... for a long while now, but he keeps reappearing in my life from time to time,' she started, watching Vincent's face contort through several emotions at once. She hated herself for having to have this conversation, especially in light of what a snake Blade had turned out to be, but she had to go on, 'I thought you were gone forever, you know, and if I had thought you were still alive, even for a moment, I never would have left you, and I will always love you,' she finished in anguish, her face a mask of horror and pain.

'Hey, hey now ... there's no need to get upset Blimey girl,' soothed Vincent softly, going to her and lifting her up to hold her tightly, 'that's history OK, before now, before our time, I don't need to know anything more than that. But why are you telling me this now? Is he coming for you, is that why we changed course? I felt the ship...' he was truly just relieved that this was all that was troubling her. A case of guilt over substance.

'Yes!' cried Blimey cutting him off dramatically, 'I am sure he is, but this time I need to take him down. Farquar has told me some secrets... that this pirate once sailed with my father, my real father, and that he betrayed him to his death. It's a very long story, and I will tell you everything another time, but if you want to leave now, I'll understand. I'll take you back to the Obscurity and you can go,' Blimey pressed her face into his broad chest and Vincent hugged her more tightly.

'I'm not leaving you,' stated Vincent, 'I just found you again! And if you are sure that it is me you want to be with, then I will face him with you.'

'Yes, of course it is you!' Blimey said as she looked up into his face, and Vincent leaned in to kiss her.

Up on the deck Betty hates Veronica had caught snippets of this conversation as the wind had sent wisps of the words to her ears through the open porthole. She smiled to herself.

Unfortunately this quiet happiness was short lived. On the horizon she could see the outline of another ship. She knew instinctively it was the Nevermore, and it was speeding towards them full sail. Betty knew what she had to do and prepared to drop anchor. The time for running was over.

The Raven coasted gently to a standstill. Feeling the ship coming to a stop Blimey and Vincent turned as one, running for the stairs that led up to the main deck. Meanwhile Betty hates Veronica had been watching the Nevermore draw ever closer to the Raven and waited. Blade hailed her as he recognized her on deck, and reaching planking distance between the two ships he dropped anchor and showing off in a completely garish fashion swung aboard. Betty hates Veronica greeted him with a stone-faced smile.

'How are ye Blade?' she asked with a sneer.

'I have come to visit my favourite girl,' was his rakish reply.

'I doubt very much that my Captain was ever your girl as you so boldly put it Blade,' stated Betty H.V with open contempt.

'Why have you always disliked me?' asked Blade, as though seeing Betty H.V for the first time and noticing her obvious distaste of him.

'Because you are a selfish moron who uses my friend, but my disdain for you is the least of your troubles now, considering what we have just learned about your... past,' she smirked, turning her head has she heard her Captain's heels upon the stairs.

Moments later Blimey emerged into the sunshine, followed closely by Vincent Blackshadow. She looked at Blade coldly, and felt an instant surge of anger, not only for her father's death, but also for herself. How could she have wasted so much time on this cad!

'What do you want Blade?' she asked, taking hold of Vincent's hand to reassure him who she was concerned for. Blimey knew that she would have to be blunt with Blade, otherwise he wouldn't be able to grasp the concept that he would soon be out of her life for good. Alive if he was lucky.

He simply wasn't smart enough to put two and two together on his own.

'Well, I guess I wanted you,' he smiled, 'but it appears that I have some competition... hello Vincent.'

'Hello James, and thank you again for my lift out of town, though I can see now that I was right to keep my intentions to myself,' replied Vincent who in truth was disappointed by this eventuality. He had actually liked Captain Blade, and did not really want to confront him.

'Yes, if I had known your mission was to come after this wench, I probably would have finished you on the spot,' replied Blade coldly, 'I thought you were a good guy Vincent... but no matter, I will still kill you now, I'm pretty awesome with a sword,' he added, laughing sarcastically before drawing his cutlass.

'Ha! Being awesome is something you earn, not something you state,' mumbled Betty hates Veronica, but no one heard her, they were all lost in the moment.

Vincent only sighed and drew his own sword. His heart was heavy for so many reasons today and he felt so tired. Yet he would face this new challenge, if only for Blimey. Blade stepped up to face Vincent, but before the duel could begin Betty H.V rushed forward, dagger in hand. She didn't get very far. Blimey grabbed her wrist.

'This is not your fight honey, it's mine,' she said gently, before turning to face Blade.

But it was too late. This movement had distracted Vincent, who turned his gaze towards the girls for only a moment. It was long enough for Blade to seize the opportunity and stab wildly and viciously at Vincent, going for his heart. Though he missed, the point of his blade cracked into the amulet that hung around Vincent's neck, shattering it immediately. Vincent looked up in shock, as the amulet fell to the ground in pieces. Vincent looked from Blade to Blimey, and then dropped silently to the deck. Without the amulet Vincent was simply a dead man.

Blade laughed heartily. 'Well that didn't take much at all, I was wondering what his necklace was fer, and why he was so pale. So you have a thing for Hollows do ye? Well I think it's time you came back to the living don't you?'

Blimey looked at Vincent's motionless body and felt pure

fury rising within her. Launching herself at Blade in a storm of anger she hit him at full speed bowling him backwards.

'You stupid arrogant bastard!' she spat at him, 'why would you think I would want to be with you? Vincent was everything that you could never be! But as if that wasn't the worst thing about you being in my life, I know it was you who betrayed my father. He died because of your treachery Blade! Farquar told me everything! You have led me down a merry path of lies and duplicity, but no more Blade. You are nothing more than a putrid piece of my past that I would sooner forget. But, lady luck still haunts you it seems, and today is not your day to die. I must deal with the situation that you have arrived and left me with. Now - get off my ship before I do something YOU regret! You know you cannot beat me you pathetic fool.'

'I never knew your father!' Blade yelled angrily in return, a look of confusion on his face, 'fine, I will go, but I will not forget this insult and I will be back for you.'

'Liar!' Betty hates Veronica screamed at him, stepping forward, dagger in hand and very keen for any excuse to take a swipe at the rogue before them.

With a look of hurt confusion still upon his face, Blade jumped across to his ship. He was a proud man and this was too much for him to take. These were also serious accusations levied against him; true it could be perhaps part of his past that, with the help of drink, he had long since forgotten. He needed to know, and the situation necessitated he get to the bottom of this quickly. Blimey was not someone who he wanted as an enemy, and so if he could prove these accusations false, and redirect her hatred this would be a powerful win for him. And with Vincent out of the picture he honestly thought he still stood a chance with Blimey. And he would have to deal with this Farquar fellow as well. What was his deal spreading rumour and libel? It was not good for his complexion.

On the Raven, Blimey flew to Vincent's unmoving form. The pieces of his smashed amulet lay all around him. Blimey knew what she had to do, she only hoped it would work. Taking her cutlass she made a long incision in his chest, just under his rib cage, and began stuffing pieces of the amulet inside the wound. Dark blood flowed over the deck as Betty H.V watched her Captain in wonder and alarm, before it suddenly dawned on her what Blimey was trying to do. She ran to grab a needle and some tough thread. Someone would have to mend that wound in a moment, and Blimey couldn't sew at all.

Through her anguish, Blimey kept stuffing the wound with pieces of the amulet, until Farquar finally pulled her away. It was the only way to break the madness that overtook her. Holding her tightly, and with surprising strength, Farquar tried to quiet her, while her First Mate, who had returned, knelt besides Vincent's body and neatly sewed up the cut on his chest, the many pieces of the amulet safely inside his body. When she was done, and Blimey had calmed, the three sat back on the deck, and kept watch over the body in front of them. Vincent's blood dried to a hard crust on their clothes and skin but they did not notice. They simply waited. It was all they could do.

Hours passed, and night approached. Still Vincent had not moved. Blimey got to her feet and walked to the side of the ship as the moon rose white above her, casting it's silvery glow around and about.

'I guess he's gone,' she said to the wind. Tears stinging her eyes, but she would not let them fall.

'Who's gone?' came a male voice from behind her, and she turned to find Vincent lying on the deck propping himself up on his elbows, smiling boyishly. Blimey ran to him, dropping to her knees as she grabbed his pale face and kissed it all over.

'Guess I got the girl after all,' smiled Vincent, getting to his feet and pulling her up with him, holding her tightly. He was soon joined by the others. That had been a close call, and they were all glad to see their crewmember back with them. Blimey most of all. But what did this mean for Vincent? With the soil of his land literally under his skin, would he ever die again?

CHAPTER TWENTY

Call of Syren

The mist had been rolling in for about half an hour when Blimey awoke to a strange song upon the winds. Turning over she sat up in bed, pulling the blankets round her. Disturbed by her movement Vincent stirred in his sleep but did not wake. The door creaked open slowly and Betty hates Veronica tip toed into the room followed closely by the ships clockwork parrot, Rawkous. Seeing Blimey was awake, but Vincent still snoozed beside her Betty H.V kept her voice to a whisper.

'Can you hear that?' she asked.

'Yes, it's quite loud. I can't believe Vincent is sleeping through it,' Blimey answered, 'where do you think it's coming from?'

'It's heavy metal isn't it? Like that band you listen to a lot ... Black Sabbath?'

'Uh huh,' confirmed Blimey, but it was as though she was still dreaming, her voice had taken on that vague kind of nuance that comes from one not yet truly emerged from slumber, 'do you think we should find out where it is coming from?'

'Why, yes of course, we should definitely follow that sound,' replied Betty hates Veronica, her voice taking on the same dreamy, monotone quality.

Blimey rose and dressed quietly, as Betty hates Veronica returned to her room to do the same. They met a few minutes later on the main deck, and Betty H.V began drawing anchor as Blimey took the helm. Rawkous and the Reverend Farquar soon joined them. Both also seemed to share their spell.

Blimey turned off the auto-pirate and steered the ship towards the magical guitar laden music that called to her. The crew of the Raven had fallen victim to what was commonly known on the Severed Seas as the Call of the Syren. Many of you may have heard of the mythological creatures known as the Sirens, written about by the ancient Greeks, but on this ocean the beguilers were not beautiful women with silvery voices but young Gods of Metal, who led many an unwary pirate astray with their solid skull jams. Yet the goal of both the Siren and the Syren was the same. The vessels of incautious travelers would be smashed to matchsticks against the rocks by which the Syren lived and then they would plunder the ship's remains, adding gold, jewels and weapons to a mountain of treasures they obsessed and drooled over until they were somewhat gooey and gross. It was in this way also that they ensured that no other would want to steal from them. Yuck. Blimey and her crew were on a similar dangerous path as many unlucky Seafarers before them, and no one could break the spell of the Syren song.

Not long into the mist-covered morning Vincent finally woke. Blimey's side of the bed was cold, and so he dressed quickly and headed up above decks – hoping for coffee. What greeted him of course was far from the caffeine goodness he had expected. Instead he found Blimey, her First Mate, Farquar and their maniacal bird staring starry eyed at some rocks that were coming upon the ship far to quickly for Vincent's liking.

Running to the helm Vincent gently pushed Blimey aside and wrestled control of the ship back. With all his strength he pulled the wheel of the helm to his right, forcing the ship clear of the jagged coastline that only seconds before they had been on direct course with.

Now ships as you know do not respond like cars when the wheel is turned sharply, and for a moment Vincent believed he was too late as the rocks encompassed his whole field of vision, but it was enough and the ship – as if in slow motion – turned away from the outcrop and towards a strange shallow bay that appeared out of nowhere. For a regular ship this would surely also spell disaster in equal measure, but the shallows present no great challenge for true pirate ships, which like the fearsome pirate Blackbeard's Queen Anne's Revenge are chosen for their speed and their agility in shallower waters.

The Raven, now out of harm's way, coasted in towards a small dock, which jutted out from the bay. The darkness that was just before them lifting slowly now that the cliffs had been passed. Watching over the others closely, Vincent kept an eye out for any strangers that might approach them. He could not hear the shredding metal tones dying away on the winds as Hollows are impervious to the Syren's call, but he was savvy enough to know that something wasn't right.

Pulling in to the dock, Vincent prepared to drop anchor and secure the boat. Something had brought them here and he was curious to find out what. As the music faded away Blimey and her crew were released from its spell. Looking down at her man, and then taking in their surroundings for the first time, Blimey accepted immediately that some kind of mischief was afoot and she wanted to know what it was. She knew instinctively that they had traveled far off course, but she could not remember how they had come to this little quay and that worried her.

Before she could open her mouth to ask the question however, it seemed the answer had arrived. A motley band if ever there was one had appeared on the beach, and were patiently waiting for them to approach. Five young Metal Gods stood before them, long of hair and scrawny of build, brandishing flying Vs, Explorers, SG's and Fenders. Three rows of guitars, three metres each across sat behind the Syrens on the sand, as well as a TAMA drum kit.

Blimey and the crew of the Raven walked down the rickety wooden dock and onto the soft white sand. The leader of the Syrens was easily recognisable by his over-bleached blonde hair, sneer and his roguish style. That, and the microphone he was casually swinging over his head. A sure sign. Acknowledging them with a nod he stepped forward.

'I am Styx, lead singer and guitarist of Resident Sneer,' he told them, 'we are Syrens, Gods of Metal. We do not normally allow pirates to land on our shores but in this case we have made an exception as you have somehow managed to escape the fate of all those before you ... and also because you have something we want,' he concluded, eyeing up the two girls with a snarl.

'And what exactly is that?' returned Blimey, 'because I can tell you right now that our parrot is spoken for.'

'We need a female vocalist and back-up singer to complete our latest album. It matters not if you cannot sing – we have Pro Tools. No 'tis the look we are wanting and your eye-patch is quite fierce,' replied Styx.

'I can't join you – I sing like a strangled turkey! There won't be enough Pro Tools to go round to save my gnarled vocals!' laughed Blimey.

'Regardless, you will stay,' said Styx.

'Ha! So you say!' Blimey stated, turning on her heel and heading back up the dock to the Raven, motioning over her shoulder for the others to follow. Yet before she even got three paces it was all over, as Resident Sneer struck up a tune and the girls, Rawkous and Farquar were compelled to return and stare dreamlike as the band played.

Unaffected, Vincent was the only one not impressed, and stood scowling at the band's efforts to control him. It took a few moments before Styx realised that Vincent was not under their ferocious guitar-shredding spell, and it distressed him so much that he actually missed his own solo. It seemed Vincent was something previously unheard of by the Syrens – a challenger.

'You cannot take the girls with this heavy metal trickery,' yelled Vincent in anger, 'now put down your instruments and fight like men!'

'Yes.... Yes! The only way to settle this is with a dual!' agreed Styx excitedly, leaning forward over his now remembered guitar solo and sneering at Vincent, 'we two shall fight for yon maidens. An axe battle, and the victor shall be the one whom the maiden's choose.'

'An axe battle?' asked Vincent, taking the idea too literally, and in his mind trying to figure out the best way to fight with such an edged weapon.

'Yes,' confirmed Styx, 'we each pick a guitar and jam until a winner is chosen. It is a battle of skill and endurance.'

'Oh,' replied Vincent, knowing that he could not possibly beat Styx in a metal-off. True he could play a tune or two on the six string, but he was nowhere near close to the posturings of these young Metal Gods. However he had no choice.

'Yes,' continued Styx arrogantly, sensing an easy win himself, 'choose your weapon – we have every guitar ever made here.'

'I'll take that 1958 Gibson Explorer,' stated Vincent.

'Good choice, then I shall go for a 1979 Gibson Flying V – a true metal choice,' returned Styx aggressively, 'you shall have one hour to warm up and then, we dual.'

'Fine, but until then my Captain and her crew go free,'

demanded Vincent.

'Yeah, fine – whatever man,' agreed Styx and with a wave of his hand withdrew the spell keeping Blimey and the others in a daze.

Awaking as if from an afternoon snooze, the girls, Farquar and Rawkous stretched their limbs and wandered over to Vincent's side, where he explained what was going down, and for the first time in her whole piratical career, Blimey realized she was not in a position to do anything. She suddenly felt powerless and angry at the thought of having to rely on someone else to get her out of trouble, but she just had to accept that sometimes we all need a little help. The songs of the Syren were as strong as Vincent's playing wasn't, and so she would have to dare to hope that some amazing kind of coincidence would save them.

As it happens the guitar that Vincent had chosen was enchanted. It had been bewitched many years before by a sorceress, whose lover had been killed by the Syrens. It was a guitar made to outplay any other that challenged it. The sorceress had been waiting for a day such as this in the hope that finally the Syrens would be defeated, but she too had passed before she got to see the day. Now she would finally get her wish, for it would go up against Styx.

Vincent picked up the guitar like it was about to bite him. To say he was nervous was an understatement. Wrapping his hand around its neck he felt a pulsing, as if the guitar itself had a living heartbeat. The body of the thing grew warm, and it even seemed to want to nuzzle him. Vincent relaxed a little, and began to pick away at the strings. The affect was instant, and a song took shape immediately.

'Wow, I didn't know you could play like that!' exclaimed Blimey.

'Me neither!' agreed Vincent amazed, 'looks like we might have a chance of beating these guys! I'll still need you to concentrate though as the final choice will be down to you.'

'Oh, yes of course,' stated Blimey completely distracted by Vincent's playing and falling under the music's spell. The others were not far behind her.

The practice hour seemed to pass in a flash as Vincent played and played while the other's listened, yet Vincent was still mindful not to let Styx hear that he could play. He wanted the element of surprise on his side, and seeing the young Metal God approaching he quickly snapped his friend's out of it.

'So Hollow, it is time, are you ready to do battle?'

Vincent sighed and turned round, and with the crew of the Raven followed Styx to the battleground. It was an arena, which seemed to be comprised entirely of giant Marshall amps stacked 30 feet high. Leads and guitar pedals crisscrossed the area, and the rest of the Resident Sneer were waiting for them.

'Plug in and play fool!' yelled Styx, jamming the nearest lead into his own guitar and delving straight into a furious solo. Blimey, Betty hates Veronica, Farquar and the parrot immediately turned to face Styx, drawn to his playing. On seeing this Vincent was incensed, and followed Styx example, grabbing a lead and plugging it in to his own guitar. Pausing for only the briefest second, he to began to play. And he was good. Damn good. A look of surprise distorted Styx's face, and it was enough to spur Vincent on - he knew he had as good a chance as any to beat the Syren.

For a day and a night they played, with Blimey, Rawkous, Farquar and Betty H.V being drawn back and forth between the two. Finally as the sun began to set on the following day Styx began to tire. He was of course only immortal and could not keep up with the endless force that compelled Vincent to win, for the love of Blimey. Styx's arm began to deaden, and he started missing notes in his last solo. He knew he was beaten and let the Flying V slip through his fingers, though the guitar strap stopped it from hitting the sand. Swinging the guitar round to his back, Styx dropped to his knees in surrender, and with his head bowed acknowledged Vincent as his successor, yet Vincent had no wish to become a Syren.

'But you must lead us, it is written,' implored Styx.

'Styx,' Vincent said bending down to help him to his feet, 'you and I both know Resident Sneer can have no other leader than you. They would not be the same. It would be like Van Halen without David Lee Roth - a disaster.'

'Very well, I accept this decision and I will stay, but you are all free to go. Please keep this guitar and remember your victory here. No man has beaten me before, and I do not wish to be beaten again. Something tells me that guitar was meant for you. But that still leaves us the task of finding a back up singer, that is if none of you wish to join us?' smiled Styx hopefully.

'I think you'd be happier without us, but I am sure sooner or later one will drift right in,' laughed Blimey, 'now if you could tell us the best way to get out of this harbour that would be grand.'

'Well it depends where you are headed, where do you sail for now?' asked Grindle, the bass player.

'It's rather a long story, but we are looking for the Thirteen Bones,' answered Blimey, 'or rather that is to say any surviving members, as the case may be.'

'The Thirteen Bones eh? Well on that score we may be able to help you track down at least one of their associates... Atticus Bacon.'

CHAPTER TWENTY-ONE

Wolves in smuggler's clothing

The city of Arkiopteriks was full of nae'r do wells and it gave Blimey a dark feeling. They had followed the directions the Syren had given them, who told them that they would find Atticus Bacon, one of the Thirteen Bones, in this port. First they had to track down the Four Brothers, a group of smugglers, who Sytx had said would know where to find Atticus. However the Syren's forewarned them not to let on right away what their intent was. Apparently Atticus was not easy to get close too, being a hide and seek champion three years in a row, so Blimey would need to gain the brother's trust before they would provide any information as to where he was hiding. Styx was a bit vague on the details, but at this point all Blimey could do was trust this information as it was their best lead yet.

The sun had disappeared a few hours ago, as Blimey and her crew wandered down the dark streets lit here and there by flickering streetlights. It was clear that the light bulbs needed replacing, but no one was game enough to go up on the town's one and only rickety old ladder to do it.

The cobbled streets were slippery from recent rain, and the air was chill causing them all to pull their coats close about them as they passed by the creaky, little wood houses that lined the street. The weather worn dwellings were for the most part dark, their curtains drawn against the night. Only one or two candles lit the windows here and there, casting a jaundiced yellow glow on their faces as they passed. Above them a nasty, angry, quite possibly grumpy-old-man was rising, and the moon was out too. It all spelt trouble with a capital 'B' for be careful. Splitting off from the girls Farquar,

Vincent and Rawkous had agreed to go hunt around for some answers in the local bar, while Blimey and Betty H.V went to the address provided by Styx.

Arriving at a skinny, two-story villa, Blimey could feel the adrenalin starting to flow as her mind began to tick over thoughts of what they might find inside that old house. She had a bad feeling about this. An icy wind struck up suddenly and wrapped its cold tentacles around some fallen leaves, hurling them brutally at anything in their path.

'Damn these autumn towns,' muttered Blimey to herself, roughly kicking at the leaves as they pooled around her feet. Looking down she saw a warm light was seeping out from under the door making the house seem safe and inviting. Sighing to herself she knew it was time to knock. Hitting the wooden door with her knuckles, Blimey waited. In the distance a dog howled as the fat, white full moon slid out from behind a cloud for a moment, lighting the street and the door in front of them, which was covered in scratch marks. It looked as if something with very large claws had tried to force its way inside at some point.

'What could have made those scrat...' Betty H.V began to ask but was interrupted by the door being opened by a very tall, rather skinny, but oddly handsome man. His long dark hair was tied back, while his beard reached down nearly to his chest.

'Yes, what do you want?' he asked roughly as light spilled out of the door behind him, making it difficult for Blimey to make out his features as she looked up into his face.

'We're looking for the Four Brothers,' she replied.

'And what would you want with them if you happened to find them?' asked the man.

'Are you one of the brothers?' Blimey responded, ignoring his question.

'Hmph, perhaps you better come inside, it's a dark night and not safe to be on the street,' he said, moving aside and beckoning for the two to follow him inside. Stepping into the light Blimey noticed a big pink scar nestled deeply in the man's dark skin. It seemed to start from his neck, before heading up under his beard and ending somewhat abruptly on his right cheek.

The three of them walked down the hallway of the small

house, past a narrow staircase on the left, and eventually ended up in a well-lit parlour. The room was dominated by a large wooden table, on which sat several bottles of wine and 4 glasses. In the centre of the table were many candles, and the whole room would have felt quite homely and inviting, if it weren't for the three werewolves sitting at the table. They turned to snarl at their guests.

'This is something ... new,' commented Betty hates Veronica quietly as she reached for her sword.

'What is the meaning of this? I only asked after the Four Brothers, I have no intention of becoming a meal for your... pets,' exclaimed Blimey fiercely.

'There's no need to be rude miss,' growled a voice behind her, and as Blimey turned to look at the man who had answered the door, his own transformation was beginning. Long, spiky and soft fur began to sprout from nearly every pore of his skin as his fingers became elongated and his fingernails developed into claws. The girls now noticed that he had been wearing no shoes when he led them into the house as his feet followed the transformation of his hands. His clothing, pulled tight by this turning, began to split at the seams as his legs turned into haunches and his body became even more muscular. Last of all his face began to change. His nose and mouth becoming more muzzle-like, the teeth becoming sharper and the ears longer.

'What is going on here?!' demanded Blimey in alarm, drawing her sword and moving to stand with her back to her first mate, who had her own weapon drawn.

'I'm afraid you both have us at a disadvantage,' gruffed the werewolf, 'the moon is full and we are unarmed.'

'What do you call them big teeth and claws of yours then, accessories?' replied Blimey, who was not ready to relax just yet.

'I know what this must look like and we are truly sorry you saw this. We try not to accept visitors on the night of a full moon, as this is when we are at our least... hospitable, and it is not good for... business... but we have been waiting for you, it's just bad timing that is all.'

'Bad timing huh? Well you could have put a note on the door or something,' stated Betty H.V, who was still in a state of shock from witnessing what she just had. Seeing a werewolf transform is not a pretty sight.

'Please, put down your swords, we are smugglers not killers, we mean you no harm,' growled one of the wolves from the table, getting slowly to his feet with his front paws outstretched, palms upward.

'Fine, but I want all four of you sitting at that table now, paws where I can see 'em. And I'm sorry I was disrespectful, I was just taken aback is all,' said Blimey.

The four wolves sat down at the table, and each picked up their glass of wine, while their other paws were placed on the table. Betty H.V and Blimey each grabbed a tall stool each, and sat down facing their unconventional hosts.

'Please allow me to introduce myself and my brothers,' said the wolf who had let them in, 'I am Bach – the oldest – and this to my left is Thomas – the youngest,' said Bach gesturing to the fair coloured wolf before continuing, 'then we have the twins, Wolff and Bohr – the consummate middle children,' he finished.

'Wolff? Are they serious?' whispered Betty hates Veronica to her Captain, thinking no one would hear her but Blimey.

'Unfortunately one does not choose ones own name before they become a werewolf,' snarled Wolff.

'Sorry, I didn't know it was a sore point,' replied Betty, smiling.

'You knew we were coming you said before, how?' asked Blimey, interrupting the conversation before it ran off any further. She needed information, not the werewolve's family history.

'Your friend, Farquar, called ahead and sent your bird to tell us to expect you,' answered Bach.

'Oh he did... interesting indeed... more so that he did not tell us, nor did the bird ... I think we'll need to watch him more closely Betty my dear, I have a feeling that's not all he's keepin' from us,' mused Blimey, her brow furrowing. She did not like to be kept in the dark - about anything.

'There'll be time to deal with Farquar later, stay focused – let's find out what else they know before he comes here with Vincent,' whispered Betty.

'We can hear you, it's these big ears you know,' growled Wolff, who seemed to be smiling directly at her. Betty was starting to think he might be flirting with her.

'So, you know why we are here then?' asked Blimey.

'Yes, you are looking for Atticus Bacon, our friend and one of the Thirteen Bones. It was Atticus that set us up in our business here. He raised us after the death of our parents. Somehow he knew what we were, even before we did. True wolves do not turn before their 20th birthday you see, and without him we would not have been prepared to face our legacy with pride instead of hiding in fear and shame. It is imperative that the townsfolk do not find out about us though. You never know what they would do. People can be so... reactionary,' sneered Bach.

'Do you know why we are searching for him?'

'Ahhh, now that we don't know, and obviously we shall not lead you to him unless we are certain that you have no intention of harming him. He is our guardian, and we will die before we see him in danger.'

'I understand, and I only want to speak to him, that is all,' answered Blimey, 'I am searching for my birth mother and believe Atticus may have information as to where she may be. She was once a pirate herself, and sailed with Atticus under the banner of the Thirteen Bones. He might yet know what happened to her, and where she has since sailed too. I know no more than this myself. Atticus is the best lead we have so far, and so I give you my word that we will not harm him... What do you mean lead us there?'

'One of us must go with you,' stated Bach matter-of-factly.

'Oh no, no... no, you don't need to do that. Just tell us where to look and we'll track him down.'

'This is not a decision open to bargaining. Either one of us goes with you or you will never find him. Tracking Atticus is not as simple as you think. We have not seen him for nigh on a year now and the scent grows fainter by the day. You will need one of us to pick up the trail, literally. It is the only way you will find him.'

'And all of you must accompany us?'

'No,' replied Bach, 'one of us will be sufficient.'

'I shall go,' stated Wolff, getting to his feet.

Bach turned to his brother, and nodded his head in ascent. 'Very well, Wolff will accompany you, but you'll need to wait until morning. Obviously he can't go out until the moon sets. Please stay, and enjoy some wine. Your friends will be at the door soon, looking for you, and you are all welcome to stay here for the night – we promise you will be safe.'

'What do you think?' asked Blimey turning to her friend.

'Looks like we don't have much of a choice,' sighed Betty hates Veronica as there was a loud knock at the door.

CHAPTER TWENTY-TWO

The smell of Bacon in the morning

Morning broke as mornings are want to do, bringing with it aching heads and an immediate dislike of loud noises. Vincent was the first to rise, thoughtfully heading to the kitchen and putting on a large pot of coffee.

The night before had, once the confusion of Farquar, Vincent and Rawkous was overcome, been rather a late one. The werewolves had been excellent hosts, putting on a rather nice spread of wine and cheese, before breaking out a harpsichord and singing songs until the wee hours of the morning. They were mostly paying for it now, with a generous helping of sore heads all round.

A light bubbling sound told Vincent that the coffee was ready. Taking it to the big wooden table in the kitchen, he let it rest for moment while he rounded up some cups, pouring a generous helping of the black gold into each. The smell of freshly brewed coffee was soon spreading throughout the house, it's fragrant tendrils tickling the noses of those still sleeping and gently waking them. Slowly, one by one they drifted down the stairs.

Taking their places at the table, everyone looked a little worse for wear but as the coffee began to work its magic, Farquar rustled up some fruit toast and slowly they returned to life. The werewolves on the other hand didn't seem to be affected at all by the previous nights over indulgence or lack of sleep. Bach, Thomas, Wolff and Bohr had returned to their human form and were all beards, smiles, fresh shirts and braces.

Pacing up and down the centre of the table, Rawkous also seemed to be a little out of sorts this morning. It must be said that he wasn't normally this annoying.

'Bird, what are you doing?' asked Blimey who could finally take his mad scrabbling no longer.

'I'm sorry Cap'n, but I think I am about to have a break down...' replied their parrot before promptly falling over and rolling onto his side.

'Rawkous!' yelled Blimey in alarm, much to the anguish of her fellow crewmates, 'bird, bird!' she continued picking him up and trying to turn the key in his back. It would not move. 'What treachery is this? Who has don't this to you, Rawkous – wake up my little mate!'

'What's up with the bird?' asked Betty hates Veronica.

'I don't know, I think he's broken,' replied Blimey looking to her first mate.

'Let me have a look at him,' said Farquar stepping forward and gently taking the bird from Blimey, screwdriver in hand. 'Hmmm – it looks like someone has tried to drown him, see – he's all damp underneath his wings ... here. I suspect there's water all in his gears too, which is causing the jam. We just have to hope it hasn't voided his warranty.'

'So, what then, can you fix him?' asked Betty H.V.

'Yes, well I will try. But it still leaves the question as to whom would do this to a poor little clockwork parrot. They were obviously trying to keep him quiet... I dare say it was not anyone here who is the culprit as he has too long dried off on the surface, and we were all accounted for last eve... hmmmm... it is a pickle for sure, Blimey,' said Farquar turning to his Captain, 'fill that bread-box there with rice, and pass it to me. Rawkous must be buried in this for three days. The rice will draw out the moisture, and I need to dry him out thoroughly before I attempt to repair him.'

'Oh my poor little bird,' lamented Blimey, sorrow filling her face as she stroked her bird's lifeless form, 'I will find who has done this to you and make them pay dearly. I'll be right here, waiting until Farquar can fix you and I am sure you'll be ok, you have to be.'

Gently, Farquar put Rawkous in the wooden box, filling it with rice and covering him completely before handing it over to Betty hates Veronica.

'Right, when can we leave this forsaken place?' asked Blimey in a huff, to no one in particular.

'I'm sorry about your bird miss, truly, and I can understand ye'd be keen to get under sail. We can leave as soon as I have packed some clothes and supplies,' replied Wolff, before turning to head up the stairs. He was not gone longer then 10 minutes. In the meantime his older brother, Bach packed some supplies in a satchel for him. Cheese, bread, semi-dried tomatoes, olives and some bottles of rather nice red wine, to remind him of home.

'Right then, see you later brother,' said Bach, as Wolff returned to the kitchen with a duffle bag slung over his shoulder.

'I'll be back soon eh, it will be nice to see Atticus again,' smiled Wolff, hugging his brothers one by one and taking one last look around his home.

'Thank you for your hospitality, and your help,' smiled Blimey as in turn they shook hands with the brothers staying behind.

Walking back down to the dock, the towns' people nodded to Wolff as they passed.

'You're pretty well known in this town then I take it?' asked Betty H.V mildly impressed.

'Haha, well, yes. It's a small town, when growing up here you tend to know everyone.'

'Doesn't that make it hard to ... hide your... condition?' she asked.

A frown creased Wolff's brow for a second before he realized that the question was one of genuine interest, and not meant to offend him.

'One learns to be discreet, yes,' he smiled.

Betty hates Veronica smiled back, before quickening her pace to join her Captain, leaving Wolff behind with the other boys.

'How are you feeling?' she asked Blimey.

'Why?'

'You know, the lead from Styx panned out. We're another step closer to finding your mother? It must be somewhat exciting to be off on another adventure.'

'Yes, I suppose. But, you know this could all go pear shaped. We're putting an awful lot of faith in Wolff, and Farquar. I don't know. We have to find Atticus, and see where that leads us...'

'Don't be so down girl! It's a start. You've just found out about a whole new life you never knew you had! You're bound to feel unsettled. I wish I had something as exciting to look forward to...' Betty trailed off.

'Hey - be careful what you wish for,' interrupted Blimey swinging her arm around her first mate's shoulders as they reached the gangplank that led up to the Raven, and made their way onboard followed closely by the rest of their crew.

'I'll show Wolff to his quarters,' offered Vincent as Blimey and Betty readied the ship to leave the dock.

'Sure, we'll be ready to cast off in 10,' replied Blimey as she walked to the helm and initiated the Raven's launch sequence.

The ship whirred into life as the main sails unfurled, the breeze catching them immediately and tickling them gently. The anchor slowly retracted and the Raven moved smoothly away from the dock and out towards the bay.

Below decks, Wolff threw his bag down on the bed and looked around his new room. He didn't know how long he would be staying with this crew, but at least his room seemed nice. There was even a bottle of Varn Clankston's 13 year old, single malt whisky on the table. Grabbing the bottle and pulling out the cork with his teeth, he took a quick swig as Vincent left him to settle in.

'We'll see you on deck as soon as you're ready,' smiled Vincent as he walked out the door.

'Sure, mate, just give me a few minutes,' replied Wolff gruffly. He was already missing dry land, and thinking that the ocean is no place for a werewolf as the boat rocked gently from side to side.

Vincent jumped up the stairs two at a time, shielding his eyes as he looked into the morning sun.

'He'll be up in a minute,' said Vincent as Blimey steered the ship on the mellow waters.

'Let's hope he's not one of them landlubbers who get's sea sick,' said Blimey as she looked up to the horizon and pointed to an approaching mass of black clouds, 'there's a storm coming.'

'Wow, that's moving towards us pretty quick!' said Betty H.V.

'What's moving fast?' asked Wolff, joining them on deck, and looking a little green around the cheeks.

'There's a storm coming young Wolff,' Farquar answered him, moving to put his hand on the man's shoulder.

'Will we be OK? I've never really been too far from land

before,' asked Wolff.

'We'll be fine, a little wind and rain never hurt anyone, but I'm afraid if you get seasick it's not going to be much fun for you. Here take this,' said Blimey holding out a small, pale-green bottle.

'What's this?'

'It's Poppy Dragon nectar, a bit of a pirate's cure-all, it will hold off the seasickness, and a bunch of other ailments for about 6 months. It's perfectly safe, and better than spending all day with your head over the side getting splattered by waves... and vomit,' Blimey explained.

Wolff tipped the small bottle to his lips, and drained the contents. He immediately began to feel a whole lot better.

'How did you find out about this?' he asked

'My father was a Shaman. My foster father I mean. He taught me about herbs, and healing cures. I haven't seen him in a long time though,' Blimey sighed.

'You're a handy lass to know then.'

'Yes, well unfortunately not everyone seems to think so. There's a bounty on my head, and many a fellow pirate would like to see my head on a spike. But it's all part of the fun,' Blimey smiled wanly, a frown creasing her brow as the wind picked up and the sun's attempt at warming the day was abruptly cut short by the approaching angry clouds.

'It's gonna be a wet one! Batten down the hatches and get ready to ride this one out!' yelled Betty to the rest of the crew as everyone scrambled to prepare for the oncoming storm.

'Sorry we couldn't have more smooth sailing for your first time aboard Wolff, but this will be exhilarating none the less – there's nothing like a gale to get the blood running!' grinned Blimey like a mad woman, as the Raven began to pitch from side to side on the rising waves.

Wolff grabbed onto some rigging, as Farquar and Vincent rushed to tie everything down. Betty H.V madly pushed buttons on the ship's control panel and locked down below decks, where Rawkous sat safely in his rice box, drying out.

The rain hit heavily, slamming down on the crew with droplets the size of pennies, soaking them through. Mixed in with the heat from earlier in the day, the atmosphere was soon cloying and humid, sliced through by the icy wind. The waves battered the sides of the ship, creeping further and further over the railing, wetting the main deck, as Blimey gripped the helm keeping the ship on a steady course as around her, the crew held on to what they could to keep from being knocked off their feet.

'Wolff – get up here! I need to see if you can smell anything, I need directions, coordinates so I can steer this baby someplace!' yelled Blimey over the din of the storm.

Looking over to the helm, Wolff made a futile attempt to wipe the rain from his face, as his long brown hair hung in dripping strands around it. As he made his way unsteadily over to the Captain, Betty hates Veronica couldn't help but give him a second glance as he passed her. She smiled as he caught her eye briefly on his way up to the helm.

'Well, whadda ya reckon? Can you pick up the scent over this storm?' asked Blimey as he joined her.

'It would be better to wait for the rain to stop, the scent will be stronger. Right now I can get traces of it, but it's fractured, old. Can you get us through this storm and out the other side Captain?'

'Ha! You just watch me landlubber!' yelled Blimey happily to the wind.

***

The sun finally broke through the clouds as the rain subsided and the wind whittled away into a light breeze, warming the crew with its toasty tendrils. They soon began to dry out, helped along by some deliciously fluffy towels that Farquar had found below deck. There is nothing like the feeling of wrapping a fresh towel around you when you're wet and cold.

'Better check below deck and make sure everything is OK down there – and check on the bird please Betty,' asked Blimey, as she kept the ship on track, 'Wolff – how's that nose of yours now? Pick up anything?'

Wolff stood up straight and put his snozz to the wind. He took a test sniff. The air was fresh and warming. He turned his head slightly to the left then to the side. He looked puzzled. He frowned. He smiled. Frowned. He moved a little to his right and scratched behind his left ear. Then he grinned.

'Got it – it's faint but it's true – set sail North East, and I will guide you from there.'

'Brilliant!' yelled Blimey as Vincent joined her and handed

her a bottle of Red Rum. Taking a swig, she spun the wheel of the helm to her right, causing the ship to come round in a wide arc. Looking at her compass, Blimey waited until they had just passed the North East before swinging the helm back round, compensating for the ships slight over steer. They were now headed in the direction Wolff was pointing.

'How far off do you reckon he is?' asked Vincent, as they sailed on throughout the day.

'At a guess I think it's about...' said Wolff sniffing the air again, 'about 420 leagues, so at our current speed we should catch them in 6 days.'

'6 days huh?' asked Betty hates Veronica reappearing from below decks, 'the bird is fine,' she added turning to her Captain and smiling.

'Well then everyone, settle in for the long haul. I'll try to pick up some speed where I can and ...' started Blimey before Betty H.V cut her off.

'I know a way we could be there within about 2 days hence,' she stated simply.

'Do you now? How so young lady?' asked Blimey, who was beginning to suspect her friend had something tricky up her sleeve. She wasn't wrong.

'Well, it was going to be a surprise for your birthday, but I guess as we need them now I can let you know early but.... I had turbo boosters fitted to the ship!' yelled Betty H.V excitedly.

'Oh hells yes!! So awesome! You know I've always wanted to get those even though they are not really by the code, who cares!' returned Blimey equally as excited.

'My argument always was that they're a 'secret weapon' really and so if you only use them in emergencies or for mischief then I don't see any problem. I reckon the pirates who don't like 'em are just jealous they don't have 'em any ways,' Betty H.V justified sagely.

'How fast can we actually go with these Turbo thingys fitted?' asked Farquar, a look of concern creasing his brow.

'Only one way to find out isn't there – punch it Betty!!' ordered Blimey as Betty H.V stepped up to the control panel next to the helm and punched in the appropriate sequence. As she did so two concealed panels at the rear of the ship opened slowly, exposing two turbo jet exhausts. At the ships bow, the mouth of the giant wooden raven also began to open further, to become the air-intake needed to get the extra air deep inside the bowels of the ship where the new mechanics were located, and which the turbo engine needed to breathe.

'When did you get the time to have these fitted without me knowing?' asked Blimey, intrigued by her mate's ingeniousness.

'Oh I can't give away my secrets,' she laughed, 'that would be no fair at all!'

The rest of the conversation was soon lost to the wind as the engines kicked in and the front of the ship rose out of the water propelled by the sheer force the jets were generating.

'I hope you can steer this thing at the rate we're going!' yelled Wolff, half elated, half scared to death.

'Don't worry – this ship and I have a special connection,' answered Blimey, 'you just keep that nose to the wind now and again and tell us which way to go and I'll steer this baby around anything in our path!'

'Right you are Captain,' responded Wolff, hiding his doubt for the moment and trusting in this girl, who right now had their lives in her hands.

***

The sun was just beginning to descend towards the horizon as the Raven finally began to slow. Blimey didn't want to come in too hot on this one. From what Wolff had told them on the way over, Atticus Bacon was an old school sailor type, who took to piracy as a way of earning enough money to survive during tough times. He had fallen in love with the sea and seen much in his time on the water, but a lot of what he had seen had hardened his heart, and as a result he had become one of the maddest pirates on the Severed Seas, prone to attacks of pure rage. He could be unpredictable, especially if he couldn't punch dance out his fury. Sometimes he spared the crew, other times he laid waste to everyone on board. He was almost beyond redemption, and at that point in his short life he would have made Blackwatch look almost sane by comparison. Atticus had been staring destruction in the face for a long time, and giving it the finger. Until he met Elizabeth Bohnes, and she had shown him a way to bury his anger and focus his energy in a new direction. That he didn't have to slaughter everyone he met if they rubbed him up the wrong way. It had been Elizabeth who had given him the four, orphaned boys to look after, a positive focus. Whether or not she had known they would grow into werewolves he could only guess. Wolff liked to think she had known.

The Raven travelled at only a few knots as it rounded a knub of rocky land that jutted out from a sheer cliff face. To their right, the rock drove straight up towards the sky. It's only residents the few crazy birds that make such outcrops their perilous home. Below waves crashed against the cliff base. Before them the horizon stretched out as far as the eye could see, with nothing in sight of any note. Wolff swore that the ship of his guardian was anchored not far off the coastline, but they couldn't see anything. However Blimey knew that didn't mean he wasn't actually there...

Atticus Bacon watched the ship coming towards him with skepticism. He was sitting up near the helm of his ship in a specially designed inflatable throne. For a moment he considered taking action, and asking his men to arm the rubberband cannons. He was about to give the order, when he noticed that the ship headed his way flew no colours, which according to the pirates code meant they should be no threat. Plus he reasoned, his own ship had been sailing with the cloaking device on for several days now, so they would not even know he was there. He scratched his chin contemplatively. He did not want to risk damage to his vessel, but he did want to find out what this new ship wanted and why it loitered so in their vicinity. It was a pickle to be sure.

It had often occurred to Atticus that his ship, which was mostly inflatable (other than the wooden exterior, sails and rope of course) and rather like a child's jumping castle, left him somewhat vulnerable. But he did love the feeling of air-filled rubber under his sock covered feet. The bouncing sensation when walking around reminded him of what he thought walking on the moon might be like. He had tried many times over the years to go for a more conventional mode of travel, but he always came back to this ship - the Carnivale. This obsession of his simply meant he had to avoid trouble as much as possible these days. He spent a lot of the time hiding rather than fighting or looting, and his crew was composed only of the most loyal men he could find. Men who could be trusted not to run with scissors, and who were similarly obsessed with inflated rubber.

Atticus himself was a bit a mystery. No longer is his prime, and well over 70 years old it was said, but strangely the man did not look a day over 20. His blond hair was as pale as corn silk, and a light spray of freckles sat on his nose, which only gave cause for his dark eyes to stand out all the more. However to be fooled by this boyish look was to court disaster, back in his time with the Thirteen Bones he had quite the reputation of being a stone-cold hard-arse, and he was still well known enough on the Severed Seas for his name to carry some weight.

'Sir,' asked Atticus' First Mate Copernicus, 'shall we do anything about this approaching vessel?'

'No, the cloaking device is still in place, I doubt they have even seen us, we shall wait... they will pass us by,'

'Very well, sir' replied Copernicus, turning to his crew and signaling for them to stop panicking, and dancing around in a panicky sort of way that was not becoming.

***

Back on board the Raven, Wolff had the scent of his once guardian, and it was still strong, though he could not see the ship. It concerned him. However Blimey seemed unperturbed.

'It's maddening – I know he's there but I can't see anything!' yelled Wolff to the winds, throwing up his hands in frustration.

'The may have a cloaking device on their ship. But don't worry, I know a trick or two to get round that bit of witchery,' smiled Blimey, as she punched at a series of buttons on the ship's console.

'She's jammin' them,' smiled Betty H.V knowingly, 'it won't matter what they got on that thing, in about a second it's all going to go offline.'

***

'Don't panic men!' yelled Atticus, 'they are flying no colours, so we wait, however ready the cannons – we must at least be prepared.'

***

'Well they know they've been rumbled,' stated Blimey turning to her crew, 'and they seem to be readying their artillery – but they're not flying any colours... I think they're just waiting to see what we do next.'

'So what's the story boss lady?' asked Vincent.

'Wolff!' Blimey called pressing a button to open the hailer on the Raven's console, 'we need you to hail Atticus, it's the only way he'll know our intentions without any doubt.'

Wolff grabbed the old, square silver microphone that had dropped down in front of him from high above. Hanging from a long black rubbery chord, it seemed to have been hidden in one of the mast-arms of the main sail.

'This ship is full of little secrets like that,' explained Betty hates Veronica with a smile.

Wolff flicked a small button on the microphone's body, turning on the mic, which immediately began buzzing like a wasp on a hot day.

'Check 1, 2... blue suede shoooessss ... baby ... check,' he said without even thinking, causing everyone on the ship to crack up laughing.

Wolff turned back to look at Blimey, who was busily adjusting some knobs on the tiny PA that had slid out from the side of the ship's control panel when she had flicked on the hailing communicator. Feeling the levels and volume were now right, she gave Wolff a thumbs up – the universal signal for 'all good' - and Wolff hailed his former guardian aboard the Carnivale.

'Atticus! Ahoy! It's Wolff, permission to approach sir!'

Back on board the Carnivale, Atticus did a double take. He could not believe what he had just heard. Calling for his spyglass, he put the telescope to his eye and looked out towards the helm of the approaching ship where he could see a small crew of people. His eyebrows rose almost imperceptibly in surprise and his mouth dropped open slightly. He blinked and refocused, but he was indeed looking at his boy, Wolff, through the lens. He had not seen in him in such a long time, and he could not fathom how here he was on another ship, mere meters away as the Raven continued its approach.

Atticus looked down at his crew with a smile as he lowered the spyglass, and picked up a brass loud speaker.

'Permission granted my boy!' Atticus yelled into it, waving his free hand in a large arc above his head. He was truly pleased to see his foster son again.

'It's my lad, Wolff,' he added, turning to his crew so that they knew their Captain had not taken leave of his sanity.

'Well that was easy,' said Betty H.V as Blimey pushed a button to retract the microphone, and swung the ship around so it was on a more direct course with the Carnivale.

'We'll be arriving momentarily ladies and gents, prepare to swing aboard!' announced Blimey as minutes later the Raven was coasting alongside Atticus' ship.

On board the Carnivale, Atticus had his crew made ready to welcome their guests, as Blimey and her mishmash crew jumped up on to the Raven's railing and each grabbed on to a boarding rope. Following Blimey's lead they swung across to the Carnivale, landing with a quiet bouncy thud on the main deck. It would be safe to say they were all a bit surprised.

'Is this ship inflatable?!' exclaimed Betty H.V trying to get to her feet but unable to find purchase on the rubbery surface of the deck. A look of concern taking up residence on her face alongside the look of astonishment that had already set up home as she kept falling over.

'Haha! I sure hope so otherwise there was something in our coffee this morning that's just started to kick in now!' laughed her Captain good-heartedly.

'Why?' is all Vincent would say as he got to his feet carefully and did his best to adjust to the unsteady terrain.

'But what happens if it gets a puncture!?' asked Betty, still full of concern. She was worried that one false sword stroke would send them all flying into oblivion.

'Why m'dear, it is made of a specially formulated compound, able to withstand even the mightiest steel,' answered Atticus eloquently stepping forward and offering his hand to help the lady to her feet, 'but I will have to ask you to remove your shoes please'.

'Thanks for the reassurance,' said Betty skeptically, finally standing straight on both pins.

Atticus stepped back and waited for his guests to find their footing before welcoming his foster son to his ship.

'Wolff! My dear, dear boy! Such a delight to see you – it has been far too long! Tell me what brings you all this way out here and how are your three brothers?'

'Father!' exclaimed Wolff stepping forward and embracing Atticus warmly, 'it is good to see you! I bring much news of my brothers, but as to why we are here... well the answer to that rests with my Captain, the lady Blimey. She has come to find you on a personal matter.'

'Ah riddles! You of all your brothers did tend to speak this way. Come! The sun sets, let us dine and you can tell me all about it!' exclaimed Atticus, putting his arm around his son's shoulders and walking him towards the steps that took them down into the ship.

As the rest of the crew followed cautiously, they took in Atticus' ship. While the outside of the ship appeared to be constructed from wood, the interior was almost entirely inflatable. From the deck to the main masts, to the helm deck. It was a clever design to be sure, and quite comfortable once you got used to walking on a surface with such give.

As they headed down into the guts of the ship, things returned to some form of normality. Everything was fitted out with delicately carved wood. Mermaids, whales, all manner of sea creatures, swords, skulls and guns adorned every inch of the wood. The floor was highly polished, and along the walls imitation gas lamps in high polished brass illuminated the way. Everything was conspicuously neat and tidy. It was clearly a well run ship, but one that had not seen a great deal of action for some time.

'Please, follow me through the next door on your right, to the Captain's lounge,' said Atticus, as he led the way.

Entering through the door as was the custom in most places, they took in the room. The first thing they noticed was the warm atmosphere even though the room itself was quite large. As the sun's last light streamed in through the brass portals it lit on everything in its path. A globe sat in one corner, opposite a long wooden bar, behind which sat a selection of whiskies, bourbons, vodka, gin, rum – almost any spirit you can think of. The bar itself was lit underneath, which highlighted a carving of a mermaid sitting on a rocky outcrop brushing her long hair. The rest of the room was simpler, but no less interesting, and was occupied by several small round tables, around which sat four comfortable, red leather chairs for each. Crystal ashtrays sat on the tables, and though they were clean now, it explained the light but stale smell of cigar smoke that hung in the air. Mixed in with this was the smell of beer and whisky that you get when you walk past any bar early in the day, when it's just opened. All in all it made the crew of the Raven feel right at home, and impressed upon them all that Atticus obviously spent more time drinking and being dashing these days than running, smuggling or plundering.

'Please, take a seat, let me get you a drink,' smiled Atticus devilishly, making his way behind the bar and pulling various bottles off the shelves, 'what's your poison?'

'Now correct me if I am wrong Captain, but Wolff here has told us on our journey that amongst other things you are rather famous for inventing a cocktail called the Geronimo, so we'll have a round of those please,' said Blimey.

'Haha! Wolff me boy, you have been telling tales out of school! Indeed I have that honour, and so if you will indulge me for but a moment I'll get said bevvy mix'ed. Perhaps in the meantime you can give me the short version of how it is you come to find me out.'

'Well it all started with a visit from Farquar here...' Blimey began, however the look on Atticus' face soon cut her short. He looked as if he had been slapped up the side of the head with a smelly mackerel.

'Farquar ...' he repeated, looking more closely at his guests as if for the first time and then spotting the familiar face. True he may have now been a little bit older, and little more ragged round the edges, but it was the man he knew. Within moments Atticus had bounded round the bar and embraced Farquar in a giant bear hug.

'Farquar! Rev! My dear friend! Where have you been keeping yourself? No one has seen you for an age, and we all thought, well, we all thought you were dead to be honest.'

'Oh my, well it will be a nice surprise for everyone when they discover that I am very much alive!' laughed Farquar, 'ahh but perhaps not for everyone. I know Blackwatch was not pleased to see me so recently,' he added as an afterthought.

'Blackwatch? That privateer scum,' sneered Atticus in disgust, 'he sold out faster than tickets to the Rolling Stones, and is living big at the expense of many a hard working pirate. He always was a noble ass-kiss'er.'

'Yes, well, he was looking to claim a bounty on Blimey here, until she showed him that it would not be so easy as he thought. It may interest you to know that she is Elizabeth's daughter...'

'Elizabeth!' exclaimed Atticus.

'Yes, that's right,' Farquar confirmed.

'But we all thought she had died, the child I mean, no one knew what had happened to her, not even Elizabeth,' Atticus went on, incredulous.

'Elizabeth knew,' Farquar began quietly, 'but she had asked me to keep the child safe. She knew that Blackwatch or Vainglorious would come looking for her, and she couldn't have her daughter in danger. I had Jea... Blimey fostered out to an old friend and his wife. Deliberately I kept her whereabouts a secret. Not even Elizabeth knew where she had gone. But it seems a love of the sea runs strong in this family, and she soon made her own way to the waves. She is a Captain herself,' Farquar finished, smiling fondly at Blimey.

The rest of the room sat in silence and let the conversation flow over them. Blimey was listening intently, as she learned more about her mother with every word.

'Well this is a fine news indeed!' Atticus said, turning to Blimey and bowing very low, 'happy news! My dear it is an honour to meet the daughter of Elizabeth and Gerald Bohnes, but what can I do for you?'

'I'm looking for my mother and I was hoping you could help,' answered Blimey simply.

'Yes, yes... well... of course for the daughter of Elizabeth I would do anything, but I would have thought Farquar would have more of an idea than I my dear,' started Atticus raising an eyebrow and giving Farquar a quizzical look, 'but if he does not know anything then I will do my best to tell you what I know. In truth I have not heard anything of her or from her for many a year, but that is not to say this is a dead end, but rather a question for those who are dead.'

'What do you mean?' Blimey asked, encouraging Atticus to explain further.

'There are those who waken in the night, who move undetected in the shadows, who listen at doors, and hear many a rumour and truth that the likes of us are not privy to. They have no heart, but are not heartless and drink a wine not born from fruit. Cold to the touch yet warm to those whom they consider friends, you must head south and follow the light of the red star to find them. They will be able to tell you where Elizabeth can be found if any of us had a clue,' Atticus finished cryptically.

'Oh,' said Blimey struggling to hide her disappointment,

'thank you Atticus, I guess we should continue on our way then, and find those that wake in the night as you say, though I cannot think whom you mean' she added getting to her feet.

'He speaks of the Night Noir,' Farquar explained.

'Nonsense - stay! Ah lass, don't be disheartened. I have no doubt that Elizabeth is out there somewhere. I feel it in my bones. And I must tell you more of the quarry you seek. You cannot simply go sailing off to seek the Noir out. No, no, they are too clever and crafty for the likes of you, or I, and they would smell your hot blood from leagues gone. Please sit, drink, eat and for tonight I insist you rest here with us. Such stories of your mother's past I could tell you and arm you well for the next part of your journey.'

Reluctantly Blimey sat back down in her chair, as Vincent reached out to take her hand. She knew he was right. She needed this information. Betty H.V smiled over at her, as Wolff slumped back in his chair and waited patiently for the drink he had been promised earlier. He was happy to sit this one out as he knew this part of the story did not really concern him, and after today he would be returning home to his brothers. He hated to admit it to himself, but he had a bit of a crush on Betty hates Veronica and part of him wanted to stay and get to know her better. Moments continued to pass, and still no drinks appeared to get made. Sighing loudly, Wolff got to his feet and decided to sort out this drinks situation. After all they wouldn't make themselves, and Atticus was now completely distracted. Walking behind the bar, Wolff got to work finishing off the cocktails that Atticus had made a start on, as the man himself set about telling Blimey the legend of the Night Noir.

CHAPTER TWENTY-THREE

The Night Noir

'The Night Noir are vampires,' began Atticus, 'but they were not always so. Their Captain was once my good friend, and we sailed together under the flag of the Thirteen Bones along with your mother, who was our Captain back then...

In fact the leader of the Noir is her former First Mate, William, who joined the Vampires in order to save the life of your mother. I did once think that they would marry, but I guess it was not to be after he crossed over to the Noir. We had been drifting for a number of days as we recovered from a recent battle. Our crew was tired and some badly injured. The smell of blood still hung in the air, which is what must have attracted the Noir. Your mother had finally agreed to get some sleep. She was a fierce and stubborn Captain, but the exhaustion was clear to see on her face. It seemed that she had not had more than an hour's sleep and then they were upon us. Out of the late night mist their ship descended upon us in the moonlight. They fairly flew aboard our ship, and within moments they had us surrounded. Their appearance was so shocking to us at the time that we froze. We could not even think of fighting. Their skin was so pale as to almost be blue, and their eyes were the colour of the blood they lived on. Then their Captain appeared, and a monster of a man he was.

'Where is your Captain!' he bellowed looking to us to point out our leader, but we were still rooted to the spot.

Then she appeared. Like a vision in black leather she stepped up from below decks. Her wild red hair roughly pulled back from her face, some loose strands picked up by the wind only served to make her look more beautiful. Her left hand rested on the hilt of her sword as she walked casually towards the Noir Captain on the main deck. She could be quite intimidating, your mother.

'May I ask who dares to intrude upon my ship, and hold my crew in such a state of immobility?' she asked, taking stock of the situation. We didn't know that at the time William was in the shadows, watching everything unfold and waiting for his moment.

'I can answer for that my lady,' said the Noir Captain, stepping forward and staring at your mother, defiant but enthralled. He had clearly decided our fate in that moment. 'We had come to dine on your men, but I can see that there is much better fair in front of me.'

'You see me and my crew as a meal? What sort of monsters are you?' asked Elizabeth without a trace of fear.

'We are those who feed on the blood of the living, we are those who travel at night and spurn the light of day, we are fast, we are deadly, we are the Vampire,' answered their Captain, bowing deeply.

'And you think that I will taste sweeter than my crew because I am a woman? Then you are as much a fool as you are arrogant in thinking you could attack me or any member of my crew while I still live and breathe,' laughed Elizabeth.

'You speak very confidently for one who is surrounded by willing killers,' answered the Noir Captain, 'but upon seeing you my intentions have changed. I will leave your crew alive if you join us as my bride.'

'And how do your men feel about skipping dinner?' asked Elizabeth.

'My men do what I will them to,' replied their Captain, smiling and clearly taking the opportunity to show his teeth, which seemed to glow white in the light of the moon, his incisors unnaturally elongated and vicious, 'and as their leader they are bound by my command.'

'I would hardly call that fair,' Elizabeth responded, noting the small smiles that passed across the faces of the Noir as she defied their Captain. She guessed that these creatures were not willingly tied to their master, though she could not guess at what spell kept them in chains.

'Fair or not they do as I want, and so will you if you want your men to live.'

Within a breath the Noir Captain had moved faster than the eye could follow, and reappeared behind Elizabeth, her head snapped backwards and his teeth hung over her throat. Still she did not show any fear.

'It is clear you are no gentleman, nor even a man of honour,' she growled in anger as she felt his hot breath on her neck.

'Indeed I am no man at all,' sneered the Noir Captain as he reared back to sink his long sharp teeth into her neck. Yet things did not go as planned for this undead fiend, as William burst forth from the shadows where he had been hiding, and with a precision born from years of experience he pierced the Vampire through the heart, the top of his sword stopping short of injuring his own Captain. The Noir Captain released Elizabeth from his grip, as she whirled round in time to see him drop to the floor. The look of surprise on his face turning to a terrifying grimace as his skin began peeling back from the bones and his life force left his body.

Elizabeth, the other men and the Vampires then looked up in alarm as William let out a blood curdling yell of horror. It seemed that by destroying the Vampire Captain, William had unwittingly taken his place and his transformation was beginning. Collapsing to the deck in a ball of pain, his dark skin took on a grey hue, as his blood cooled and all warmth left his body. His dark eyes took on the red of the other Vampires and his teeth grew sharper and somehow longer. His heart stopped and it looked as though he had passed from this world. Elizabeth dropped to the deck on her knees beside him, and though her hand recoiled from the icy touch of his skin, still she pressed her hand to his chest.

'His heart has stopped!' she yelled to no one in particular, rolling him over fully on to his back, and pushing down onto his chest with both hands, trying to resuscitate him. Then she felt a cold hand on her arm.

'It be no use my lady, he is ... like us now,' said a Vampire who appeared suddenly at her side.

Elizabeth looked up at him, defiant tears threatening her eyes.

'What do you mean?'

'It is part of the curse we live under. If you kill one of us you must take their place, and as he has taken our Captain, so now he must become our Captain,' he explained.

'But surely one of you could be Captain? You don't need to take him? Is there nothing we can do?'

'I am truly sorry m'lady. It is how it must be. How it has

always been, as far as I know.'

'So he will be a killer, like you? He is such a good man, he would rather die than drink blood to live,' stated Elizabeth, getting to her feet and looking down at the still prostrate form of William.

'But if you or any of your crew were to kill him then you will take his place, and we cannot kill a fellow Vampirate. He is our Captain and we are bound to follow him, as we were the Captain before him, but your friend does not have to take the same path as we have been on until now. He can take us towards a new destiny. We do not thirst for living blood, but we do need it to survive. There are other ways. It was only the will of our old Captain that took us down such a destructive path, but as you divined he saw us more as slaves then a crew who sailed alongside him, we are glad to be free of him.'

'I understand,' replied Elizabeth in sad acceptance, as she watched William stirring on the deck.

Getting to his feet, William looked confused as the eyes of the entire ship followed his every move.

'What happened? I did kill him didn't I?'

'Yes Will, you saved my life, but you are ...' Elizabeth explained.

'Now a Vampire,' finished Will, looking down at his grey skin and then reaching up to touch his teeth gingerly, 'so what does this mean for me?'

'You are now our Captain,' answered the other Vampires in unison.

'And I can't turn you down and change back?'

'No, it is part of our curse, though I hear that if you do not drink the blood of the innocent you can be returned to human form some day, other than that I do not know much more of our history, I only know the rules that we are bound to live by. For instance we cannot go out in the day as the sunlight would burn us, but these things we will gladly teach you. It will be nice to have a good man as our Captain.'

'OK, then I have a chance to return to human,' stated William suddenly filled with hope, 'I will not accept this fate. I have no wish to live without the sun on my face and the love of my life at my side,' he added looking pointedly at Elizabeth, as time suddenly seemed to slow to a crawl and the rest of the men faded into the background – this moment was for these two.

'Will, it will be dawn soon and you must get to safety. We will meet again soon I am sure my love,' said Elizabeth, stepping forward and cupping Williams face in both her hands, 'I dare not have admitted this but now there is need more than life can say, I love you William and I will see you restored to human form before I leave this world. Then if luck be on our side, perhaps on that day we can marry.'

'I will hold ye to that as a promise.'

'Then hurry my love, pack your things and be gone before dawn approaches. The sooner we find a way to break this damned curse, the sooner we can start this new life together.'

In a flash of speed no human could hope to muster William fled below decks, returning minutes later with his things. He embraced Elizabeth and kissed her with a passion that only a condemned man can gather. William and his new Vampirate crew then returned to their ship, and in a blur of movement were soon lost to the night.

That was 15 years ago now, and since that time William has been looking to discover a break for the curse so he can return to Elizabeth and start life anew. I am sure he will know her whereabouts as sure as I am that he would not have given her up so easily.

In truth I have not spoken to either William or Elizabeth for many years now, but that is not to say that William and the Night Noir will not be easy enough to locate. Some time ago I had a tracking device fitted to their ship. Only for practical purposes you understand. You never know when you might need to find someone in a hurry...'

CHAPTER TWENTY-FOUR

Catch them if you can

The sun was beginning to rise, casting a pale orange glow on everything it touched. As the first rays crept over the horizon, the vessel Blimey and her crew had been tracking for the past week suddenly disappeared into the ether and with that, off their scanner again. This was the seventh time in seven days that this had happened. Always at sunrise. Blimey was getting sick of the damn ether hiding stuff from her and leaving her feeling adrift, frustrated and with no focus for the following 13 hours or so until the sun set and they could pick up the ship's signal again. At least they knew they were following the right ship.

She turned to the bird sitting on her shoulder and nuzzled his chest gently with her nose. It was good to have him back in action. After he had dried out Farquar had been able to repair him, but unfortunately Rawkous couldn't remember yet who it was that had tried to drown him.

Looking back to where the Night Noir's ship had just vanished, she asked Rawkous to fly up to the crow's nest and take a quick look around. She knew he wouldn't see anything, but she had to be sure. She still found it hard to believe that they could hide a whole ship in the blink of an eye each dawn without a cloaking device. No, some trickery was afoot.

Vincent joined Blimey at the helm, offering her the cup of coffee that had been sitting quietly on the deck, minding its own business, and waiting for her to notice it for the past five minutes.

'Again hey? Look, never mind, but drink this before it gets any colder, we'll pick up their trail again at sunset,' he stated the obvious.

'Yes, maybe the bird will find some trace of it though,' replied Blimey.

'Where do you think they go to?' asked Betty hates Veronica, joining the conversation.

'I don't really know,' mused Blimey, 'I mean all we know is that every morning they disappear and then at nightfall they re-appear miles away and we play catch up again. But they can't have dispersed like mist, and there's no way that thing has turbos or anything like that installed, they just don't travel far enough during the night. And those models could never handle that sort of pressure.... There is a chance that it could have been fitted with a teleportation device, but that doesn't explain why it keeps reappearing in the evenings, but only within a days sail...'

'Do you think they know we're following them?'

'No ... I think if they did they would have turned to meet us by now. We're in a bit of spot this time my friend. We daren't use the ship's turbos or we loose our advantage. Remember they are still dangerous, and I would prefer them not to know we are here ... just yet.'

'Their ability to make their ship disappear at will without a cloaking device is indeed perplexing,' interjected the Farquar, joining them on deck.

'Yes, but we must catch them, we're so close,' added Blimey.

'I know, and we will,' soothed Vincent, 'but I don't think there's much we can do until nightfall, so let's get something to eat and then some rest, I have a feeling we'll have a big night ahead of us.'

The day passed slowly and uneventfully in a haze of naps and lazy cups of tea on the deck. Farquar had even tried to take everyone's mind off the pending evening by trying to teach Rawkous how to appreciate wine, a talent the bird would never need but one that kept everyone laughing and went a short way to dispersing the anxiousness that pervaded the Raven.

The hours dragged by until finally the sun began to set, and as the last traces of the orange glow disappeared below the horizon the ship Blimey had been chasing materialised again and its tracker started blip-blip-blipping.

CHAPTER TWENTY-FIVE

A dark meeting

'Thar she blows!' yelled the Farquar in a jolly fashion as they finally caught sight of the ship they had been chasing for days.

'I can see,' hissed Blimey, turning in alarm and putting one finger up to her lips to shush him, 'if what we have heard of them is true then they will hear you from here! However, my friend, I do think this time we may be able to catch them, they aren't so far ahead at all. Betty get us there!'

'Aye, Captain' replied Betty hates Veronica who already had them at full sail, and was now making further adjustments to increase their speed but keep them running quiet.

'Be ready to board when we catch them everyone, but always remember what they are and what they are capable of,' warned Blimey sternly, 'keep behind Vincent, he will lead us. They can't harm him.... he's not their type,' she smiled sarcastically, before turning to Vincent and hugging him tightly. She only hoped that the Noir's faith in their own abilities would make them vulnerable if they could sneak up fast enough and close enough.

'Do we have any other means of defending ourselves Captain or is this more of a suicide mission?' asked Wolff, appearing out of the shadows and winking at Betty. In the end he had decided to stay. He was enchanted with Betty hates Veronica and was pretty sure she liked him back. He wanted to see where this might lead rather than returning to his brothers. He had never met a girl quite like her before, and never felt such an instant attraction.

'Oh you better believe it my good sir,' answered Blimey with a sly smile, 'I've had Rawkous hard at work for the past few days stringing up ultra violet lights on the masts of the ship. One snap of my fingers and the whole place lights up like its midday, they would be wise not to mess with us.'

'I like a lady who's got all her bases covered,' smiled Wolff, appreciating his Captain's forethought.

The moon rose high into the night sky as, under the cover of a convenient mist, the Raven drew silently up alongside the Vampirate's vessel. Strangely nothing happened, though the crew of the Raven were prepared for almost anything. The children of the dark made no move against them, though it was not clear if this was because they had not yet awoken from their slumber, or if knowing that their pursuers were a basic food source had something to do with their inaction. Sometimes you just want your meals delivered.

Blimey felt uneasy as the silence continued long after they had dropped anchor as quietly as possible. She did not want to board the Vampirates' ship, and would have preferred to meet them on her own turf. Her crew all had their eyes on her waiting for her decision as to how they would approach their quarry. She did not want to put them in danger, but did she have a choice? She was confident that she could activate the ultra violet lights on the Raven from the Noir's ship, but there would be many more places for them to hide on their own vessel, she was sure of it, and so it was bigger risk. At least she could lock down the Raven so there was nowhere to go.

The moments ticked by, and still nothing happened. Blimey knew they would have to go over. Turning to face her crew she signalled for Rawkous to come to her, and on a wisp of the wind that blew he glided down to her shoulder.

'Keep an eye out sharpish bird, and if we perchance should fall, you know what to do.'

'Yes m'lady,' he answered her quietly, knowing that he was to stay on the ship and what she had entrusted him to do. It was quite a lot of responsibility for a parrot, but he could handle it.

Blimey then signalled to the others to follow her, and as one they began climbing the rigging on the Raven's three masts. Once they had reached around half way up, each grabbed hold of one of the boarding ropes and with a deep breath they jumped off into space, free falling for a moment before the rope pulled taught and swung them as one aboard the Vampirate's ship. They landed on the main deck of the Noir's ship with a dramatic thud, Vincent immediately taking the lead position with the rest of the crew behind him. This seemed to finally cause some kind of reaction from the Noir, who within seconds had the unwelcome intruders on their ship surrounded.

'You fools!' laughed the Noir closest to Vincent, 'do you think we did not know you have been following us for days? It is but a game to let you catch us, and also we are quite hungry,' he leered bearing his sharp teeth.

'Your arrogance betrays you,' returned Vincent calmly, 'do you in turn think we would not come armed to defend ourselves against you? Look to our ship there, each mast is covered with ultra violet lights. One snap of my Captain's fingers and you're toast – literally!'

The vampires seemed to bristle. This was not something they had been expecting at all. The humans could be bluffing of course, but did they want to get burnt to a crisp finding out? A moment later and the point was rendered moot as the Captain of the Noir came flying through his men, stopping inches from Vincent. He was slightly taller than the Hollow, though his skin was as dark as Vincent's was pale. They were similar in build, both being quite skinny and muscular. William's hair was a dark brown, and much longer, but it was the eyes that really separated the two. Where Vincent's were solely black, William's were blood red. Where Vincent was dressed head to toe in black, William was dressed in dark grey tweed trousers and flowing white shirt, with a tweed vest buttoned over it. He looked more like a gentleman who was headed out for an evening of cards than a Vampirate.

Their noses were almost touching, as the Vampirate tried to figure out what he was dealing with here. The intruders beyond the man standing in front of him smelled like human to him, but this other's scent was different. After a second he was able to place it.

'What do you want Hollow?' he smiled, looking past him to size up the rest of the crew.

Behind him Vincent sensed movement as one of the Vampirates made a grab for Blimey. Vincent moved faster than the eye could follow, snapping the Vampirate to one side and sending him crashing to the deck.

The other Noir hissed in anger, but before they could move their Captain signalled for them to stand down. He had just noticed Blimey for the first time, who had moved forward and was now standing proudly beside Vincent.

'You move faster than any Hollow I have known sir, I did not know that you could possess such skills,' William said quietly, understanding instantly that he was up against an equal and not just another deadhead.

'Yes, well those of us who can do such things don't advertise it, it would not bode well for us ... as you can imagine,' responded Vincent calmly.

'And who is this girl you move so quickly to protect? What do you want of us?'

'She is my Captain, and my love, but what may interest you more William, Captain of the Noir, is that she is the daughter of Gerald and Elizabeth Bohnes.'

This news had the effect that Vincent had hoped for, and William staggered back slightly as though he had been hit.

'Elizabeth ... Gerald... Bohnes? But that is not possible, that baby died.'

'Unconfirmed rumours my boy, that is all,' said Farquar stepping forward, and giving William another shock, 'but I can assure you that she is who Vincent says she is.'

'Farquar you old salt! Where did you come from?!' exclaimed William forgetting himself momentarily and running to embrace his old friend.

'Does he know everyone on the Severed Seas?' hissed Betty, leaning in to Blimey's ear.

'It does seem a bit strange that he knows everyone we have encountered so far, but he has not said anything. I am beginning to wonder...' answered Blimey, forcing her attention back on the reunion that was taking place before her.

'That's not important right now my friend,' Farquar continued speaking to William, 'but if you will grant us some of your time all will become clear, and I think you owe your men an explanation. They are looking quite ... famished,' he added warningly.

'Yes, of course ... Men,' said William turning to his crew, 'I have some good news and some bad news. Unfortunately these people are not breakfast, but rather the companions of an old friend of ours. You will all remember Farquar?'

William's men bowed slightly to Farquar out of respect, but you could see the disappointment in their faces. They had not had a fresh meal for some time. Their Captain would not allow them to feed as often as their previous leader had encouraged, and though they accepted this, there were those among them who missed the old days.

'Now, come to my quarters and tell me why you are here,' said William turning back to Farquar and gesturing for Blimey and her crew to follow him below decks.

'Can you guarantee the safety of my crew?' Blimey asked suddenly, realising that if they went below decks her only weapon back on board the Raven would be rendered useless.

'I give you my word,' replied William with a smile, showing off his long incisors. She is so much like her mother, he thought to himself, no longer doubting that she was Elizabeth's daughter.

Below decks oil lamps flickered in the hallway, barely doing their job and casting a dirty yellow haze over everything their shallow light touched. In the gloom the hall looked as though it continued on forever, disappearing into the darkness. Somehow the ship felt bigger on the inside. To the right and left a myriad of doors lead off to different rooms, but William stopped at the third on the right and turned the door handle sharply to the right. The locking mechanism dutifully released the door and it swung inwards. The room was not much better lit than the hallway, but at least their eyes had now adjusted and they could take in some of the details. Directly to their left was a small, carved, black wood table on which sat a number of bottles filled with a dark liquid. Around the table were four plush, black velvet chairs. In the left corner of the room was a large bed, hung all round with heavy, black velvet curtains. To the right of this was a round portal, then as their eyes followed the natural turn of the room they could see a desk, on which sat a number of items any Captain would be expected to own. A globe, compass, map charts, logbook, ink, quills. There was also a chair at the desk of course, again plush, black velvet. Someone obviously had a taste for dark shaded soft fabrics.

'Please take a seat,' said William dragging over the chair from his desk and taking a seat himself on the edge of his bed, 'I am sorry I cannot offer you a drink, but we don't often get ... living visitors.'

William stared intently at Blimey, still trying to come to terms with who she was, as Farquar spoke first.

'I suppose you are wondering why we have come to find

you William, it has in truth been many years. Our old friend Atticus told us where we could find you. He has been ... watching you ... he likes to know where you are at all times. Do you understand what I am saying?'

William nodded. He indeed knew about the tracking device, but as it had seemed to do no harm, he had left it where it was. He liked Atticus to think that he was the cleverer of the two, though this was certainly debatable.

'The short version is that Blimey here is Elizabeth and Gerald's daughter. After Gerald was murdered Elizabeth requested I foster her out to a trusted family so she could hunt down Gerald's killers, with you. Everything was going well for the girl's first 19 years or so, but I lost track of her a few years ago when she ran away ... to become a pirate no less,' Farquar continued, with a small smile, 'I finally found her again sailing under the flag of Miserablesod on the Avernus, but it seems my presence only caused more trouble. When he found out whom her father was, he accused her of mutiny and threw her overboard. I managed to find her again, just before Blackwatch came to claim a bounty on her head actually – yes, I can see your face harden William, and I didn't want to believe he was still alive either – but somehow Vainglorious has found out about the girl, and has employed Blackwatch to hunt her down.'

'And so what do you want from me Blimey? I am afraid we Noir are better pirates than allies,' said William, with a suddenly tired air about him, 'besides, given our aversion to sunlight we are not much good during long drawn out battles.'

'That is Miss Blimey to you,' she corrected him, 'and I don't need your allegiance, I need information,' she continued, getting to her feet and crossing the room, 'I am looking for my mother, and Atticus lead us to believe that you may know where we can find her.'

'I see ... so you think you are capable of fighting Blackwatch *and* Vainglorious on your own, and finding Elizabeth as well? That would be a tall order for any sea farer let alone a woman as young as yourself.'

'Don't patronise me, Captain, I have met Blackwatch on more than one occasion already, and beaten him back to his own ship in disgrace, and this Vainglorious does not scare me. In fact it sounds like I have business of my own to settle with this man. From what I understand it was he who ordered the murder of my father,' returned Blimey fiercely.

'Yes, that news is well travelled, but from what I hear, Blackwatch will be better prepared next time he meets you, and so I would not count on another outcome being so easily in your favour,' said William, 'and Vainglorious throws more gold towards your capture each day. He wishes to see you brought in before the year is out.'

'Then I too will be better prepared,' said Blimey, 'I thank you for this forewarning ...' but she did not get to finish her sentence, for there was the loud explosion of cannon fire heard up on deck.

'Damn it! What can this new devilry be!' bellowed William, flying from the room in a blur of shadow.

The others were on their feet and following him within seconds, pelting up the stairs and bursting up onto the deck in time to see another explosion rock the Noir's ship metres from the Raven.

'Whomever these late night visitors are, they're not very friendly,' yelled Blimey to her crew over the noise, as she looked out across the deck and watched the madness, smoke and flames around them, 'come on, let's find out what's going on here,' she added breaking into a run and making for the side of the ship. Hitting the banister hard, she looked out into the chaotic night, lit by the fire that had caught the main sail of the Noir's ship. Through the bellowing black smoke she could almost make out the flag of the opposing ship.

'Where is the fickle wind to clear the smoke when you need it,' she whispered to herself, leaning further out over the side of the ship. As if in answer the smoke parted briefly, and the flag became clear. They were under attack from the Nixe.

CHAPTER TWENTY-SIX

Meeting of minds

Captain James Blade stumbled down some cobbled stairs and pulled open a heavy wooden door. Stepping into the dark bar it took his eyes a moment to adjust to the gloom. His ears were greeted by the low murmur of several shady conversations, but he was not there to meet anyone. He was here again to drink away the shalacking that his pride had taken at the hands of Blimey, and the revelation that her father had been the Captain he had once betrayed in exchange for a small fortune and a place on Captain Blackwatch's crew. To his 10 year-old self, at that time, this had been a smart move.

Now he had lost Blimey, someone he had hoped perhaps one day to marry, it was a decision he was now regretting. True he had never been a good boyfriend, often getting drunk and cheating on her, but he had intended to settle down one day. In his mind he was the bad boy who would come good eventually, and she was his girl, no one else was worthy of being with her. Of course Blade had never considered asking Blimey if this was what she wanted too. He just assumed she would want what he did, a mistake many men before him had made about women, and a mistake many still made.

Blade sat down heavily at the table, and didn't bother to look up as the serving girl came over to take his order. When his bottle of Gynwhysky arrived, the only movement he made was to lift the bottle to his lips as he worked to drink away all memories of the past. As the bottle began to empty, Blade felt the hurt turn to anger and transform itself into a dark betrayal. He was not to blame for Gerald Bohnes' death - that one was on Blackwatch, he had merely led Blackwatch to his former Captain. It was not as if Blade had plunged the sword in himself. It was totally unfair of Blimey to blame him for that. And what of this new man, this Vincent Blackshadow? Where had he really come from? It was not his fault he had killed him either. He was simply defending his honour! Of course Blade could not know that Vincent had actually survived.

No, he decided, he should not have to shoulder the responsibilities for the deaths of these two men, who just happened to be important in Blimey's life. That was her fault. If only she had done what he wanted, then there would be none of this mess and he would be sailing off into the sunset with her right now. Of course Betty hates Veronica would have to go - Blade knew she could not stand him, and after a while that would cause too many issues, but he was sure he would be able to convince Blimey to dump her best friend. Perhaps they could even trade her to another ship for some whisky and wine, after all with him as the Raven's new Captain they would not need her.

As Blade drank on his schemes became darker, more unbalanced, and he began to convince himself that if he could only get rid of Blimey's First Mate, then all would be well and they could live happily ever after. He was so lost in his fantasies of being the Raven's new Captain that he did not notice the hooded figure who sat down across from him at the table until the figure reached out and grabbed the bottle, taking a swig from it.

'Hey!' yelled the startled Blade, as he looked up, 'oh it's you,' he added smiling as the figure sitting opposite him pulled back their hood and revealed herself.

'He's not dead, Blade,' said the woman.

'Who's not dead?' Blade slurred slightly as he leaned back in his chair.

CHAPTER TWENTY-SEVEN

Ship of lost souls

'What do we do?' yelled Betty hates Veronica over the noise of the fighting, 'should we get back to our ship and get out of here before the Nixe hit her too?'

'We can't leave the Noir,' answered Blimey, 'I don't have the information I need yet. I think the Raven will be safe. The Nixe are deliberately aiming for the Noir's ship or they would have hit her too by now.'

'Well, if you're sure,' said Betty H.V not sounding too confident.

'What do we do then boss?' asked Wolff, stepping up to his Captain's side.

'We need to find out why the Nixe are here and stop this nonsense before both crews slaughter each other. Follow me!'

'Where are we going?'

'We're going to board the Nixe's ship of course and have a word with their Captain,' smiled Blimey.

'But how are we going to get over to their ship? It's not as if they are alongside.'

'Not yet, but they will intend to board soon enough, tell me Farquar of the Severed Seas who seems to know everyone, while we wait for them to come closer, what do you know of the Nixe?'

'Oh I could not possibly know everyone, but it is true my chequered and polkadotted past has led me to cross paths with many different characters on the Seas,' said Farquar not missing Blimey's inference, 'the Nixe however, are true underworld figures and not the usual riff raff that we may come across. They are known as sea demons, and will do almost anything to claim a prize they deem worthy of their attention. They know nothing of logic and laugh in the face of reality... they are vicious, obsessive ... nutters really,'

'But what do they want with the Noir?' asked Vincent, 'are

they not demons as well?'

'That I cannot say with any surety,' answered Farquar, 'but I have never seen the Nixe so bold. This strikes me as being more than about looking for a simple collector's piece.'

'We'll be soon finding out, here they come to board! It's imperative that I get onto the Nixe's ship before they get to the Noir. Their Captain just happens to owe me a favour and I think it's high time I called it in,' said Blimey to everyone's surprise.

They were just about to climb the rigging in order to swing across to the Nixe ship, when William caught up to them, grabbing Blimey by the arm and holding her back.

'Where do you think you're going then? I cannot protect you if you try to fight them. They are demons, creatures not of this world. Even the Noir cannot fell a demon ...'

'Don't worry about us William,' said Blimey pulling her arm free, 'the Nixe will not touch us, you have my word,' she bowed slightly to emphasize just how gallant she was being, though her gesture was cut short by a red canon ball smashing through ship's sail above her head, and the sudden influx of Nixe onto the Noir's ship. They had moved faster than she had anticipated, and William's interruption had delayed them long enough to allow the Nixe the advantage.

'Damn my hide!' swore Blimey as they were quickly surrounded, and the Noir faced off against the demons of the sea.

A cold wind blew in from the east, and the smoke began to clear now that the canon fire had stopped, while from above a light rain began to fall dampening the fires on the ship, which soon subsided to a smouldering glow. Out of the dark stepped what appeared to be a woman, but she was a little too tall, and her limbs were a bit too long to be human. Her eyes stood out an eerie pale green against her darkish blue skin, almost as if they were glowing in the moonlight. Her black hair hung down her back in loose curls, cascading from under her tricorne hat, and the moon glinted off her black leather chest plate, which was polished to within an inch of its life. The plate itself was carved with an anchor. She wore light wool trousers of navy blue, rolled up over black leather lace up boots that came to her calves. She had an unmistakable air of defiance and authority that marked her out as the Nixe Captain.

Stepping forward she scanned her captives briefly and smiled with satisfaction, however as her eyes lit on Blimey her expression changed to one of surprise, followed by annoyance.

'Blimey! Step forward,' she demanded, 'what are you doing here? You interrupt my sport – and not for the first time.'

'The last time was an accident – I told you that, Lorelei,' Blimey smiled as she stepped away from her crew and the Noir, and bowed to the sea demon.

'Perhaps it was, as you say, an accident, but you can have no business here now, we have a private matter to settle with the Noir, and I trust you will not interfere,' warned Lorelei.

'I have business of my own with the Noir, Lorelei, and insofar as your business does not cross mine then I shall not get involved. May I ask what is it that you want with them?' asked Blimey calmly.

'Not that it is any business of yours, but I am here for their Captain, and will take him by any means necessary, even if that means taking you down with his crew.'

'Lorelei, we have known each other a long time, and I trust that you can be more candid with me than that, please tell me what you can want with their Captain as my business is also with him,'

'For the sake of the debt I owe you I will tell you, but mark my words it is unfortunate that you have been caught up in the details of this transaction as I will not spare anyone in it's foreclosure,' warned Lorelei, before continuing, 'Captain Blackwatch has taken my daughter, and in exchange for her safe return he has demanded I deliver the Captain of the Noir to him before sunset on All Hallows Eve,'

'Then I can understand your ferocity, but what can he want with William?'

'Apparently he knows the whereabouts of the leader of the Thirteen Bones, and places this knowledge above all else for the present.'

'Elizabeth,' William whispered under his breath.

'Yes, Elizabeth,' repeated Lorelei to the stunned William, who had thought he had not been heard.

'But what does he want with her?' asked Blimey, playing it down as it was obvious that Lorelei did not know her own connection to the Thirteen Bones, nor of the bounty she had on her own head.

'I assume there is a price on her head, or it is some kind of vendetta, I am not to sure of the details and I do not want to know them, all I am interested in is the safe return of my kin.'

'But what if I help you get your daughter back, and then you don't have to do this,' bargained Blimey, stalling so she could think. She was pretty sure if the Nixe decided to take William there was not much she could do about it, but she needed him to find out where Elizabeth was herself.

The Noir looked at each other uneasily. In their minds there was no point in fighting, the Nixe had the advantage and would easily slaughter them, and they did not understand why this Blimey was complicating a simple situation.

Blimey turned to look at William, whose handsome face was set in grim acceptance, and in a moment her decision was made. She could not let the Nixe take him, and her best chance for finding her mother, with him. She would have to go instead.

CHAPTER TWENTY-EIGHT

No news would be better news

Bessie ignored Blade's questions and threw up a tentacled arm, signaling for the barman to bring her a drink. He knew what to bring her as they had pre-arranged it when the barman had called her to let her know Blade was there. A little theatre never hurt anyone and it had the desired affect.

'They know you here I see?' said Blade impressed as the barman set down a fine single malt whisky in front of Bessie.

Bessie ignored this statement too, wrapping her right tentacle around the glass and lifting it to her lips to take a sip.

'What do you want Bessie?' sighed Blade finally, tiring of Bessie's games. She was sorely interrupting his drinking time.

'I thought you might like to know that Vincent Blackshadow is still alive,' she said.

'Not possible, I saw him die,' answered Blade who had no patience for this nonsense.

'Well I have it on the best authority that he lives and is sailing with that wretched Blimey.'

'Why should I care Bessie?' asked Blade, swigging from his bottle and trying to hide the anger rising inside his head.

'Oh Blade,' Bessie burst out with a laugh, 'it's no secret you're in love with Blimey – and that she has scorned you for this Vincent.'

'Did you come here to mock me? If you have then consider me mocked, now please leave.'

'No, no, that would be a pointless exercise, I can mock you any time. No, I have come on behalf of my fiancé, Captain Blackwatch, he is pulling together quite a force to go after Blimey. She has ... ahhh ... shall we say insulted him one time too many, and now he is quite serious about making her pay for it, but if you wanted to join us I am sure some bargain could be made in order to save her life and return her to you,' Bessie suggested, knowing full well that Blackwatch would never agree to this, but also how to play on Blade's emotions, his rejection and his longing for redemption.

CHAPTER TWENTY-NINE

A change of plan

Back on the Noir's ship, Lorelei looked at Blimey with a sad smile. She had, true to the stories about her, offered to help save the life of someone she had never met if it meant saving the life of someone who was important to her. Lorelei had to admire this, yet she was also sorry that this time she could not help. All that was about to change, and in a way none were expecting.

'I'm sorry Blimey, but I have no choice, I must deliver the Noir Captain in exchange for my daughter.'

'But what if you could give Blackwatch something even more ... valuable to him?'

'No you can't! Please don't do this!' yelled Betty hates Veronica suddenly, darting forward and grabbing Blimey by the wrist, causing everyone to flinch at the unexpected movement. Immediately the Nixe raised their weapons.

'Please, Betty, I know what I am doing,' said Blimey quietly, gently pulling her arm away from her friend and gesturing for everyone to calm down.

'What does she mean, you can't do what?' asked Lorelei slowly, intrigued by the passionate outburst.

'I know you think you have to take William because of the information he has, but the end game for Blackwatch will be the same if you take me instead. He is looking for Elizabeth, but he is really looking for me ... I am her daughter. '

'How is this the possible? Blimey this better not be a game. Are you telling the truth?' asked Lorelei in disbelief.

'I am telling you the truth Lorelei, and if you take me instead of William I guarantee you he will return your daughter and reward you handsomely as well. You won't have to do anything more. Then I will deal with Blackwatch, he has meddled with my family for the last time.'

'Are you sure this is what you want Blimey? I cannot ensure your safety after I hand you over – you could be going to your death,' said Lorelei.

'If it will keep William and the Noir safe, and sees your daughter returned to you, then yes, this is what I want.'

'Blimey, don't do this, it is me that Blackwatch wants, let me go,' said William stepping forward and dropping to one knee in front of his friend's daughter. Looking up at her he smiled sadly, the look on her face told him there was no changing her mind, 'you truly are Elizabeth's daughter. She would be very proud of you,' he added.

'Please Captain, get to your feet and thank you for your kind words, I know you understand why I need to do this, Blackwatch would kill you as soon as he is done with you – he knows your weaknesses, I am sure of it,' said Blimey quietly, helping William to his feet and kissing his cheek, a little overwhelmed by his statement. She turned to her crew, 'Betty, you must take command of the Raven now, you know her best, I will return soon enough, but in the meantime, stay out of trouble OK?'

'Yes Captain.'

'William, I will be back for you, and I will find my mother.'

'Of course,' bowed William.

Lorelei signalled to her crew and in a blur of blue the Nixe returned to their ship, leaving Lorelei for the moment with Blimey as she said goodbye to Vincent.

Vincent stepped forward and cupped Blimey's face in his hands, tilting her face to his as he kissed her. And everything he felt in that one moment poured out in that one kiss – the fear of loosing her, the longing, the pride he felt that she was his girl, his admiration for her and of course at last, his love for her. Pulling away finally he looked into her eyes.

'I can't let you go alone, I'll follow you,' he said simply.

'Oh Vincent, I'll be fine,' said Blimey with a wink, 'you don't have to follow me, just wait and see, I'll be back before the new moon rises,' she said taking his hands and then letting them fall away gently as she turned to go with Lorelei.

Blimey turned before Vincent could reply, she didn't want him to see the pain in her eyes. She would not cry, but it took all her strength to keep those tears at bay. For all her bravado, she didn't know what would await her when she was handed over to Blackwatch, and she was afraid. She couldn't let her crew see that though, least of all Vincent.

'Come, we must go now Blimey, I hope you're right about this,' said Lorelei as they headed for the boarding plank and walked back over to the Nixe ship.

Blimey took one last look back at her friends and smiled, held her hand up and waved goodbye. She didn't know when she would see any of them again despite what she said. Once aboard the Nixe ship, Lorelei went to the helm and gestured for Blimey to join her.

'Well now Blimey, you're about to see something no mortal has ever seen before!' and with that Lorelei threw a black and silver lever next to the helm wheel, and with a sound that was suspiciously like dolphin chirping, the engines of the ship came to life. The clockwork circuitry of the control panel lit up, and clicked and clacked beneath painted glass as Lorelei twisted a smaller leaver sharply to the right. The main sails of the ship unfurled with a sharp snap of canvas, and Blimey couldn't help but gasp at their beauty though her heart was heavy.

She could not but be impressed by the Nixe ship, and as it pulled away from both the Raven and the Noir's ship, she took some time to take in the details of the vessel. The stern was oddly sleek and round, it suggested the ship could travel forward and backwards with relative ease. The sails were painted as though hung with a thousand stars against the black canvas, while the rest of the ship was painted a dull, dark blue, with angels and anchors carved into the mainmasts. The main deck was painted a wonderful shiny black so that in the darkest night it reflected the stars from both the sky and the sails giving you the sensation that you were floating through space.

'To remind us that the universe is all around us,' explained Lorelei as she noticed Blimey's awed expression, while with her hands she expertly set their course as though she had done this a hundred-thousand times, which for all Blimey knew, she had. Under just the wisp of a breeze the Nixe ship sailed away into the night.

On board the Noir ship, Vincent and Betty stood arm in arm as they watched their Captain sail away with the Nixe in sad silence, while Wolff and Farquar stood talking with William.

'What do we do now?' asked Wolff finally, breaking away from the hushed conversation, and breaking the silence. Vincent and Betty turned towards him.

'We follow them,' said Vincent decidedly.

'But how?' asked Betty, turning to look up at Vincent.

'I will always be able to find her,' smiled Vincent, 'and besides she's set a tracking beacon on board that ship, that should help us a bit.'

'How can you know that?'

'You think my girl would be mad enough to go running off with a bunch of sea demons and not give us a way to follow her? Ha! Don't be ridiculous, she wants us to follow her, she thinks of everything!' exclaimed Vincent.

'Back to the Raven!' yelled Betty joyously as she realised what Vincent was saying.

'Well William, it looks like I am off again,' said Farquar, 'I'm sure we'll find you again soon enough.'

'That won't be necessary Farquar, I will give you the information she requires, and there will be no need for her to come back for me.'

'It doesn't work that way William,' answered Farquar distractedly, and for the most part unconvincingly.

CHAPTER THIRTY

What did you have in mind?

'What did you have in mind then Bessie?' asked Blade as he took another swig from the bottle.

'Obviously I can't discuss the details here, Blade, but come with me and sail with your former mentor. Together we will capture Blimey and reduce her crew to a massacred mess.'

'Fine, fine, when do you sail?' he slurred.

'Tomorrow morning, you will collect me from the port and then from there we will meet Blackwatch in the sea of Trascorn.'

'Do you not have a ship of your own?' asked Blade.

'You know very well what happened to my ship,' hissed Bessie in anger, 'and I intend to get the Raven back!'

'Yes, of course,' laughed Blade with the alcohol kicking up a gear and sparking his sense of humour.

'Blade I warn you, if my fiancé did not need you I would slit your throat from ear to ear!'

'You're a treasure Bessie, really you are.'

'One day Blade, one day you will not laugh at me so!' replied Bessie, anger in her voice, as she got to her feet and stormed out, leaving Blade laughing into his bottle of Gynwhysky at the table.

Storming out into the street Bessie took a deep breath and turned right, heading towards the house she was staying in that night. She did love Blackwatch a great deal, but he was always underestimating her. She didn't see why he had to involve that wretched double crosser Blade in anything he was planning against Blimey. Surely she should have been enough. Sighing loudly she roughly adjusted the scabbard on her hip and started off up the street towards the setting sun.

Blade meanwhile had finally gotten control of himself, leaning back in his chair he took a swig from the bottle and nodded to the barman. His head was spinning slightly, and not from the drink. He had only just been thinking about how he could go about getting Blimey back when the opportunity had virtually appeared in front of him like a gift from Santa. It was almost too good to be true and Blade wondered if he could really trust his former Captain to play ball, or if this was simply a long wind-up to bitter disappointment and perhaps even his death?

The bottle finally empty he got out of his chair, and wobbling slightly headed back to his ship. He had to get her ready to sail in the morning, and in her current state he doubted Bessie would even step foot on board. He'd let the crew be pretty slack somewhat of late, and the Nevermore was in need of a good mop and polish.

CHAPTER THIRTY-ONE

In over your head

'What do you call your ship?' asked Blimey as Lorelei steered her through the calm seas.

'The Eudoxus, but she's more than a sailing vessel.'

'What do you mean?'

'You're about to find out! Crew prepare to dive!' yelled Lorelei.

'You mean underwater? This ship is going underwater?' asked Blimey uncertainly.

'Yes!' laughed Lorelei, 'in about three minutes time.'

'Do you wear some sort of breathing apparatus or something?'

'No, we have no need of it.'

'Well, I know you sea demons may not have need of air to breathe underwater but I'm going to have to decline joining you if that is the case, I need air to live.'

'Relax Blimey, look we're not really sea demons, we just let our enemies think this as it gives us the advantage, in reality we're Planarians, and we too need air to breathe underwater, just wait and watch and I promise you, you are in no danger.'

'Planarians! Well, well I never would have guessed that – so that means you are able to ...'

'Yes, we can restore any part of our bodies if we lose it in battle, and the process only takes a few minutes, we can also live for hundreds of years but there are not many of us left now,' Lorelei sighed.

'Why, what happened to you all?'

'For many years people tried to capture us and discover how to use our bodies so they could live longer, horrible experiments were carried out but they could not figure it out, thankfully,' Lorelei explained, 'to escape this persecution we started the rumour that we were sea demons, and as such could not induce long life in anyone – only eternal damnation of their souls - Ha! But we became overconfident and were hunted for different reasons, to stop us from the horror our people were causing. Our weakness was discovered, and similar to the Vampirates, if you were to cut off my head you would extinguish my life. I don't know why I am telling you this, but I trust you Blimey, you have been a good .... friend to me.'

'You're secrets are safe with me Lorelei,' smiled Blimey, 'but now show me how we are to go into the deep with this ship, I am intrigued!'

'Well then hold onto your hat, and hit that green button there!'

Blimey did as she was told and immediately the sails wrapped themselves up neatly while the masts on the decking began to lower into the deck itself. Once they were about two thirds of the way down a series of clanking sounds could be heard as amazingly the ship began to transform. Along both sides, from the bow to the stern, metal sections expanded out covering the sides and blocking out the moonlight. A third section then interlocked with the other two over the top, with the mainmast just touching the top of it as it went past. The final section, a clear glass dome, then emerged from the stern, and slid out over the heads of Blimey and Lorelei. They were soon enclosed within the ship.

'That is fantastic!' exclaimed Blimey with admiration, 'I've never seen anything like it – it's a submersive! Oh but how do you steer this thing? We can't see forward now?'

'Ah, but we have thought of that of course! Push that small button there with the looping arrow on it,'

'Oh this is so much fun, I wish I had sailed with you a long time ago Lorelei, so many things I have never seen!'

'I'm glad you like the ship Blimey, I am quite proud of her – now push the button!'

Blimey did so and the whir of clockwork could be heard again, only it sounded slightly louder this time and seemed to be coming from under their feet. The helm on which she and Lorelei stood slowly began to turn on a rotating platform that encompassed not just the wheel but also all the circuitry of the navigation system. When it came to a stop through 180 degrees it began to rise up, while a spiral stair case leading back down to the deck below appeared. They could now see out over the stern, and where they were going.

Grabbing what looked like a brass funnel on a tube Lorelei commanded her crew, 'reverse propulsion! All forward stop!'

As they had still been moving in the direction they been travelling before the ship had transformed itself, they were heading what was now backwards. Many of her crew ran below decks, and the hum of a large engine could soon be felt through the ship.

'There's no wind down there and the currents are too set in their ways to be of much use to us, so we have to rely on mechanical power below the waves,' explained Lorelei as they could feel the ship slowly coming to a halt. Lorelei grabbed the communications system again but this time put it to her ear. After listening for a few seconds, she put it to her mouth and spoke again.

'Forward stern, five knots and prepare to dive on my mark.'

The Eudoxus began to move this time in the direction it had come from, but as Lorelei swung the helm it came around in a wide arcing circle, and was soon facing the direction they needed to go. Once they were on course, Lorelei grabbed the comms device and yelled 'Dive!'

Immediately the pitch of the engines increased, and though she couldn't see it, Lorelei explained to Blimey that deep within the ship several specially built compartments were opening and flooding with water. This in turn made the ship much heavier and caused it to sink beneath the waves. She also explained that once they were below the surface they would pick up more speed.

Blimey watched through the thick glass of the observation deck at what was now the bow of the ship, as the water began to rise alarming fast around the Eudoxus. She held her breath as the water came up over the glass, and soon they were completely submerged. Down they headed, deeper and further away from the pale moonlight, and now they could see nothing in front of them. Lorelei flicked a small switch and light appeared to pour out from the front of the ship, lighting their way. Inside the submarine a dirty orange light lit everything so they could see their way around the ship.

'What do you think then Blimey?'

'She'll do nicely!' laughed Blimey.

'Right, let's get on then!'

As Lorelei maneuvered the Eudoxus through the underwater labyrinth, Blimey stood and watched their progress through the observation window. She noted the way the light of the moon glowed on the surface of the water above, while they passed fish of all kinds, octopi, starfish, jellyfish, corals of all colours – things she had never been able to see before, which were lit by the light projecting from the ship. She smiled to herself in the wonder of it all.

About 10 hours into their journey beneath the waves, long after the sun had risen again, Blimey saw something that wiped the smile away and replaced it first with a concerned frown and then as what she was seeing dawned on her, rage took over.

'Lorelei,' she called, trying to remain calm, 'do you see what I see? The water turns red with blood, what could be happening here to cause that?'

'I see it, yes, it gets darker as we approach, it looks like we're coming up on a slaughter of some kind.'

'Where are we?'

'We are near the Cove of the Dead, home to the Tecausians. According to the lore of my kin they hunt the Scylla for food, driving them into the cove and then attacking them with long silver spears. The Scylla are a peaceful race of sea nymphs who live under the waves. They are mostly harmless, and I don't know why they keep returning to cove, but they do and against the Tecausians they are defenseless. Some of the Scylla are captured and sold on the black market to be held in private aquariums, but they don't last long separated from their own kind and they fade away and die.'

'Barbarians,' said Blimey quietly.

'I always thought it was just a story,' said Lorelei sadly.

'Well it looks real enough to me!' said Blimey through gritted teeth as through the red water above them she could now see the Tecausians in diving suits attacking the Scylla. She could also hear the Tecausians' laughter echoing through their metal diving helmets. Yet they had not noticed the Nixe ship below them in the dark and the deep.

'We have to do something!' Blimey cried out, as her heart beat faster and she could feel the anger blazing in her head.

'Of course my friend, I will not stand for this disgusting

behaviour to continue in my ocean, but we must remain quiet so as not to disturb the battle, I want to surprise them,' Lorelei said angrily, grabbing the commlink and addressing her crew, 'prepare for battle!' she ordered in a quiet fury that was more terrifying than a raised voice would have been.

CHAPTER THIRTY-TWO

Anywhere you go I will follow

Betty hates Veronica gripped the helm of the Raven and swung it hard to the left, while at the same time stabbing at the button that dropped the anchor. Immediately a loud clunk was followed by a series of clinking gears, as the anchor dropped into the sea and pulled the ship to a stop. The rest of the crew turned to her in surprise as she hadn't indicated they would be taking a break anytime soon.

'Damn and blast!' yelled Betty as she looked down at their expectant faces.

'What's the matter?' asked Wolff.

'I've lost her. The Nixe ship. It turned back towards us suddenly and I thought we were cooked for sure, but then the signal faded and she just disappeared.'

'Have you checked the radar?' asked Vincent.

'Yes, twice. I even rebooted it, but it's working fine. You don't think they could have gone to the underworld Farquar?'

'No, no, there's no such place,' said Farquar, but he sounded about as convincing as a second-hand ship salesman, 'I expect Lorelei probably just has a cloaking device on her ship.'

'No, I checked for that. If that ship had an active cloak on we'd know it,' explained Betty, pointing to a small round object on the control panel. It looked almost like a snowglobe, but instead of fake snow and a castle, inside were the innards of a rusty old clock they had found in a recent diving expedition, affixed to which was a tiny screen and a blue light.

'I like it, what does it do?' asked Wolff leaning forward for a closer look, on the screen he could see the image of a tiny dagger.

'She calls it the Cloak and Dagger, it's designed to pick up changes in the atmosphere that occur when a cloaking device is activated. Apparently just after a cloaking device is turned on a number of ions are displaced and this machine can detect that. When it does the image changes to a cloak, and if you push that little brass button on the side ... well then you can still track the cloaked ship by following the ionic path it leaves behind.'

'My lady certainly is clever!' exclaimed Vincent proudly.

'OK, so no cloaking device, where did they go then?' asked Wolff.

'Farquar, any ideas?'

'Well I did hear that ... but surely she wouldn't show that to a human.'

'You heard what?' asked Betty H.V with a hint of frustration.

'The Nixe ship is rather special,' explained Farquar, 'in that it can sail underwater as well as over it, it's submersible, and so the only reason I can think of as to why we can no longer track them is that they have gone underwater.'

'But Blimey can't breathe underwater! She'll drown!'

'She'll be quite safe. The ship becomes enclosed, she'll be perfectly fine, and quite dry too.'

'I'm not feeling any better about this,' growled Betty H.V, 'we should never have let her go alone!'

'Lorelei would never have let you go with her,' said Farquar, 'she wouldn't do anything to put her child at risk, and showing up with all of us in tow... well it wouldn't look good.'

'You seem to know an awful lot about this Farquar, is there anything else you want to share?' asked Betty H.V testily.

'You credit me to much,' said Farquar loftily, 'bits and pieces of lore I know yes, but the rest is supposition based on common sense,' he added before stalking off to the bow and staring off into the distance.

'What are you about Farquar?' Betty whispered to herself, as she turned to the control panel next to the helm and made some adjustments.

'What are you doing?' asked Wolff stepping up beside her, looking from her to Farquar and back.

'I've added some parameters to the radar, so we should be able to track the Nixe ship underwater now.'

'That's actually very cool,' said Wolff, leaning in a bit closer.

'Thanks,' smiled Betty hates Veronica, turning round and

almost falling into Wolff as she hadn't realised he was standing so close. They were almost nose-to-nose, and you could feel the electricity crackling between them.

'Step lively there, sailor,' said Betty awkwardly, completely caught off guard by how she felt with him standing so close to her, but refusing to let it show. Catching the scent of his skin, she couldn't help but thinking he smelt delicious, and blushed violently.

'Ahhh, sorry,' smiled Wolff, stepping to the side.

'Now,' said Betty taking a deep breath, and turning back to the radar, 'here we are! I've picked them up again, let's get this bird flyin'!' she yelled to the crew as she pressed the button to retract the anchor.

The Raven was soon moving again at good pace across the waves, but Betty was careful to keep their speed below 15 bows. She didn't want to give their position away and she didn't know much about the technology on the Nixe ship, nor to be honest much about the Nixe themselves. And though she doubted it, for all she knew they could have superpowers.

Betty was also starting to worry about having Farquar with them. He seemed to be manipulating the situation to his own personal ends. After all, as Betty recounted to herself, he had been responsible for Blimey getting thrown off her old Captain's ship, and then she was sure he had somehow gotten them captured by the Syrens. And now her Captain had been taken by a crew of sea demons, who they were tracking as they sailed towards who knew where. She had a bad feeling about this. Farquar seemed to know much, but never revealed enough.

'How are we lookin' now?' asked Vincent joining her at the helm.

'Good, good,' said Betty absently, as she stared at Farquar, who irritatingly was still standing at the bow, looking out over the sea.

'You don't trust him much?' asked Vincent, following her gaze.

'I don't trust anyone,' Betty smiled, shaking her head and looking back down at the radar. Tapping the instrument panel she made some subtle adjustments to the sails, and turned the ship slightly West.

CHAPTER THIRTY-THREE

The sea of Trascorn

Bessie waited on the dock in the cool early morning air. The sun was yet to rise, but her eyes had long ago adjusted to the dark. Neither Blade, nor any of his crew were anywhere to be found. Reaching into a leather pouch that was attached to her scabbard belt, she pulled out a delicate silver pipe. Putting it to her lips, she puffed away thoughtfully. As the vapour disappeared into the morning air, she paced casually back and forth, and wondered what she was doing. Was she just Blackwatch's messenger girl now? Or was she still his equal partner? Either way, whether it worked out with Blackwatch or not, she would hedge her bets to ensure she would be OK.

At first she had been surprised at how easy it had been, and how keen certain people were to work with their enemies if they thought it meant they were saving their friends - despite the obvious gamble they were taking. Ever since she had drowned Blimey's parrot, she had been working behind the scenes to guarantee that no matter what happened, she would stay the golden girl. As long as that parrot could keep a secret, she'd be OK.

After a few minutes lost in thought like this, she no longer felt like waiting for Blade or his crew to awaken. They were wasting time. Walking towards Blade's ship's gangplank, she decided it was probably time to find out. Stepping onto the main deck of Blade's ship she strode towards the helm, pressing the button to retract the gangplank. Bessie had no problem with taking Blade's ship while he slept, whether he or his crew were even on it or not. Taking the wheel in her left hand she leaned down to start punching in the launch code. Unlike the Raven, the Nevermore had no kill switch, Blade being too lazy to install one, and so getting her underway would be a cinch. The ship sprang to life immediately, with the main sails unfurling in the early morning breeze. The rising suns rays cast a wonderful orange glow on the sails and the main deck, as Bessie raised the anchor. It was as the ship was easing it's way out of the harbour that a bleary-eyed Captain Blade came stumbling up onto the deck from the Captain's quarters.

'Hey what gives!' he exclaimed, and then clutched his head in obvious pain, 'oh it's you, Bessie,' he added almost instantly as his vision cleared and he realised he was really too hungover to argue.

'Go and get dressed Blade,' sighed Bessie as she looked on Blade with disdain. He was missing his shirt and was only wearing some loose cotton trousers.

'My ship, my rules Bessie, you don't get to take command just because old Captain angry-britches sent you OK? Right now I feel more like a hot cup of coffee than pulling on some scratchy old clothes, my skin just couldn't take it at the moment.... I'm feeling a bit sensitive,' Blade responded wryly, smiling his most charming smile and leaning against the helm deck banister.

'Very well Blade, but we will meet Thadius as planned, I will not be late on your account,' answered Bessie refusing to look at him. It was well rumoured that Blade could charm his way out of anything, and she was not going to let him distract her.

'Can I get you anything ... at all?' he asked, looking up at her. He ran his fingers through his long shaggy hair and brushed it to the side. The movement forced Bessie to look at Blade quickly, and she was annoyed to see he was still smiling in that infuriatingly charming manner. And that she found it attractive.

'Coffee, please,' said Bessie curtly, turning back to the helm.

Out of the corner of her eye she saw him turn and walk off, and sighed with relief. She was not used to dealing with such cheeky unruliness and it unnerved her.

Blade meanwhile stumbled back downstairs to his quarters and threw on some clothes. White shirt, dark wool vest and heavy black wool trousers. Not bothering to put on his boots yet he splashed some water on his face and examined himself in the mirror. He looked tired, he thought. The drinking was starting to catch up to him. Perhaps he should lay off the juice for while. He wandered down the hall to the galley, knocking loudly on the doors of his crew as he went.

'Come on you scoundrels! Rise and shine!' he laughed heartily, and immediately there was a scuffling in each room as his small crew got up and at them.

Reaching the galley he turned to the kitchen's control panel and pushed a large red button labeled coffee. Soon a bubbling percolation could be heard and the smell of roasted beans filled the air. Blade's crew began to drift in and help themselves to a cuppa. They didn't even seem to notice that Blade was with them and not steering the ship, which was clearly moving. It took a few moments but finally Blade's first mate, Sixpence Harred, caught on.

'But who's flying the ship Boss?' he asked, concern creasing his brow and a sinking feeling hitting his heart. He really hoped it wasn't that Blimey girl. He had really liked that girl and didn't think his boss had treated her very well.

'Headless Bessie,' answered Blade shortly.

'But she has a head though,' pointed out another of the crew, a tall thin man named Raymond Cutts.

Blade looked at Cutts and smiled, 'that be true lad, that be true, but for loosing her head in a game of cards she will forever be known as Headless Bess – though I wouldn't go sayin' it to her face – she'd as soon as cut off your head as cut out your tongue.'

'Did you know she was coming like?' asked Harred, sipping his coffee and rubbing the stubble on his face.

'In truth yes, and I should have said something last night but we seemed to be having such a merry time I forgot.'

'Sounds about right, so spill the beans Captain.'

'Well we've been commandeered by Bessie there,' he said pointing up, 'and Captain Blackwatch in order to bring in Blimey. There's a huge bounty on her head and we're in for half a cut of the score if we capture her alive, and Bessie is after gettin' her ship back. The Raven was once hers you know. We'll be meeting Blackwatch in the sea of Trascorn before we head off to track down Blimey, together.'

'Are you serious Boss? But I thought you and her ...?'

'It's not your place to think Harred,' said Blade suddenly loosing his usual jovial demeanour. Picking up his coffee he stormed off angrily, back down the hall towards his quarters.

'So much for finding out where we're going then,' Harred

mumbled under his breath, before walking off himself, leaving the rest of the crew to look at each other awkwardly in silence.

As he stormed up the passageway, Blade only paused to get his boots as he stomped on back up to the deck, where Bessie was still running the ship herself.

'Good to see you run a tight ship here Blade,' said Bessie sarcastically as he burst into the sunlight.

'I'm not in the mood for your sass now Bessie, what do you mean?'

Bessie was taken aback slightly by Blade's sudden change in attitude. Gone was the charming boy Captain and in front of her now stood a weary man who was out of patience, more with himself it seemed than anyone else.

'I just mean that your crew have been beaten to the deck by their Captain, it's just unusual, that's all,' explained Bessie, with the hint of a smile. She needed to calm Blade down. He was easier to manipulate when he was happy.

'Yes, well, perhaps they are not as in tune to the movement of the ship as I am,' he smiled, sitting down on the stairs that led to the helm deck and taking a large sip of his coffee.

'Perhaps,' said Bessie deciding it was best to change the subject, 'we are a day's sail from Trascorn, and Blackwatch has seen to it that we won't encounter any trouble on the way. He has received word that Blimey has been picked up by the Nixe as planned.'

'The Nixe?' asked Blade, consternation crossing his brow. He knew a little of the lore around these sea demons, and was not sure why they would be involved in what seemed like a simple track and capture.

'Yes, we have something of value to their Captain, and so she kindly volunteered to go and pick up Blimey and deliver her to us.'

'Then why do you need me?' asked Blade suspiciously. He smelled a rat and it was getting more pungent by the minute.

'In all honesty Blade I don't know, Blackwatch sent me for you, so here I am. I guess you'll find out soon enough,' answered Bessie.

'A days sail you say,' mused Blade getting up and walking up the stairs to join Bessie on the helm deck.

'Yes, at our current speed.'

'Well then, we'll have to do something about that,' smiled

Blade, 'would you please step aside Bessie?'

Bessie blushed as Blade gently lifted her hand from the helm and kissed it. Composing herself quickly, so he wouldn't see this had thrown her, she nodded curtly and moved away.

Blade took the helm and leaned over to the ships main console. Pushing the comms button he ordered his crew up to the deck.

'What do you have up your sleeve Blade?' asked Bessie, watching him work with mild admiration.

'This ship has some secrets yet,' Blade smiled, walking around the helm to address his crew as they assembled.

'Men! We sail to meet Blackwatch in the Sea of Trascorn, it is a days sail as the crow flies at our current speed. Those of you who have known me a long time will know that this is unacceptable, and so we have no choice.'

'No choice!' yelled the men in unison, who knew what was coming.

'We have met the conditions of the code, all ahead Turbos!' yelled Blade.

'Turbos eh?' smirked Bessie, 'I never would have thought you would have those hidden away on this thing.'

'Yes, well, you will find the Nevermore is as full of surprises as I am,' Blade smiled, full of himself once again as he flicked back a small black cover to reveal a red button on the console. A faint cacophony of cogs and gears could be heard as two panels opened at the ship's stern revealing two jet engines, which immediately purred into life.

'I bet you are,' Bessie said under her breath as she tilted her head slightly to one side and crossed her tentacles, watching Blade work. His hands moving furiously over the console as he punched in the coordinates for Trascorn.

'Ready men?' yelled Blade standing up finally as he prepared to launch the ship.

'Aye Captain!' they responded as one.

'Then may Brid have mercy on our souls!' he shouted happily, slamming his hand down on the red button. The ship lurched forward with a howl and in moments reached a ridiculous speed. Bessie tried as hard as she could not to look impressed, but eventually couldn't help it, letting out a small scream of joy as the wind rushed in her face. This was what she lived for. This was her life.

CHAPTER THIRTY-FOUR

The Scylla

Lorelei swung the Eudoxus sharply round and positioned her at the outer edge of the ring of the slaughter that continued above them. Before she could attack the Tecausians she needed to ensure the Scylla were ready for it and able to escape to safety. This would be tricky. She called one of her crew to her and explained her plan.

'Lydia, I need you to go out there and get the Scylla to move to the far end of the cove, but they need to do it in such a way that they look cornered. You'll need to use all your skill to hide amongst them so you're not seen. The Tecausians will form a ring around you thinking they have the upper hand. Once I have broken their line, I will need you to lead the Scylla out to sea and tell them to swim for it.'

'Yes Captain,' said the girl.

'Good luck,' Lorelei said, resting her hand on Lydia's shoulder briefly, before she turned and headed for the ship's airlock, 'now then Blimey, we wait until my girl here has cleared the area and then we'll strike in a manner they will never be expecting!'

Blimey watched out the viewing window as the girl emerged from the airlock with two small brass air tanks on her back, which fastened around the chest allowing her arms to move freely. Then a slim hose attached to the tanks lead up to a clear facemask that covered her entire face from forehead to chin. It was fitted to the head with rubber straps that buckled at the back of her head. A very simple set-up, but effective for short underwater missions. As Blimey watched the girl slowly disappeared into the water, becoming invisible, starting from her feet and rolling up her body until finally her head was gone.

'That's some nice diving gear your crew have there Lorelei,

you must tell me where you got it,' marvelled Blimey as she thought she had figured out what had happened.

'Yes...' said Lorelei absently as she watched the progress of her crewmember outside of her ship.

The Nixe girl swam up towards the surface as high as she dared, and then turned away towards the inner circle of the cove. Telepathically, Lydia called out to the Scylla in their own tongue and told them that the Nixe had come to their rescue. Through their terror the instinct to survive was still strong, and Scylla began to move as she had indicated. They knew it was a gamble to trust an unseen voice but they had nothing more to lose.

Back on the Eudoxus, Lorelei watched all this play out. She watched as the Scylla moved further into the cover, followed by the Tecausians who indeed formed a blockade hemming them in. The Tecausians were right above the ship, still unaware that they were being watched. Grabbing the internal comms, Lorelei pulled it to her lips.

'Prepare for emergency surface!' she hissed into the device, as she turned to Blimey, 'you better hold onto something – this is going to be a bit rough.'

Blimey held fast to the helm deck balustrade as she heard the suddenly thunderous sound of the ships internal mechanisms springing into life, expelling the water they had taken on earlier and forcing it out and downwards. The effect this had on the Eudoxus was instant, and while the Nixe crew knew what was about to happen and showed no more interest in the process than a painter takes in watching paint dry, it took Blimey completely by surprise. The ship pitched suddenly skyward and seemed to fly out of the water like a whale cresting as it chases the sunlight. Reaching peak height the ship then landed with an almighty smack on the water sending out a shock wave. The sudden displacement of water sent the Tecausians every which way, dislodging the brass helmets of some and forcing them to surface.

Seeing the Eudoxus prepare to surface was just what Lydia had been waiting for and she told the Scylla to dive with her so they could escape the blast wave that she knew would result from the ship smacking down onto the surface. She would then be able to lead them under the ship and away from the fresh battle that was soon to follow.

Back on the Eudoxus, Lorelei wrestled furiously with her ship and brought it round hard left. Punching at the ships main controls, the ships glass roof began to retract. She then signalled to her crew to get ready for boarding. She knew the only course of action the Tecausian's would take was to try and capture her ship as she pushed a further button to retract the ship's metal casing.

By now the Tecausian's were recovering from the unexpected interruption, and signalling to each other, they spread out to surround the Nixe ship. Lorelei watched their progress and smiled. This wouldn't be a fair fight really, but she was never one to back down from a bully.

'What happens now?' asked Blimey as she watched the Tecausians surround the Eudoxus.

'They plan to board us, but let them come,' said Lorelei calmly, as she felt her ship rock slightly. The first of the Tecausians had grabbed on to the ship, and she could now hear them making their way up the side of her.

'Crew – let them think they have captured us! Do not fight until I give the order!' yelled Lorelei.

'I hope you know what you're doing,' said Blimey, smiling.

Lorelei was just about to answer when the first of the Tecausians landed on the deck. The man looked around angrily, while the other Tecausians piled up behind him, and then started to spread out. Lorelei's crew instinctively moved back towards their Captain. Noticing this, the Tecausian approached her as it was obvious she was their leader.

Blimey pulled her cutlass out of its scabbard, and let it hang loosely at her side.

'What is the meaning of your attack woman?' said the leader of the Tecausians, advancing on Lorelei threateningly.

'You cruelly hunt and kill the Scylla when you know they cannot defend themselves. I am here to see that you stop this, for good.'

'Who are you to judge our traditions?' screamed the man enraged.

'What tradition?' snorted Lorelei indignantly, 'there is nothing about what you do that even lightly smells of tradition, if there was any stench to this at all it would be that of cowardice. Your actions reek of nothing more than greed and cruelty.'

'Whatever, it is no matter to us what you think, we will deal with you as we do the weak and delicious Scylla, those of you who are lucky will welcome death, those of you who are captured will become our pets, and it will not be an easy life you will lead,' smirked the Tecausian leader.

'As you wish, but I must warn you that it is your families who will also suffer if you choose this path of violence, please remember to tell them that I gave you a choice,' said Lorelei and signalled to her crew, who drew their own weapons. This took the Tecausians by surprise, but they didn't show it for long, 'are you sure you wish to fight?'

'Ha! You cannot touch us, we will destroy you!'

Lorelei looked at the Tecausian leader with pity in her eyes, and opened her mouth wide letting out the blood curdling war cry of the Nixe.

'Kill them all!' screamed the Tecausian leader in response.

The Tecausians and Nixe rushed at each other in a flurry of limbs and screams. Swords and spear guns clashed in a silver blur. Not one to be left out Blimey sprang into the fray, cutlass swinging with vicious purpose as she went for the leader of the Tecausians. The noise of the battle rang out harshly against the peace of the blue sky. As the Nixe fought on, one by one the Tecausians fell until all but a few were left, mostly lying injured on the deck. Finally they dropped their spear guns in surrender.

Lorelei and Blimey stepped over the bodies of the fallen as they made their way over to where the Nixe crew had piled the Tecausian survivors.

'I did warn you,' said Lorelei, 'and now I must finish this. I will summon the Signathus who will watch over your village and make sure you never hunt the Scylla again. I trust you know who I speak of?'

The Tecausians looked up pathetically and nodded their heads sadly, before looking down again in shame.

'You could never have beaten us,' continued Lorelei, 'we are the Nixe, sea demons who cannot die, see there, even those of us who are injured badly still stand, and any wounds they have sustained will heal shortly too.'

The Tecausians said nothing, but they did not look happy to have been defeated. Lorelei walked up to the helm deck and pressed a silver button on the ships command console. From the side of the ship a brass speaker was dropped into the water. Once the speaker reached a depth Lorelei was happy with she pressed a further sequence of buttons on the control panel, and the speaker started emitting an inhuman noise. The only ones able to hear this monstrous noise were the Signathus.

'Who are the Signathus?' asked Blimey as Lorelei returned to watch over their prisoners.

'The Signathus are a powerful clan of sea ghosts,' Lorelei explained, 'they appear as huge skeletal creatures that resemble a blue whale, and they bring plague and destruction to any village they cross. I have been friends with them for … let's just say a very long time. They will watch over the Tecausians for me, and make sure they never hunt the Scylla again, lest their village be struck down with plague and they all perish.'

'Cool,' said Blimey nodding her head.

After a few moments the water around the ship began to swirl like boiling water. The ship moved erratically, though everyone managed to keep their sea legs, and a guttural roar soon filled the air. Out of the waters sprang several terrifying beings, and they were just as Lorelei had described them. Skeletal ghosts, huge and terrifying. Lorelei spoke to them briefly in a language that no one else seemed to be able to understand, but when she was finished the largest of the Signathus nodded solemnly and looked down at the Tecausians. One by one the Signathus picked up the remaining Tecausians with their transparent skeletal flipper arms, and transported them back towards land.

Lorelei watched them go, and then turning her gaze out to sea, she could see Lydia bobbing in the water amongst the Scylla, who would now be safe to swim in the cove any time they chose. She smiled to herself, but this happy respite was short lived as she knew they would have to get back on course now in order to meet Blackwatch and hand over Blimey before the deadline. Lorelei knew she really didn't want to hand her prisoner over, no matter how willing Blimey was to exchange herself for her child. It was a decision she knew would haunt her if she went through with it. But what choice did she have.

'I need to come up with a way to get out of this,' Lorelei mumbled to herself under her breath as she watched the Scylla disappear into the distance.

CHAPTER THIRTY-FIVE

Two sides to every Blade

Captain Blade's ship, The Nevermore sliced through the salt water with Headless Bessie at the helm. Blade had been kind enough to let her pilot the ship while he sat in a colourful deck chair and sipped on a glass of red wine. Bessie was clearly enjoying herself. From what Blade understood she had not commanded her own ship since she had lost the Raven to Blimey, and it was obvious to him that she missed it.

From time to time Blade stole an admiring glance at Bessie, who despite her scarring and tentacles was still a real beauty. Against his better judgment Blade found himself attracted to her and wondered why he had never felt this way about her before. Clearing his throat he made an effort to focus on the path ahead. He couldn't afford any more emotional entanglements right now. There was still Blimey to deal with, and anyway Bessie was betrothed to Blackwatch.

'We're about 10 minutes away now!' called Bessie happily from the helm.

'Aye Captain,' said Blade getting to his feet and winking at Bessie, who caught off guard blushed despite herself, before he turned to his crew, 'men! We'll be at the Sea of Trascorn in 10!'

Blade's crew sprang into action. There were a million little things to do before they dropped anchor, and Blade had given them specific instructions not to show him up in front of Blackwatch. As they approached the coordinates Bessie had provided they could see Blackwatch's ship, the Riffraff anchored and waiting for them. Blade could just make out Blackwatch talking to a tall skinny gentleman whom he didn't recognise on the deck.

'Who's the stringbean?' Blade yelled up to Bessie.

'That's Vainglorious – he's bankrolling this whole thing.'

'Why do we need someone to bankroll this?' asked Blade with a puzzled expression on his face.

'Well, you know Blackwatch – there's always money to be made somewhere, Vainglorious has a bone to pick with Blimey ... or her mother... or both, I can't recall exactly,' lied Bessie, who obviously knew more than she was saying but she didn't want to share more information than she had to.

'Right, but I'll still get the girl right?' asked Blade, who was starting to have a bad feeling about this whole adventure. Something here wasn't right. He was beginning to think that he was being conned.

'Oh sure, of course,' smiled Bessie reassuringly, as she powered down the ship's engines and put her back under sail.

'Ok Bess, but I'm trusting you on this OK?'

'It will all work out fine Blade, don't worry,' Bessie lied, as she brought the ship expertly around next to the Riffraff and dropped anchor. After all she was still Blackwatch's girl at heart.

'Prepare for boarding!' yelled Bessie, as Blackwatch turned to acknowledge the Nevermore.

Blade's crew then ran to place the gangplank in between the two vessels, as their Captain turned to address them.

'Men, stay here but keep an eagle eye out, stay on your toes. I'm not expecting trouble, but at the first sign of anything untoward I want you to get the ship out of here and save yourselves.'

'We ain't leavin' ya Captain, you say this every time you get a whiff a trouble, and every time we stay and fight,' smiled Harred.

'Well you can't say I didn't try to keep you out of it,' laughed Blade as he stepped up onto the gangplank behind Bessie who was already half way across, 'but seriously lads, something doesn't feel right here so keep astern,' Blade added in a gruff whisper before he sauntered off to join Bessie on Blackwatch's ship.

'Aye,' said Harred to no one in particular as they watched their Captain go. This was going to be a long day.

CHAPTER THIRTY-SIX

The clock strikes twelve

'Where are we headed Lorelei?' asked Blimey stepping up to the helm with a cup of coffee in her hand.

'The Sea of Trascorn, Blackwatch is waiting for us there.'

'I've never been there, sounds wonderful,' smiled Blimey.

'I don't want to hand you over Blimey,' said Lorelei grimly.

'Don't worry about it, I can take care of myself.'

'Perhaps not this time, Blackwatch has Bessie and Vainglorious with him, you would be vastly outnumbered.'

'Everything will be fine,' said Blimey smiling, 'you just worry about getting your daughter back, I'll worry about me.'

Lorelei wasn't so sure though. Blackwatch was not one to fight fairly.

'How far away are we?' asked Blimey interrupting Lorelei's thoughts.

'A few hours, no more, we'll be there by midday.'

The Eudoxus sailed on through the morning under fair skies, carving through the water like a hot spoon through ice cream with nothing to interrupt the calm beauty of the day. The smell of salt water carried on the wind sweeter than any perfume as gulls circled in the sky. They were getting close. After a while Blimey could make out a few small black dots on the horizon. Instinct told her it was Blackwatch, but she didn't know whose the other ships might be. It made her feel slightly uneasy, but she let that pass. This was no time to get the jitters.

A strong southerly gust blew cold across the deck, causing the crew to pause for a moment, caught off guard as it hit the sails and pushed them along, increasing their speed significantly.

'The wind must know something you don't Blimey!' called Lorelei from the helm as she braced to keep them on course.

'She always does!' Blimey called back. She smiled to herself as she let the moment wash over her. Regardless of what happened, she knew that as long as she stayed on the sea she would be fine.

Bessie watched the Nixe ship approach with one hand on the shoulder of the kidnapped Nixe child. The girl was about 12 years of age, slender and almost boyish. Her blue face was dappled with gold freckles beneath her almond shaped eyes and cherubic child's mouth. She kept her expression impassive with some effort. She had strict instructions from her mother to stay quiet and compliant.

'Your mother must love you,' Bessie said bitterly.

'Why would you doubt it?' asked the girl.

'Blackwatch set her a near impossible task, finding Elizabeth Everlone, famed leader of the Thirteen Bones. Though I guess she may not have done it and is just here to fight for you, but that would be a very silly move on her part as she knows what would happen to you.'

'You couldn't kill me, Bessie,' said the girl confidently.

'Perhaps,' said Bessie surprised at the girl's conviction, 'but it would not be up to me to do so, you know that.'

'None of you could kill me,' said the girl.

'What do you mean?' asked Bessie looking down at her, intrigued.

'My mother let you take me, she knows I am quite safe.'

'But she cannot have ... what do you mean you are quite safe?' asked Bessie, but there was no time to answer. The girl smiled faintly as she watched her mother's ship approach.

Blackwatch picked up his spyglass from where it sat on his ship's control panel, next to the helm, and looked out at the approaching ship. He had never seen it in the daylight and it truly was an amazing sight. The sun glinted off the gold masts, interwoven with sapphire and glass. The sails had become almost translucent in the sunlight, and the front of the ship featured a carved black seahorse with pale blue eyes, which contrasted beautifully with the brightness of the rest of the ship. Blackwatch took a deep breath, almost against his own will. It was nothing like he had expected.

Blade and Vainglorious joined Blackwatch at the helm as the Eudoxus pulled alongside the Riffraff and dropped anchor. Lorelei appeared at the side of the ship and clicked her fingers. Immediately a gangplank extended creating a bridge between her ship and Blackwatch's. Lorelei stepped up onto the plank and straightened up to her full height. She looked like Pirate Queen. With a small wave of her hand she signalled to her crew to stay behind, then she turned to Blimey and nodded. Blimey nodded back and jumped up onto the gangplank behind Lorelei, her hands tied behind her back loosely, as together they made their way over to Blackwatch's ship.

Jumping down onto the deck, Blimey came to stand beside Lorelei. Turning her head slightly to her right, she whispered out of the corner of her mouth.

'I need to ask you a favour Lorelei, when you have your daughter, take her and leave, don't fight – let them think they have won. I need to find out what the story is with Vainglorious, and I'll need some time to do that.'

'Are you sure?' asked Lorelei, 'I know we could take them down together.'

'Yes, please, do this for me and I will consider our debt settled.'

'Very well, but it goes against everything I believe in,' said Lorelei before turning her head to the front and looking back up at Vainglorious and Blackwatch as they approached.

'What is this you bring me Lorelei?' asked Blackwatch coldly, 'I asked you to bring me Elizabeth Bo.... Everlone in exchange for your daughter!'

'Something tells me you will be just as happy with this ... asset,' Lorelei replied.

'Who is she?' asked Vainglorious turning to Blackwatch.

'I am the daughter of Elizabeth ... Everlone, as you call her,' said Blimey, 'I understand that I will do quite nicely in exchange for the return of the Nixe girl.'

'Really?' said Vainglorious stepping forward and running his hand down the side of Blimey's face. She did not flinch, but his touch repulsed her, 'well isn't she a pretty little thing, except for the eye-patch of course, that is a little unfortunate but aside from that ... yes ... I think she will do nicely.'

'So you're happy then sir?' asked Blackwatch with some faint hesitation.

'Oh yes, she's a much younger model isn't she?'

'Why yes sir, she is,' squirmed Blackwatch ingratiatingly.

'Then you will honour our agreement?' asked Lorelei seizing

her moment and stepping forward.

'Why yes, of course, Blackwatch be a dear and return the little blue girl to her mother.'

'Are you sure sir? She is good leverage, it might be worth...'

'Blackwatch don't be stupid, I want no more trouble with this woman and her demon race - return the girl forthwith!' said Vainglorious raising his voice.

'Aye sir,' said Blackwatch uncomfortably and motioned for Bessie to bring the girl forward and hand her over.

Lorelei bristled as Bessie marched the girl over, her hand clamped on the girl's upper arm.

'Let Acionna go Bessie,' she warned, 'she can walk on her own.'

'Very well,' said Bessie, letting the girl go.

Acionna ran to her mother and threw her arms around her waist as Lorelei looked down at her and stroked her hair.

'I have no further business here, do not darken my door again, Blackwatch,' she warned as she took her daughter's hand, and turned to leave, taking care to look behind her to make sure no one was thinking of doing anything stupid, like following her. Jumping back up onto the gangplank between her ship and the Riffraff, she made her way back onto the Eudoxus and retracted the gangplank.

'Sail us from their view, and then prepare to dive!' she instructed her crew.

On the Riffraff Blimey stood in the mid-afternoon sunlight refusing to give anything away. She showed no emotion, and made no movement. She was like a statue, while the others stood and stared at her.

'Why am I here Blackwatch?' she said finally as it became clear that someone had to speak first.

'Why my dear, I intend to marry you,' said Vainglorious, leaning in and kissing her cheek.

Blimey recoiled slightly.

'I have no wish to be anyone's bride,' she said quietly, 'is this really the only reason I was brought here?'

'Well, yes,' said Blackwatch.

'You should have known this was not going to happen, I'm not going to marry this aristocratic scum.'

'You will not have a choice.'

'Bring it on, Blackwatch,' Blimey smiled, suddenly freeing

her hands and reaching for her cutlass.

'Now that's enough of this nonsense,' said a familiar voice stepping out from the shadows. It was Captain James Blade.

Caught off guard, Blimey turned suddenly in his direction. As she did so, Blackwatch nodded at one of his crew, who burst forward and smacked Blimey on the back of the head with the butt of his gun. Instantly she dropped to the deck, knocked out cold.

'What new treachery is this Blackwatch, that was not part of the deal I was sold,' said Blade in anger.

'Oh yes, you are so predictable Blade, and gullible, this was all too easy thanks to you.'

'So that is all you wanted me for? To distract her so you could knock her out? That seems to be ridiculously complex for a task so simple,'

'Simple? You know as well as I do Blade that she would never willingly agree to marry Vainglorious, and she is far too skilled as a fighter, she would have mangled us all. Plus the opportunity to make a fool of you was too tempting to refuse.'

'Blackwatch, she was promised to me and I am taking her with me!'

'Blade, go home, you are in over your head ... as usual,' smirked Blackwatch.

'I was told that I would get the girl,' said Blade like a petulant child, even though he knew that he had been completely duped, 'well at least it's good to see you're as good a liar as you ever were Bessie, a pity as I was actually starting to like you.'

'It was not my idea Blade,' said Bessie apologetically, though she was surprised at herself for saying anything at all.

'There's no pride in being Blackwatch's lapdog, Bessie,' said Blade angrily.

'I am not his lapdog!' screamed Bessie, enraged.

'But of course you are,' Blackwatch laughed, causing Bessie to blush and storm off towards the bow away from them all. She was tired of being disrespected by this gaggle of men.

Blade took the opportunity to make his own exit, turning on his heel and heading back to his own ship in angry frustration, thoroughly humiliated. How could he have been so blind and stupid. He needed some time away. He needed to get sober. He needed revenge on them all, and he would have it.

Bessie watched him go with a touch of sadness. It had been fun sailing with Blade for that short time. More fun than she had had in a long time with Blackwatch. Blade seemed to appreciate the freedom of the sea in a way that Blackwatch had not for a very long time, and she missed that reckless abandon. She also felt guilty for tricking Blade, and in hindsight his presence was truly unnecessary. It was just another example of the way Blackwatch let himself be led by his ego and desire for cruelty. Bessie was getting tired of it, and as she looked out at the open ocean, as the Nixe ship disappeared in the distance, she wondered if she did still love him or if it was time for her to make a fresh start on her own. As the wind picked up her hair, a tear rolled down her cheek, and she wondered as she wiped it away angrily. Perhaps if she tracked down Blade and apologised she could sail with him for a while and enjoy herself.

CHAPTER THIRTY-SEVEN

Two days in the brig

Blimey woke up on a hard bed with a scrap of a blanket draped over her. Her head was throbbing and she found she couldn't move it too far without searing pain forcing her to lie back down. Opening her eyes again after a moment she could see that she was in a small barred cell within the ship's hold. It smelled of dampness and the sea. Closing her eyes again, she felt down her side and realised that she was not only still fully clothed, but that her weapons had been left with her. Now this was interesting. Obviously they were either fairly certain that she would not try to attack anyone who came down to see her or ... but they couldn't surely? Leave her down there on her own for who knows how long?

The question was answered with a creak as the door to the hold opened. Despite the pain in her skull, Blimey jumped up and pulled out one of her guns, pointing it through the heavy, black iron bars.

'Who goes there?' she demanded, and then instantly regretted it, putting her hand up to her head and grabbing onto one of the bars to steady herself.

'My name is Kitterine miss, I'm a seamstress, I've been sent to do your dress.'

'Step over here into the light,' said Blimey lowering her gun.

Kitterine did as she was asked and Blimey could see that she spoke the truth. She wasn't part of Blackwatch's crew. In fact she seemed quite terrified. She had a half finished dress slung over one arm and a basket in the other.

'Please, come and sit down here,' Blimey indicated to a chair, 'now tell me, how did you get here and what did they tell you? Me for my part, I have been taken prisoner by Blackwatch, and I am to be married against my will to that aristocratic barbarian, Vainglorious.'

'I came with Blackwatch, he brought me here to do your dress and that is all I am meant to say,' said Kitterine, obviously not willing to give up any further information.

'Then you have a key to my cell, otherwise how would you be able to do the fitting...' mused Blimey, 'but they would be expecting that,' she continued to herself under her breath, 'or are they counting on that fact that I would never attack an innocent ... that must be it, and damn it they are right, I can't hurt this poor woman.'

'Yes miss, but they assured me that ...'

'That I would not hurt you? Yes, well sadly for me they are right, I will not,' Blimey smiled at her own trap.

'Well Miss, while I am known as the best dressmaker in all of Hallvard, I myself am not here willingly either, and no amount of money could make me take part in this ... Vainglorious holds my husband and children captive. I said to him I wanted no part in this evil thing, you see I'm old enough that I remember your mother and her parents, and what he did to them is just terrible, terrible. But he said he will only free my family if I create your dress.'

'There seems to be too much hostage taking and threats being made around here for my liking,' said Blimey addressing Kitterine, 'I understand, can you tell me when I am to be married? I will help you if I can but I need information if I am to figure a way out of this for all of us.'

'In two days Miss, they aim to do this thing quickly before word gets out and your supporters rally to your rescue.'

'Two days, can you get the dress ready by then?' asked Blimey.

'I think so Miss, I already have the bones of the dress ready, and I don't have much of a choice.'

'OK, we've got two days to get this dress ready, and that means two days for me to think of a way out of here ... you said you were against this marriage, would you help me if I can be sure to keep that secret?'

'That I can Miss, that I can,' said Kitterine smiling, as she unlocked the door to the cell and Blimey stepped out, taking a seat on the chair herself as her head continued to pound.

'You'll have to forgive me, I received a nasty bump on the head yesterday, was it yesterday? I am not quite myself.'

'You take your time Miss, there's plenty I can do. Here, now you best eat something, there's some nice bread and cheese in this basket here along with my sewing kit.'

'Thank you, that's very kind,' said Blimey, looking around her and resting her hand on the hilt of her sword, 'if only I could hide my weapons in the dress, then no one would suspect I had them when I walked down the aisle.'

'Oh Miss, that's easy, I helped my own mother sew your mother's dress,' smiled Kitterine.

Over the next two days Kitterine worked on the dress while she and Blimey chatted to pass the time. Kitterine told her something of her mother and her grandparents, things that she never knew, while Blimey regaled her with tales of her adventures on the sea. As dawn approached on the day of the wedding, finally another person appeared in the doorway to the brig. It was Blackwatch.

'Get back in yer cage girl,' he laughed as he stepped into the dirty yellow light of several candles.

'As you wish Blackwatch, but I want assurances from you that you will send the seamstress home, she has finished the dress as promised.'

'And what do you know of it?'

'Well I know she is not part of your crew, I know that you hold her family hostage, and I also know that if you do not honour your agreement with her and release her family then many more people will hear of this than you intend.'

'So what if I don't, and I just kill them instead?'

'Blackwatch, I am to be Vainglorious wife, do you not think that this will give me some influence? You may think that you are indispensible to him at the moment, but I can assure you that if you cross me I will make your life a greater hell than you can ever imagine!' Blimey stated calmly.

Blackwatch looked at her as if he was seeing her in a new light. So, she intended to use this marriage to gain power over him through Vainglorious. He could not risk that, but he also saw that for the moment he was trapped and he could neither kill her, nor let her go.

'Very well Blimey, I will return the seamstress and her family to Hallvard tonight.'

'Do it now, and I want you to bring proof to me that they are safe Blackwatch.'

'As you wish Blimey,' said Blackwatch through gritted teeth, before turning on the dressmaker, 'you woman, leave the dress and if you know what's good for you, you'll get back up on deck now, it's time for you to go.'

CHAPTER THIRTY-EIGHT

Speak now or forever hold your peace

Blimey stood in the dark hallway below deck on Captain Blackwatch's ship and looked up at the stairs that lead up to the main deck, where she would be going any moment now. Looking down at herself she almost started laughing. She was wearing the wedding dress that had been tailored for her. It was all petticoats, satin and lace, and not something she would have chosen. It was a horrendous exercise in medieval princessary.

Grabbing a handful of the dress she swished it back and forth before letting it drop. Straightening up she adjusted her eyepatch out of habit, and then rubbed the back of her head painfully. There was still a large bump there from where she had been hit four days earlier. Vainglorious had organised his last wedding as far as she was concerned. Blimey turned to her left sharply as she sensed movement behind her. It was Blackwatch. He was there to make sure she didn't try anything tricky.

'It's time to go lass,' he said looking her up and down with a menacing smile.

Without a word Blimey hitched up her wedding dress angrily as he jabbed his cutlass into her back, and stomped up the stairs. As she stepped out into the open air, the ship's lone bagpiper struck up the wedding march, which rang out across the sea, annoying the seagulls who were cresting on the waves trying to catch a quiet moment.

'Keep going and don't try anything stupid now,' Blackwatch ordered in a low voice, jabbing her again to emphasize his point.

'You'll pay for that Blackwatch,' Blimey snarled.

'Not this time lassy,' Blackwatch laughed.

Blimey stepped forward and stalked down the deck past Blackwatch's crew, who each in turn either smiled or smirked at her as she passed. She grimaced inwardly but her faced remained a serene calm. She would not show Blackwatch, his crew or that aristocratic prat Vainglorious that she was even slightly rattled. She didn't have a plan as yet, and while Kitterine had indeed managed to hide her cutlass and her guns within the voluminous dress she wasn't quite sure what would happen when she reached the makeshift alter at the ship's bow. She shrugged ever so slightly as she tried to snap her mind into gear. Come on Blimey girl, think of something!

Then she saw it, behind Vainglorious and a short way off in the distance, hidden beneath the blinding afternoon sun. A familiar shape outlined against the sky – the Raven, with the clearly recognizable outline of Betty hates Veronica standing at the helm. Blimey struggled to keep from grinning like a madman as she walked towards her captor. She didn't want to give the game away as she would have to wait until she reached Vainglorious, and Blackwatch left her back. All eyes were on her right now and so the Raven should be able to sneak right up to Blackwatch's ship unnoticed until the last minute. Only a few more steps.

As she looked towards her ship again, she noticed Betty hates Veronica nod ever so slightly. Three steps to go. Two. One. She had reached Vainglorious, who roughly grabbed hold of her upper arm, as Blackwatch did indeed step aside, melting into the shadow of the nearest mast. Vainglorious didn't want him anywhere near the formal ceremony, even though Blackwatch had protested that this is when he would be at his most vulnerable. Vainglorious had laughed. Surely this mere slip of a girl would be no threat once she knew she was beaten? Blackwatch had disagreed, but as he had been paid he really didn't care enough to press the matter further. Now he was just enjoying the show.

Blimey let Vainglorious grab her arm and pull her closer to him, knowing this would work to her advantage. The closer she was the harder it would be for him to retaliate. Headless Bessie looked at them impassively from behind the makeshift altar. Vainglorious had requested she conduct the ceremony, which she was qualified to do, but beneath her cold exterior she was feeling uncomfortable. As much as she despised Blimey, she didn't want to marry her off to Vainglorious. The man was arrogant and ethically questionable, and he was an Aristocrat – her natural enemy. She was only doing this because of Blackwatch. It seemed so important to him to be part of Vainglorious' inner circle. She couldn't really understand it herself – why did he want to be so involved with the aristocracy. From what she had seen when Blackwatch had taken her to meet Vainglorious, the nobles on the Isle of Hallvard kept their people in a constant state of oppression. They were worked to the bone, and lived in squalor while the aristocracy lived in luxury. She hadn't been impressed at all, though clearly Blackwatch had seen something he wanted there. Power and money were all he seemed to care about.

'Begin,' Vainglorious ordered, snapping Bessie out of her thoughts.

'Dear... we are gathered here today to witness the marriage of Lord Jacob Vainglorious to .... Jeanne Bohnes....' Bessie trailed off, 'wait – is your father Gerald Bohnes?' she asked, looking as though someone had just slapped her in the face.

'Yes Bessie, he was, what of it?' asked Blimey stonily lifting her chin high in defiance.

'No, no, that's not true, you can't be his daughter. He's my father, though I never knew him...' she trailed off.

'He was my father Bessie, he died just after I was born. In fact it was your betrothed who murdered him, stabbed him right in the back as Farquar tells it,' Blimey said acidly.

She looked at Bessie square in the eye. It felt to her that Bessie was telling the truth, and perhaps she was her half-sister. Bessie was older than her, and it was obvious that her father would have had other relationships before he met Elizabeth, but what good would it do her to try and play on Bessie's emotions now? Her crew was standing by to help her escape. This would have to be another item for the 'maybe later' agenda, which she sighed inwardly, seemed to be growing longer every day.

Bessie on the other hand looked stricken and gripped the altar with both hands, her knuckles white. She shot Blackwatch a look of pure menace, the anger seething off her skin in waves, though he himself remained unmoved.

'You mean he killed my ...?' but Bessie didn't get a chance to finish this line of questioning.

'Enough of this!' Vainglorious interrupted angrily, 'this is my wedding day and it will not be hijacked by some nonsense family reunion. You two are obviously sisters – any fool could see it in your faces!'

Blimey and Bessie looked at each other and both took a step back to examine the other in more detail. Although Bessie's dark skin and hair contrasted with Blimey's fiery red locks and pale Celtic skin, they had the same green eyes, and the same nose, they were roughly the same height and build – aside from Bessie's pale blue tentacled arms of course.

Vainglorious was becoming impatient, but this minute break in the ceremony gave Blimey an opportunity. This was no time to get sentimental, and regardless of whether she believed this new genealogical revelation or not, she could use this information to her advantage.

'Fine, I will accept that we look alike, but what does that mean for you Vainglorious? Does Bessie know that it was you who ordered the murder of our father? And that it was Blackwatch who carried out the deed?'

'Him?!' demanded Bessie snapping out of her funk and looking up at Blimey.

'Yes, that's right, Vainglorious ordered it and Blackwatch hunted our father down and then treacherously ran him through when his back was turned, he is a coward and it was he who killed our father!'

Bessie looked from Blimey to Vainglorious not knowing what to do. This was a lot to take in, and the way she saw it, she had two choices. Either she could stand here paralysed by this new knowledge or she could do something about it. She was well over this wedding nonsense anyway. Looking at Blimey pointedly, she kicked the altar aside and pulled out her cutlass, turning to her left and running straight for Blackwatch.

'I'll see you in hell Blackwatch!' she screamed, surprised at her own fierceness as she flew towards him. Caught off guard, he stood rooted to the spot, but it only lasted a moment before he stepped aside at the last second and shoved Bessie to the ground. She landed with a thud, remaining motionless for a moment, embarrassed and in pain.

At that same moment Blimey turned to Vainglorious and

smacked the heel of her palm into his nose, breaking it. Blood immediately began to pour from his snoz, and he let go of her arm, putting both hands up to cover his injured face, which was a mask of terror. He could not believe that someone would hit him like that!

Blimey smiled and pulled roughly at the skirt of her wedding dress, ripping it away from the corset. Underneath she had been wearing trousers all along. It's amazing what you can get a seamstress to do when she hates your fiancé. Blimey silently thanked that wonderful lady. Next she reached for her cutlass and one of her guns.

'Ha ha!' she yelled happily, and she watched as the crew of the Raven jumped down onto the deck of Blackwatch's ship, 'you've had it now Vainglorious – I'm taking you out!'

But Vainglorious was already off and running. A true coward, he had no intention of hanging round for a battle. Reaching the side of the ship he jumped over it lithely and landed in the water next to a small honeymoon boat, which he had anchored there waiting to take him and his almost bride to a nearby Island after the almost ceremony.

'Never mind,' said Vincent appearing suddenly at her side, 'he can't get far.'

'I know,' said Blimey smiling, leaning up to kiss Vincent on the cheek as he pulled her close, 'and we've got our own troubles to deal with right now. It looks like Blackwatch's men have finally figured out what is going on,' she added as they moved in to surround them, while Vainglorious' other guests made a quick getaway.

'Nice to have you back Captain,' smiled Betty hates Veronica, joining them as Blackwatch's men moved in, forcing them closer together.

Blackwatch approached them, sauntering over with a smirk firmly glued to his face. Bessie was still lying on the deck, forgotten for the moment by everyone it seemed, she cried softly to herself as she propped herself up on one tentacle.

'Vainglorious has run away, I've been paid a fortune in gold, and now I get to take you down... this might just be the perfect day!' Blackwatch announced jovially.

'What about Bessie?' asked Blimey.

'She'll come round,' Blackwatch replied, his smile faltering for just a second before recovering in a Cheshire cat like manner, 'but not before I run ye through!' he added making a grab for his cutlass and swinging it wildly in Blimey's direction. This was all the signal that anyone needed, and immediately they sprang at each other. Swords clanged and guns fired as the two crews fought on. Blimey's crew so obviously outnumbered, but they relished the challenge.

'Just like always,' yelled Betty hates Veronica, as she fought off two of Blackwatch's men at once.

On the other side of the ship Blimey and Blackwatch were engaged in a one on one for the moment as both their crews left them to fight it out, yet it was obvious from the beginning that Blimey was the better fighter of the two. Blimey fired a cherry bomb at Blackwatch's head, a warning shot across the cranium, causing him to stumble as she parried his cutlass out of his hand. Blackwatch looked at her in shock and then did what any blackhearted coward would do – he ran for his life and disappeared into the mêlée.

Before she could give chase however, Bessie approached Blimey from across the deck as if in slow motion, as the battle continued to rage around them. They smiled at each other through the smoke and the noise, as though both knew it would come down to this eventually. As they drew closer their smiles settled into grim acceptance. It was clear now that they were sisters, but it didn't change the fact that they had been enemies for so long.

As their swords clashed, Blimey spoke.

'You can't seriously stay engaged to Blackwatch now Bessie, as much as I hate to say it, you deserve better.'

'This is not about that fool, I want my ship back, nothing more.'

'I can't give you the Raven Bessie, she's been mine for a long time, I won her fair and square, but perhaps I can give you another ship.'

'What do you mean?'

'I happen to know the whereabouts of a fine ship... the Obscurity – have you heard of her?'

'Etype's ship – yes.'

'Well it's no longer his... let's just say he ran into some life difficulties with her and now she is in my possession.'

'Really? well it looks like I underestimated you.'

'So what do you say?' asked Blimey as they circled around

each other, continuing to clash swords.

'If this is true, that would do nicely, I do miss having my own...'

But Bessie was cut short by the sudden appearance of Blackwatch behind Blimey. Before she even had time to turn Blackwatch had run his sword through her back, up to the hilt. Blimey cried out in pain, but she could not move. She was trapped on the blade.

'Just like your father,' Blackwatch whispered menacingly leaning into her ear, before roughly pulling his cutlass free. Blimey gasped and dropped to the deck in a heavy heap as Bessie looked down at her and then up at the man she had thought she loved, the same man who had killed her father and now her sister too it seemed.

'Blackwatch! This is against the code! You truly are a coward – and to think I was to marry you!' Bessie said angrily as she approached him. Blackwatch raised his sword as he prepared to fight.

'This should be as easy as ... well, stabbing someone in the back!' he laughed.

Bessie lifted her own weapon, but she had different ideas. As Blackwatch brought his blade around for a circular shot, Bessie simply reached out with one tentacled arm and caught Blackwatch's own arm, stopping it in mid-air and holding it firm. Retracting her muscles she started to squeeze until Blackwatch felt the bones in his arm grating against one another. Screaming out in agony he dropped his sword. At that same moment Bessie brought her own sword round, slicing into Blackwatch's upper arm and ensuring he could not hit her. Then she brought the sword back round and ran it through Blackwatch's ribs, just missing any internal organs. Pulling the sword free again she wiped it on the sleeve of his shirt, as he doubled over in pain.

'A quick death is too good for you,' Bessie said quietly, as she put her sword in it's scabbard and with both tentacles picked up Blackwatch and took him to the side of the ship, dropping him overboard, 'let the sharks have at you,' she added.

Turning back to the battle, Bessie took in the scene. Most of Blackwatch's men lay dead or injured, as Blimey's crew fought on, unaware that their Captain had fallen. This madness needed to stop now. Bessie roared in anger and flew at the remaining crew, cutting down each of Blackwatch's men as she crossed them until they all lay slain. As this was happening Blimey's crew watched in awe, the only other person they had ever seen fight with such ferocity was Blimey herself. Speaking of which, they had not seen her for some time – where was she? Then Vincent spotted her lying propped up against the main mast, clearly badly injured and in a great deal of pain.

'Jeanne!' he called out, dropping his weapon and running over to her side and taking her in his arms. He was joined shortly by Betty, Farquar, Wolff and Rawkous.

'Is she OK?' asked Betty H.V, kneeling down with a frown of concern on her face.

'She's lost a lot of blood, and this wound ... well it is a fatal blow,' answered Farquar.

Vincent looked up at him and then back down to his beloved. She was too weak to speak, to weak to move, but she was hanging in there.

'What can we do?' he asked.

'Make her comfortable, tell her you're all here so that she knows that you're by her side as she passes into the next world,' said Farquar.

'I refuse to give up on her like that!' yelled Betty, getting to her feet and turning on him, 'you know something Farquar – you've known all along this would end like this, but I don't believe you would let her die like this! Tell me what you know!'

But Farquar ignored her and walked away, towards the helm, leaving Betty to stare after him. She had never felt so helpless.

'Farquar!' she demanded, but still he ignored her. Once he reached the helm he simply started punching a series of buttons on the ship's control panel.

Meanwhile, Bessie approached the others and looked down at her sister. She felt nothing, just an impassive coldness – it was not hate, nor even mild dislike. She was just empty. She had just found out that not only did her fiancé kill her father, but it now looked like her sister would die by his hand too. She was numb.

'Can I speak to her?' Bessie asked, kneeling down.

'Uh sure, of course,' said Vincent quietly.

'Blimey... Jeanne ... I'm so sorry ... about Vainglorious, Blackwatch... everything. Don't worry about the other ship, I think I'll just keep this one,' she said, smiling sadly and not a little awkwardly.

Blimey opened her eyes, and whispered to her, 'I saw you disarm Blackwatch, you could have taken me out the whole time but you chose to follow the code, you fought well my sister,' she smiled.

'Yes, well, this doesn't mean I like you...' but Bessie was cut off by the sound of water rushing skyward.

'What is that!' exclaimed Wolff, running to the side of the ship.

'That my dear Wolff, would be the Nixe coming to save your Captain ... I took the liberty of calling them,' explained Farquar walking back over.

CHAPTER THIRTY-NINE

Just in the Nixe of time

'How did you get here so quickly?' asked Bessie, frowning.

'We've been anchored below the waves here for the better part of three days,' said Lorelei as she leaned forward and examined Blimey's wound, 'ooh this is a nasty one, she doesn't have long, she's lost a lot of blood, look at how pale she is, almost grey...'

'Underwater?' asked Betty hates Veronica, her curiosity getting the better of her as she put two and two together.

'Yes,' answered Lorelei shortly.

'Can you save her?' asked Vincent tensely, in his mind this was no time for chit chat.

'I can't make promises, but if you want me to try you'll need to step back and let me have some space. Just lay her down there,' said Lorelei.

Vincent did as she asked, before moving back to give her some room.

'What are you going to do?' asked Betty, peering over Lorelei's shoulder as she knelt to rip away the sleeve of Blimey's bridal corset.

'There's only really one thing I can do at this stage my dear, I'll have to give her a transfusion of my own blood.'

'WHAT!' exclaimed Betty, 'but you can't do that, what will that even do?'

'Well, as Farquar knows we are Planarians, and we can heal ourselves. If I give Blimey my blood, she will heal but she will inevitably also inherit some of our... properties.'

'What do you mean properties?' asked Vincent.

'We are immortal, but I do not think she will become so, though she will live a long life. If her body is suitably matched to our genotype, then she will mutate and her skin will become slightly blue. She will also become impervious to most wounds, being able to heal herself – however some... extreme injuries may not be healable.'

'Immortal? And Farquar knew about this?' asked Betty hates Veronica, turning to face the demon.

'Yes, of course,' said Lorelei who opened a big black bag she had brought with her, and began taking things out.

'You planned this!' hissed Betty, turning on Farquar.

'No, he didn't, he just knows... things,' answered Lorelei distractedly, without looking up as she set up her machine. It was a beautiful contraption of turquoise glass, brass and light.

'But how can we trust him, ever since he's shown up we've been on a collision course with this moment – he knew we could have avoided all this!' Betty raged.

'It's not that simple,' Lorelei groaned as she found a vein in her arm that would do and dug in a long thin glass tube, 'now this won't hurt too much my friend,' she whispered to Blimey as she inserted a similar tube into Blimey's arm and pressed a pale green button on her machine. Blimey took in a deep breath and let it out between clenched teeth.

'Yes sorry, that was a bit of a lie,' added Lorelei as the machine sprang into life and began pumping blood slowly from one girl to the other.

'How long will this take to work?' asked Wolff, who was watching fascinated.

'A minute, no more, but then she will need some days to recover as we very nearly lost her. The longer she lives with my blood in her the faster her body will learn to heal.'

'So she will live then?' asked Bessie stepping forward suddenly.

'Yes, I think so,' smiled Lorelei, looking up at her, 'ahhh you must be her sister.'

'What .. how could you know that, I only just found out myself!'

'It doesn't matter what I know, or how I know it, but no one could mistake it – you really do look so much alike.'

'Why does everyone keep saying that!' Bessie responded angrily, stamping her foot like child throwing a tantrum, 'you don't know anything about me, couldn't do, and you know what? I would like you all to get off my ship right this instant! Don't worry about all this mess. Blimey will recover better on the Raven anyway, and I wish to get out of here as soon as I can. I have my own business to attend to,' she finished.

'Bessie, are you sure this is what you want?' asked Farquar, concern creasing his brow.

'Blackwatch was still alive when I threw him overboard Farquar, I wasn't thinking straight, I was angry, and if he has survived then I must find him and he will pay for what he has taken from me. Vainglorious as well. That fool has been pulling everyone's strings for too long.'

'Can we move her though?' asked Vincent, looking down at Blimey, whose breathing had stabilised. The wild flow of blood from her wound had also ceased, and the colour was returning to her cheeks, but it was clear she had lost consciousness.

'I think that'll be OK, but she'll need a few days bed rest and quiet to make a full recovery,' smiled Lorelei packing up her machine and getting to her feet, 'but it is time I left you to figure the rest out for yourselves, I have business of my own to attend to and Bessie is looking anxious to get going on her own quest,' Lorelei looked at Blimey fondly, 'tell her that any time she needs ... well Farquar knows how to find me,' and with that she turned and ran to the side of the ship in a blur before flying into the air and landing on her own ship.

'And that's also our signal to leave,' said Vincent bending down to gather Blimey up in his arms, kissing her lightly on the forehead.

'Thank you,' said Bessie, returning to her more usual steely demeanour, 'I'm not sure about all this sister stuff, but tell Blimey that I consider our score settled.'

Vincent nodded, and together they made their way back over to the Raven. Farquar hung back for a moment to speak to Bessie, as Betty hates Veronica eyeballed him suspiciously on her way to the side of the ship.

'You don't trust him much, at all, do you?' asked Wolff.

'I ... I just think he knows a lot more than he lets on, and I think that keeping us in the dark is dangerous,' Betty answered, caught off guard as she didn't think anyone had seen her giving Farquar the evil eye.

'That may be the case, but he hasn't led us astray so far.'

'That is a matter of opinion,' Betty answered in a huff and kept walking, leaving Wolff slightly embarrassed and confused.

Back on the Raven, Vincent took Blimey upstairs and put her to bed in the Captain's quarters, before heading back out on to the deck.

'What now?' he asked.

CHAPTER FORTY

Blackwatch gets away

After Bessie had thrown Blackwatch into the water, he knew he didn't have long before the sharks would come for him. He was bleeding quite badly from where she had run him through. As he swam for his life he was filled with pain, anger and loss. But mostly anger. How dare his fiancé, former fiancé, treat him like this? After all, he had stood beside her after she had been turned into that tentacled freak. She owed him! Blackwatch howled in anger as he swam on. He had to catch up with Vainglorious, who he could see rowing off in the small boat not to far away.

After nearly 10 minutes in the water chasing Vainglorious, who refused to slow down or stop, Blackwatch finally caught up to him. Vainglorious was not happy to see him. He began paddling furiously in an attempt to make the boat move faster, but it was too late as Blackwatch grabbed on and pulled himself over the side, into the boat.

'Get away Blackwatch, there's no room in this boat for you and you're getting water everywhere!'

'Like hell there isn't Vainglorious you rich bastard! This is all your fault, I told you we should have had more men on the ship but no, you didn't want your snooty wedding polluted!'

'Go back to your own ship Blackwatch!' screamed Vainglorious in a rage.

'I will not, besides, it will have been claimed by Bessie by now, she's always wanted it. No, no, you will take me to land where you will purchase for me a more powerful vessel or I will kill you now!'

'You don't have the mettle,' spat Vainglorious.

'You want to wager your life on your arrogance?' asked Blackwatch springing at Vainglorious and holding a dagger to his throat while the boat rocked back and forth alarmingly under the weight of the sudden movement.

'Fine, fine, I will do as you bid, but this is where our partnership ends Blackwatch, I want nothing more to do with you, now get away from me, you are bleeding all over my jacket!'

'Oh yes, so I am,' said Blackwatch lightly, grabbing at the scarf at Vainglorious' waist and wrapping it firmly around his own wound to stem the bleeding, 'thanks for reminding me, I might have bled out and left you all alone,' he smirked.

Vainglorious growled to himself, and returned to the task of steering the ship towards the port where he had planned to take his bride. There he could be rid of Blackwatch forever and make his way back to his house and servants. The wind had thankfully picked up and once they hoisted the sail on the little boat, it didn't take them long to reach the island of Lyere. Following the curve of the land they reached a shallow bay and pulled into port. Once they had docked and paid the parking tax, they made their way to the Stuffed Goose, one of several luxury hotels that dotted the small island. There Vainglorious begrudgingly paid for a room for Blackwatch, and attained the services of a local surgeon, who stitched up Blackwatch's wound and dressed it. Vainglorious then retired to his own room, and got changed out of his wet and blood soiled clothes.

'How did it come to this!' he cried wringing his hands at the ceiling, before dropping his hands to his sides and sighing loudly. Moving over to the window, he picked up a delicate crystal flute and poured himself a glass of champagne. Looking out towards the sunset he sighed again and sat down in a comfy chair, letting his mind wander. Touching his bruised nose gingerly, he knew it was broken. Perhaps he should have let the surgeon look at it. Oh well, there was always the morning. Had it been a mistake to try and marry the girl? I mean she was obviously too strong to be broken in a few days of confinement, and she was too feisty to control. Look what she had done to his nose! It might have been better to continue to pursue her mother, and simply have done away with the girl as he originally planned. She was very attractive though, despite the missing eye, and admittedly he had been swept away by her beauty. Never again though. Now he would put a price on her head so large that anyone would be fool not to claim it, and if he spread the news wide enough he might attract the attention of her mother, who might show up to bargain her life for her daughters. As he dipped deeper into this ridiculous fantasy, Vainglorious smiled to himself in triumph. In his mind there was nothing that could not be achieved if you had the money and the means. He would have this Blimey's head on a spike, and that of her bastard sister too, for foisting that incorrigible pill Blackwatch on him. Yes both of them would pay for ruining his special day.

Blackwatch meanwhile was settling into his five star room, paid for courtesy of Vainglorious. He had just climbed into his luxurious bed, clothed in a silk bed gown, with a glass of red wine wrapped in his fingers and a good book laid across his chest. Safely hidden in a wooden box under his bed was more than enough gold to purchase a new ship. He had asked Vainglorious to pay for the room for the next month. He figured that would give him long enough to recover properly and then he could be on his way with a new ship and a new crew. He would hunt Bessie and Blimey down in style.

CHAPTER FORTY-ONE

The other side of betrayal

Bessie looked around her new ship in disgust. It was covered in dead things. Dead men, blood, discarded weapons, bits of the ship had been damaged and destroyed. She had her work cut out for her. It was a mess and she refused to sail on her own in such disarray. Growling to herself she got to work, throwing dead men, and anything else that she didn't need, over the sides. Then she got to work swabbing the deck, making light work of it, as she was able to use both tentacles to hold a mop each. She knew she could have gone after Blackwatch then and there, when he was vulnerable. She could easily catch him with his own ship under her sail, and she had a fair idea of where he was headed, but she was also tired and as she looked around at her now clean ship she realised it might be nice to be on her own for a while.

Leaning on one of the mops, she looked out to the sea. She loved the gentle wash of the waves against the side of the ship. Looking up into the darkening sky, she nodded sagely to herself. A gentle breeze picked up her hair and swung it around her face. Smiling to herself, she looked down at her boots and shook her head. She would have to go somewhere. It would not be wise to stay at this location longer than tonight. Blackwatch might be injured but he still had contacts, and at this point she wasn't sure he wouldn't try to get his ship back. Perhaps she could sail North for a spell.

Not tonight though. Tonight was between her and the sea. Pullling a bottle of whiskey from a small bar near the helm, she also grabbed a square crystal glass and folding chair and dragged it back down to the deck. Unfurling the chair, she flopped down in it exhausted, pulling her jacket tight around her. The air had gotten chilly. Pouring a measure of the single malt, she put the bottle down on the deck and saluting the moon she downed the spirit in one gulp and closed her eyes. A happy smile on her lips.

It must have been about an hour later that she was disturbed by a familiar faint rippling sound. Another ship was approaching, and was not too far off. Jumping up, Bessie ran to the helm and pressed a sequence of buttons that would allow her to arm the cannons from the helm deck. Then picking up the spyglass next to the console she looked out across the waves. A ship was indeed nearly upon her but it was a ship she recognised. It was the Nevermore, and true to form a drunken Captain Blade was at the helm. She could see him swinging a bottle from side to side as he steered the ship. He was clearly on his way over. Was he expecting to find Blackwatch? Bessie was sure that as far as Blade knew, everything had gone to plan and Vainglorious had married Blimey, leaving Blackwatch to a night of drunken celebration. Is that what Blade was planning on? Was he trying to avenge himself against Blackwatch or trying to rescue Blimey? Well, she would find out soon enough.

For his part Blade was indeed good and drunk, and angry. He had been shamed and humiliated beyond anything he had ever considered bearable. His intention was in fact twofold. Firstly, to do away with Blackwatch (and if he could, that aristocratic loser, Vainglorious), and then to rescue Blimey. He knew now that she would never forgive him, and he couldn't blame her. Not only had he, in her eyes, assisted in the murder of her father but also in her own imprisonment. Yet he still felt he had to try to redeem himself somehow. Even if all it meant was that he could sleep at night without being plagued by guilt.

Coming up on Blackwatch's ship, the Riffraff, he was surprised to see Bessie standing on the side of the ship waving a strop of white material. What did this mean? Was he rumbled? Surely if that was the case Blackwatch would have opened fire upon him by now. And why was Bessie standing up there like that? It was almost as if she was on her own. But that wouldn't .... Blade turned to his men suddenly and signalled for them to stand down. Curiosity got the better of them and they rushed to the side of the ship. When they saw Bessie standing on her own, seeming to wave a white flag at them, they turned to each other in confusion. Blade's First

Mate ran to his Captain, they needed orders.

'What's she like then sir?' he asked.

'I don't know,' said Blade slowly, 'this is not at all what I was expecting. She signals surrender, perhaps she is on her own and some terror has befallen Blackwatch and the crew?'

'I'd wager it's a trap.'

'That is not entirely out of the question as well,' Blade responded thoughtfully.

'Right, what then be our orders Capt'n?'

'Let me go aboard and see where she stands, at the first sign of ...'

'Yes, I know, I know, this is becoming a habit of yours Captain.'

'Have I ever steered you wrong?' asked Blade with a smile.

'No, I guess not.... Yet,' answered Sixpence, taking the helm, while Blade called out to his men.

'She surrenders! Wait here while I go aboard and mark out the terms of this peace,' he called.

Sixpence turned the Nevermore towards the Riffraff and pulled her alongside, close enough for his Captain to swing across.

'Bessie!' called Blade as he stepped up the rigging to get enough height, 'I'm coming over, stand down!'

'Aye Blade,' she called, smiling as she jumped down to the deck and waited for him to appear.

She didn't have to wait long as Blade thudded down onto the wood of the deck. Bessie turned away from him and returned to her seat, picking up the whiskey and giving Blade a moment to take it all in.

'Where is everyone?' asked Blade, confused.

'They're dead,' said Bessie simply.

'What happened here?'

'You can guess,' smiled Bessie.

'Blimey?'

'I like to think that I had a hand in it somewhat.'

'And Vainglorious? Blackwatch?'

'Ah yes those two .... those cowards escaped unfortunately,' Bessie growled.

'So what happened really?'

'Well, why don't you put your men at ease, grab a glass and I will tell you.'

'OK, sure,' Blade smiled, now he was on familiar territory. A drink with a pretty lady was more like his style. Running to the side of the ship he called to his crew.

'She's on her own! I'm going to stay here for a bit, and you ah, get back to what you were doing,' he yelled to his men.

Behind him Bessie rolled her eyes, but she couldn't help but smile. Blade was a cad, though a charming one. She knew exactly what his men would think of this.

On the Nevermore, Sixpence clapped his hand to his forehead and smiled at his fellow pirates.

'Take the night off lads,' he called and went up to the helm. Taking a seat on a small crate, he lit a candle and pulled a small book out of his pocket. Even though his Captain had given him the night off Sixpence intended to keep watch. He had been in this position before, and he new things could go badly wrong any minute.

As Bessie poured Blade a glass of whiskey, he sat himself up on a nearby barrel, and stared at her intently. In the moonlight, and away from the influence of Blackwatch, she seemed to have relaxed finally. All the anger was gone, she was tired obviously, but at peace. He found it overwhelmingly attractive. And as she began to speak, re-telling the events of the past day, he hung on every word. He realised he had never felt like this before. It wasn't just the whiskey. It wasn't quite love or lust. It was a simple longing to touch her, hold her, kiss her. Blade blushed to himself at the thought, and hoped she hadn't noticed. Though now he realised there was another issue to bridge.

During the course of her discourse, Bessie had also revealed that Blimey was her half sister. He recalled his amazement, the recognition that it had to be true, but also the horror at the realisation that it was he who had led Blackwatch to kill their father. If Blimey would not forgive him, how could he expect Bessie to believe him. He had only been a child at the time. An impressionable boy from a poor family, who had taken to the sea in order to raise enough money to look after them. And Blackwatch had promised him a small fortune for one piece of information. The whereabouts of Gerald Bohnes. He had also promised to take him on as a full crewmember, not just a simple cabin boy, with a chance to train as a pirate and one day Captain his own ship. He had believed it all, joined

Blackwatch's crew and served his apprenticeship, but he had also lived with the shame and regret of betraying his former Captain. Perhaps that's why he drank so much. Oh the insight of the damned! Silently Blade cursed his childhood mistake again. Would he ever be free of this burden? He was about to find out. Bessie had finished her tale, and was about to ask a question that was the physical equivalent of a punch in the face.

'So Blade, tell me about your role in the death of my father?'

Blade turned pale and stared at Bessie in shock. Blimey must have told her. That was the only explanation. But why then had she let him on board? Did she plan now to kill him? What could she want?

'That was a long time ago Bessie, I was only a child,' he managed to say finally.

'Tell me,' she said simply.

'Why do you want to know Bessie? You know Blimey despises me, she has obviously painted the picture before I have had a chance to wield the brush, what do you want me to say?'

'Blade, if there is one thing I have learnt in my short time on this plane of existence, it is that there are two sides to every tale. My sister is impulsive, sometimes she is too quick to judge and right now she is hurt and angry. In her eyes you have betrayed her in the worst possible way. I am giving you a chance to reveal yourself as something other than the villain, don't you want a chance to do so?'

'But why would you do that?'

'I like you Blade, a scoundrel you may be but at heart you are a decent man, I have seen it and now I am giving you an opportunity to expose it yourself.'

'Thank you, this is something that has weighed on my heart these past months, and it would be good to tell someone,' he began.

'Then tell me,' smiled Bessie encouragingly, getting up to pour Blade another drink.

'My father had left when I was around five or so, I think, he went off to sea, it was the only job he could get. He never returned. Then later my mother got sick, when I was about 10 she got really bad. Up until then she had worked in a tavern and I can remember sometimes I would sit behind the bar and play with the empty bottles, but she couldn't work anymore, couldn't even get out of bed some days. So I said I would go to work, to get the money we needed, to get her the medical attention she needed, and I joined your father's crew as a cabin boy. He treated me well, and paid me above the standard wage, but it wasn't enough. Then one night, as I waited by the ship for your father to return, Blackwatch approached me. He had seen your father with a dark haired girl, one of Vainglorious' servants in a nearby tavern, and he wanted to know what Gerald was up to. Of course, I did not know, but Blackwatch seemed to know something was up. He has always been a dark schemer ... sorry,' Blade broke off as Bessie winced.

'No, you are right, he is Blade, which is why I am done with him ... please continue.'

Hiding his surprise at this not unwelcome news, Blade went on.

'Yes, well, he knew something was afoot, and he bid me report to him about what went on with Gerald and his crew, he promised to pay me a small fortune, which he did, and he also said he would take me on as his apprentice, and that one day I should have my own ship. What can I say? I was very young, and I did not fully understand the consequences of my actions. I didn't know that Blackwatch intended to kill your father, and by then it was too late. I hope that you can forgive me?'

Bessie looked at Blade and took all this in. She found she didn't blame him, nor hate him, but she did see an opportunity for his redemption.

'So you want to make this right then?' asked Bessie after some thought.

'Why yes, of course!'

'Well then Blade, we have a day or so to prepare and then we go a hunting!'

'Hunting for what... or rather for whom?'

'Blackwatch of course!' laughed Bessie, jumping up.

'But you wounded him, how far can he have gotten?'

'The beauty of it is that I don't know Blade, but I have all the time in the world to find him - we are alive!' she yelled, swigging whiskey from the bottle and then handing it to Blade, who looked confusedly between the glass in his hand

and the bottle, before absently throwing the glass over the side of the ship and swigging from the bottle himself. He liked where this night as going, and could let this play out for a bit. Besides he was too drunk to go anywhere right now.

CHAPTER FORTY-TWO

Over the edge

The Raven sailed on as Blimey recovered from her wound and regained her strength. Eventually she was well enough to sit up in bed, and she requested a hot cup of coffee to welcome in the fourth day. Sipping it slowly so she wouldn't burn her tongue, she noticed that her skin had taken on a slight blue hue, while her natural freckles had taken on a gold hue. Frowning slightly, she reached for one of the drawers next to her bed and pulled it open clumsily. Reaching inside she grabbed a small mirror and sitting back in her bed she held it up to her face. Yep, also blue with gold freckles. What had happened to her? Turning the mirror face down on her bed she looked towards the door, which was now filled with the welcome form of Vincent Blackshadow.

'How you doing?' he asked in concern.

'I'm a bit.... blue?' she answered, looking up at him as he walked over to her and sat on the bed. She was still frowning.

'I know.'

'What happened to me? I remember Blackwatch stabbing me in the back, and then ... where's Bessie?'

'Bessie took off after Blackwatch in the Riffraff, she said you're even now or something? That woman is a bit weird.'

'My sister.'

'Yes, sorry.'

'I thought I was dead,'

'So did we, it was a bit touch and go, but Farquar called in a favour from the Nixe. They can heal themselves indefinitely, and well, you got a transfusion of blood from Lorelei, so you're a bit ... Nixian now, hence the blue skin and all. She's not sure how long the effects of her blood will last on you, she doesn't think you'll be immortal, but you will live a very long time and you're body will heal itself if you are ever wounded.

The pale blueness will persist though.'

'Oh, that makes sense. Right,' Blimey's frown deepened, and she shook her head to clear it, 'where are Farquar and Lorelei now?'

'The Nixe are long gone, but Lorelei asked me to pass on her thanks, she says she is forever in your debt for rescuing her daughter and if you ever need her she'll find you. Farquar on the other hand is on deck chatting to Wolff and Betty.'

'I guess it's time I got up then,' said Blimey flinging back the covers and getting to her feet. She noticed a strange tingling in her skin, but chose to ignore it. Pulling on her clothes, she smiled at Vincent, 'well?'

'You look beautiful,' he said handing over her eye-patch from where it had been sitting on her side table.

'Thanks Vincent,' she smiled kissing him quickly on the lips, as she tied the patch in place and then pulled out her hair so that it wasn't trapped beneath the leather strap.

'Come on,' he said grabbing her hand and leading her onto the main deck.

'It's nearly evening,' she said with surprise as the sky was starting to glow orange.

'Hey! Welcome back sleepy head!' exclaimed Betty hates Veronica jumping up from her seat and running over to her friend, wrapping her up in her arms for a big hug.

The rest of the crew turned and smiled, as Blimey wandered over. They were all seated on the deck enjoying a sneaky rum in the sunset.

'So where are we?' asked Blimey, looking up into the sky. It was not yet dark enough to see the stars, by which she could get her bearing.

'We're about three days sail from the border, the Land Beyond the Dead lies hence, we figured we needed some kind of plan while you were recovering, and Farquar suggested we might find the Noir there, and William could then impart the location of your mother,' explained Betty hates Veronica as fast as she could.

Vincent walked up behind Blimey and wrapped his arm around her waist as she looked off into the sunset. Looking down at her friends as they happily sipped their drinks while the night air rolled in, she realised that for all the company in the world she had never felt so isolated. Covering Vincent's arms with her own, the cool of his skin was a welcome reminder that she was not alone.

'Ok then Blimey, where are we going?' he whispered into her ear as he followed her gaze out over the waves.

'Over the edge of time and space, into the Land Beyond the Dead,' she replied looking up into his face, 'to find William, and then my mother, just like you planned.'

CHAPTER FORTY-THREE

The Land Beyond the Dead

'Coming up on Lucien falls,' called Betty hates Veronica as she watched the sea coming to an abrupt end though the spyglass.

'OK prepare to go over!' called back Blimey as she punched madly at the control panel and kept a firm grip on the helm.

'Can she make it?' asked Vincent only slightly nervously.

'She's got a few tricks up her sleeve. I have no intention of just dropping over the edge of the world my love, but we will make quite a splash!'

'How long Betty?' called out Wolff as he climbed down from the rigging, Rawkous perched on his shoulder. For some reason the parrot had taken a shine to him and followed him around the ship like a small, red, feathery puppy.

'I should say about two minutes – Blimey! Are you ready for this? What do you want us to do?'

'Tie yourselves to something solid, that way if anything goes wrong at least you'll stay with the ship, there's some rope on the deck for you.'

'OK, everyone anchor yourself to something, we go over in one minute!' called Betty, as she continued to prepare the ship for whatever was to come next.

'What about you my love?' Vincent called to Blimey.

'I'm already secured to the helm – don't worry, I'll be fine!'

The falls were coming up on them fast now, Blimey could just see the white foam and spray leaping up as the water rushed down into a chasm hundreds of feet below.

'Here we go – don't look down! 3, 2, 1!' she screamed above the thunderous noise of the falls, but the ship didn't go over the edge and down as expected.

As she counted down Blimey hit the button for the ship's turbos and the sudden propulsion sent the ship straight on instead of following the path of the water down. They were now sailing through mid-air over a thousand feet up. It was quite a drop. Blimey hung on to the helm like a mad woman, keeping the Raven on a straight course. What she knew, but that the others couldn't see is that she just had to make sure the ship cleared the valley the falls ran into. Water poured into the valley from both sides, and if she could make it to the other side they would once again be in the water, and sailing into the Land Beyond the Dead. Tense moments passed as the wind flew past them, freezing the blood and chilling the bones, but the Raven stayed in the air, the turbos doing their job of shooting them across the ether.

'Not much further,' Blimey mumbled under her breath as the ship continued on, and then in a blinding flash everything went white.

As the new world began to take shape about them the first thing they noticed was that darkness had fallen, but there were no stars in the sky and no moon to guide their way with it's pale light. It clearly wasn't night, but rather they had crossed into the Netherworld. The Raven drifted along on a sea that was as calm as glass. The only ripples to be seen were created as the ship carved through the water. It was eerily silent. The crew untied themselves and walked to the bow of the ship to get a better look at what they were sailing into, as Blimey stayed at the helm.

'What now Farquar?' called Blimey, 'you led us here, I assume you have a plan for finding the Noir?'

'Hmmmm, yes, well all you need to do is play Mull of Kintyre on these bagpipes here.'

'But I don't play!'

'Then it's a good thing I do,' said Wolff stepping forward to save the day and taking the bagpipes from Farquar, 'just where were you hiding these?'

'I have my secrets,' smiled Farquar knowingly.

'Certainly you do,' said Blimey, raising an eyebrow.

As Wolff hit the first notes, a ship appeared on the horizon, speeding towards them over the water. Blimey grabbed at the spyglass next to the helm and put it to her eye. Looking out she could see the Noir ship thundering towards them, faster than humanly possible without any wind to drive it. The Raven drifted on gently, as the Noir ship came upon them. Without waiting for it to slow William had appeared out of nowhere, running full speed along his ship until he reached the bow, and then without a break in his stride he launched himself into the air and landed with a thud on the deck of the Raven.

'Stop that infernal racket now or you will wake him!' he yelled angrily, waving his arms madly across his body. Instantly Wolff stopped playing and the sound of the bagpipes drifted away in a mournful whine. He looked confused.

'Wake who?'

'How did you even get here?' asked William ignoring Wolff and looking pointedly at Blimey, 'you should not be on this side of the veil, only those who are dead can cross over... my god! You didn't pay the ferryman did you?'

'Ferryman? What? No! We followed the tracking device on your ship, and Farquar filled in the rest.'

'Well, you cannot stay here obviously, if he wakes you will all be dead.'

'I promised you I would return for you William, I intend to find my mother, and I need you to tell me where she is,' stated Blimey firmly.

'Yes, I guess you do...'

'What does that mean? Are you angling for some kind of bargain? I have already saved your life, and that of your men, what else can you want from me?' asked Blimey, annoyed that he would play these games with her now. Perhaps she had misjudged this man.

'No, no you misunderstand me,' he continued on quickly, 'your mother ... I don't need to tell you where she is Jeanne, and I don't need to take you to her, she is already here with us.'

'How? Where?'

'She did not want you to see her, she was with us on the night that the Nixe attacked.'

'On your ship with you? But that means that she ....'

'Is a Vampirate, yes, she didn't want you to know, she was ashamed.'

'Then she turned to be with you... and that is why she hasn't been seen for so many years?'

'Yes,' said William, 'we tried for many years to find a way out of this life for me, so we could be together, but we were wasting so much precious time, with every year she grew older as my body refused to age a day... in the end this was the only way we could be together without watching her life spin away into dust. We were married shortly after. '

'There is no shame in wanting to be with the person you love,' said Blimey sagely, as she turned to look over her shoulder at the Noir ship expectantly, 'so Elizabeth is on your ship now?'

'Yes,' answered William simply, following Blimey's gaze over to his own vessel, which was moored next to the Raven.

There she was at the railing, looking over at her husband and the little party of people standing on the deck of the strange ship. A pale vision in an ornately embroidered green dress, her hair tied back with a leather strap, except for a few strands round her face. She smiled faintly on spotting the young woman, who she could be in no doubt was her daughter. She waved hesitantly, and then moving back a few steps she ran forward suddenly, jumping high in the air, over the rail and landing on the deck of the Raven. Smoothing down her dress she walked towards Blimey, and once she was close enough she grabbed her by the shoulders, letting her hands drop down Blimey's arms, pulling her hands out to the side and then letting them drop gently.

'You take after your father,' she said quietly, tracing the edge Blimey's eye patch with a long pale finger and smiling.